THE
MARSHKEEPER

E. L. WERBITSKY

To Jon
for his endless encouragement

and

Jennifer and Johnny
for their inspiration

"The world is a dangerous place, not because of those who do evil, but because of those who look on and do nothing."

— ALBERT EINSTEIN

CHAPTER
ONE

Cal felt the shove first. Then his shoulder joint crumpling against a locker as the door vents sliced into his cheek. He ducked out of the headlock, just as a fist whaled into the locker, inches from his head. Even as the taste of blood and dirty metal filled his mouth, Cal recognized the flabby arm and cloud of BO descending over the hallway.

"Get—off me, Jardo," he grunted, wiping back the strands that'd slipped from his hair band. "What the hell?"

But his protest only widened the grin and darkened the Franken-brow leaning over him. "You're a…a cretin, Hughes. A loser."

Jardo's older cousin leaned in, stinking of sweat and stale tobacco. "Next time you try and torch the school, make sure you g-get the right building, jerk-off." His finger jabbed into Cal's chest. "N-not the restaurant across the street."

For a second, Cal didn't look at the greasy-haired goons. He just stood there staring down at his trembling hand, numb by the raging rumors, the stuff people were saying about him. Then he let his gaze drift up and lock onto them.

The ogre-sized cousin startled back. "C-come on, Jardo, let's get out of here before the f-freak blows."

Taking a deep breath, Cal smoothed his tee shirt, shoved back the tails of his plaid shirt and combed his fingers through his hair—too long if you lived within Jardo's reach. Dabbing his bloody cheek with the back of his hand, he headed to class and sidled into the last row just as the bell rang.

Breathe, he reminded himself. It was Friday afternoon. Every kid in school sat ready to dash off and start the weekend. Except here, in Mr. Schlenz's class. Cal looked around. Not a single eye fidgeted toward the clock or down to a hidden cell phone. With his usual theatrics, the teacher staged the lecture like a one-man Broadway show, his voice thick with a German accent, his shaved head covered by a wig of wild silver hair.

Cal tuned it out. History? Come on. It'd all been said before. Sure, you could drum up dates and places, but who could say why stuff happened, why people did what they did. No one knew. Well, *almost* no one.

Behind a tumble of bangs, he fixed his eyes two rows over. Second desk. In spite of bright pink highlights streaking her hair, new ink coiled around her upper arm and more chains than he could count, Star McClellan bore a crazy close resemblance to her younger sister. Yet she refused to talk about her, about what happened.

Cal shifted his gaze through the open windows, beyond the idling busses to the marsh simmering in a haze of mosquito-filled humidity. Maybe it was too painful for her. Or maybe Star sensed what he already knew: the story of what happened out beneath the muddy waters was a lie.

Minutes later, the sound of the final bell rattled through the building but not before Schlenz assigned an essay on Albert Einstein. "Tree hoondret fifty words. No more. No less. Dizmissed!" He pulled the wiry wig from his head and with it, the theatrical gravity of his voice fell away. It made his next words sound flat, almost ominous. "And Calvin, see me before you leave."

As his classmates shuffled out, Cal averted his eyes. He didn't want to see their energy, the maelstrom of color that came at the sound of his name. He'd seen it all before. He knew what they thought of him.

Star glanced over her shoulder; her copper-colored eyes too careful to linger more than a moment on him. *You're — in — trou — ble*, she mouthed, her tongue lifting on the last syllable. Then she sauntered away, the swing of her tiny skull-shaped earrings keeping the beat, a toss of red hair swaying over her back. People talked about how resilient she was. But the dark makeup and tough-chick attitude didn't fool Cal. To him, her pain was as plain as the wave of bruised-blue energy shivering around her.

With his classmates gone, Cal approached the podium, not bothering to brush back the stubborn strands of hair that had again drifted over his cheek.

"Calvin, I didn't see your term paper on my desk. It was due today. Worth a third of your final grade. Problem?"

Cal shoved his hands in his pockets. For a moment he listened to the rev of the buses, inhaled the diesel-fueled exhaust pouring through the open windows. But he said nothing. He didn't have excuses to give.

"I know it's been a rough couple of weeks, so I'll give you a break." The teacher winked, still looking a little crazed holding his Einstein get-up. "You have the weekend to finish the paper but make it an oral report so you can share it with the class. Got it?"

Always a catch. The last thing he needed was more work— more attention. But as Cal filtered into the hallway, crowded with stares and whispers, he didn't care. All he could think about was diving into the pool and letting the pump of adrenaline obliterate the boundary between his body and the water. It offered the ultimate rush, the perfect release. Shoving open the locker room door, he knew he'd never needed that feeling —or lack of it—more than now.

"Yo, Cal. Over here."

He found Bill Emerling preening in front of a mirror, his body outlined by a slick silver suit.

"Cool, huh? The guys who used these at the Olympics blew away the competition. Glides better than human skin, they say."

"Looks expensive."

"Shit, yeah. But, hey, it's the latest gear. So, you guys better watch out!" He turned to his teammates who roundly ignored him, then started up on Cal. "Man, where'd you dig up *that* piece of crap? I didn't know the thrift store sold swim trunks. And who's that French guy on your tee shirt—*Les Paul*?"

Cal shrugged off Bill's bravado as easily as he pulled off his vintage guitar shirt. It was white noise coming from a guy who scraped through try-outs, whose lane time lagged behind the rookies. Some of the other guys, though, weren't up for Bill's bullshit.

"Look out. Emerling's got a new suit."

"Guess we'll have to sprout gills to catch him."

"Or fins!"

Bill spun and flexed his middle finger. "Assholes."

As the banter kicked up, a teammate peered around the corner. "Cal? Coach wants you."

Instantly, the laughter dried up. Cal re-zipped his jeans and splashed bare-foot across the tile floor, aware of conversations drizzling away like water down a drain. By the time he got to the coach's doorway, he wished he could drizzle away, too.

"Mr. Thornley?"

"Yes, Cal. Come in, come in." He indicated a chair near his desk, then glanced over to the case of trophies lining one wall.

He pointed with his chin toward the largest one. "You remember that meet, don't you? You're the reason we won it. Broke the school record for butterfly and shattered the regional time for backstroke." His smile faltered. "Exceptional swimmers are the reason I enjoy coaching—"

Thornley went on and Cal tuned out, ignoring the explanation moving through the pasty lips, the eyes that wouldn't look into his own. After all, people could say stuff they didn't mean, but they couldn't hide what they were feeling—at least not from him. Right now, all he saw was selfish energy radiating around the coach in an arc of tarnished yellow.

"—so, you see, I've done what I can for you, but there are forces out there not to be messed with—namely the Board of Education."

"Can I still practice with the team, you know, stay in shape for the next meet?"

The coach's mouth gaped. "Perhaps I haven't made myself clear. The Board wants you benched until this matter is resolved. Off the team." He straightened a manila folder on his desk with a stern tap. "Doesn't look good. One of our swimmers entangled in this arson thing."

"But I had nothing to do with... Look, just because I was there... I mean, the cops are saying a lot of stuff but it's not—"

"Ut, Ut," the coach said, extending his arm, motioning illegal procedure. "The Board president was insistent. After all, Zoe McClellan *is* a generous benefactor of our sports program here."

Star's aunt. Why wasn't he surprised?

"It's out of my hands. And *believe me,* this is hurting me as much as you—maybe more. Our division is tough. We need every win." The coach's voice trailed off as he stepped from the office and into the locker room. "And I thought we were going to go all the way this year..."

Cal sat there, disappointment sickening him like a lethal

poison. He waited until the slap of wet feet disappeared from the locker room, then headed back to collect his clothes. Some of the JV swimmers started filing in, careful to give Cal space, skirting around him like he was a leaky container ship oozing nuclear waste. He pulled on his shirt, grabbed his sneakers, then tossed the contents of his locker into a gym bag, ready to bolt.

"Hey, Cal. Hang on a minute."

Cal's head snapped up, hoping for news of a reprieve. But it was just that new kid, Orrin Parker.

"Tough break, man. Team needs you." His pale hands fingered a swim cap onto his head. "Coach caved."

Cal nodded, then looked harder, concentrating on the outline of the muscular body for so long, he might've left with a punch to the gut. But Cal couldn't help himself. It was amazing. This guy, who with his goggles and swim cap looked like a jacked white frog, had no visible sign of energy—at least none Cal could detect. He just looked—normal.

So, this was how everyone else swam through life. Listening, watching, then simply guessing whether someone meant what they said. It was cool. Uncomplicated. You could believe the best in a person without second-guessing the cloud of colors around them. How simple. How normal. How human.

CHAPTER
TWO

The swim team. Why the hell couldn't they take something else, like the privilege of going to chemistry class? Cal scanned the empty schoolyard. Buses long gone; walkers dissipated. He stood alone in front of the flagpole listening to the snap and ripple of the flag above him, feeling the whip of his hair against his neck. The wind stirred the heap of ashes across the street, lifting the scent of burnt ash into the air. His eyes followed the charcoal smell. The remains of Houdini's Grill stood like a blackened skeleton against the blue October sky, its vacant windowpanes hollow eye sockets. He shook his head. A tumble of bangs fell over his eyes, partly obscuring the view. But it couldn't obscure what he knew: that the authorities were wrong about what happened there. Just like they were wrong about Alula McClellan.

He wiped the sweat from his brow, pulled back his hair with a small band, and hoisted his gym bag to his shoulder. Turning from the schoolyard, he drifted along the back streets until he reached the end of Fox Sedge Avenue. There the boardwalk began its long zigzag over the marsh before dropping off on the North side where the muddy water stretched along every backyard and usually into them.

He reached his house on the far side of Creeping Cress Court, dodging a stagnant puddle at the end of the driveway. Trudging up the side steps, he let the screen door slam behind him then pulled the strap of his gym bag off his shoulder. It dropped to the floor with a thunk. That's when he saw the note stuck beneath the candy dish:

Cal: Court clerk called. You're due at Oakwood Cemetery by 4:00 p.m. It's the best of your options. Don't be late. Mom

The boneyard. Great. He dropped his head into his hands. How could something he had nothing to do with screw-up his life so completely?

"Tough day?"

And now Eva. Despite her question, there was nothing sympathetic in her tone. She came up from the side door, her boots hitting hard against the oak steps.

"Had quite the day myself," she continued. "Of course, you deserved what you got, while I had to put up with all sorts of crap because I happen to be related to the notorious Calvin Hughes."

Wanting no part of the argument Eva was working herself up to, Cal got to his feet. "I'm gonna go jam."

"Oh, right. That reminds me—"

Something in the curl of Eva's lip forced Cal back into his seat. She seemed to sense his worry and played with it, leaning over the table, sifting through the sweets at the bottom of the candy dish, fishing out the last package of sour gummy bears —his favorite—before tearing at the wrapper.

"Turk came by yesterday." She popped the bears in her mouth one at a time, smacking her lips as she chewed. "Said something about rehearsal...you blowing it off...him being pissed..."

"Yesterday? Why didn't you tell me sooner?"

His sister shrugged.

"Eva, I coulda caught up with him, made the end of rehearsal."

"Then maybe Turk should break open his piggy bank and buy a cellphone."

"He's saving for a sound system for the band."

"And that's *my* problem?"

"Did you at least tell him where I was, why I wasn't at rehearsal?"

Her eyes made a suspended roll. "Hmmm... I don't recall."

"Look, why didn't you just tell him I was tied up in court?"

"Why don't you, if you're so proud of it!" she snapped. "Besides, everyone on this side of the planet already seems to know where you were last night. If Turk wants to keep tabs on you, tell him to get a police radio and tune in."

Cal met Eva's accusing green glare with crushing silence. Right there, he wanted to tell her everything, that yeah, maybe he was a freak, but not for any of the reasons she imagined. He thought differently and felt differently because he *saw* differently and it made him do things that no one else would do unless they saw and felt the things he did.

Instead, he got up, pushed his chair aside and strode out the side door. With a quiet fury, he walked toward Alder Lane and Bittersweet Road. But by the time he reached the wetlands, he began to stall. The steady creak and groan of the boardwalk seemed to beg him to stop. Picking up a flat pebble, he rolled it in his palm then winged it across the marsh, skimming the water with four rapid-fire skips. Nice. Still had it. He smiled and slid down the bank—checking for carp, foraging around for crayfish, lingering at his childhood playground even as the sun faded and an odd mist crept over the muddy water.

After a while, he climbed back onto the boardwalk and leaned against the wobbly rail. He smiled again as he watched the pond snails and the trace of slimy patterns they left behind inching toward deep water on their fall pilgrimage. His smile fell away. If he were a snail, he wouldn't need to go a step further. He was already in deep water—way over his head.

He grabbed another pebble, more of a rock, and chucked it into the green water.

Okay, so maybe he knew how the fire started—it didn't mean he set it. Still, rumors traveled fast here, like the flash floods that raced through the marsh during spring rains. Lieutenant Gavin had already told half the town the "Hughes kid" was guilty. One of those no-good punks from the North side. His son, Tom, had butted heads with Cal a bunch of times, and the good lieutenant was quick to throw that smoldering heap of circumstantial evidence on the case as well.

"You don't always need fingerprints to crack a case," Gavin liked to say. And in places like West Shelby, Cal knew you didn't need wind to fan a fire.

He started walking again, his palm brushing over the plants and weeds that lined the boardwalk. Fall was full on. He could smell the decay, plants dying all around him. His fingers grazed a cluster of rushes crisping to a rich brown, then past the sedges drying like golden straw. And the water soldiers? No point looking for them. They were long gone with the summer, sunk deep below the marsh until next year. At the honk of a goose, Cal's gaze lifted skyward. The herons and egrets had already checked out. After the Canadian geese left, the blue jays would brave the bitter winter here alone.

For a moment, it grew quiet. There wasn't a stir in the air, a soul in sight. For the first time that day, that week, that month,

Cal felt his world ripple with a tranquil vibe. Closing his eyes, he breathed it in as if it were the last gulp of oxygen on earth. Here, he felt as close to normal as his life would ever allow.

Strange, then, that it was here it'd all fallen apart.

He was just a kid—five years old—drawn by every buzz and croak gurgling up from the late August marsh. A kid's paradise. Cal smiled, remembering the endless scavenger hunts, the muddy water, his muddier clothes. One day, as dusk settled over the water, he spied one of the season's last water soldiers and reached for it. He heard a huff, looked up and saw a hooded figure foraging around down the marshy creek. He couldn't tell who it was but remembered the determination of the slender hands as they searched through the reeds along the shore. As he scooped the lily from the water, he looked over. Though he couldn't see the face, he suspected it wasn't smiling back.

Hours later, his parents found him, unconscious, sprawled on the boardwalk, confused. At first, he thought the strange light around his family was some trick of their flashlights. But from then on, the clouds of colored energy wavered around them—around everyone—telling him things he didn't want to know, forcing him to tune into a dimension he didn't want to see.

He never told anyone what he saw. Easier to be normal that way. Or pretend to be. Not long after, the tremors started. Cal glanced down, flexed his fingers. His hands were still now, but any second, they could start trembling. Early on, his parents tried therapy for him, medicine, herbs, even new age remedies. Nothing worked. Soon enough, the name-calling started up. By middle school, he'd been in more fights than he cared to remember. Now, on a good day, he was just glad to be ignored. And though he never picked anything from the muddy waters again, Cal found he still loved to be out on the marsh.

Reaching the South side, he paused at the fork in the path. Instead of heading east toward town and every other place he'd ever needed to go, he veered right onto a dirt trail. Old-timers used it as a short-cut to Ackley's Bend but as Cal brushed aside the overgrown brambles, he guessed it'd been a long time since anyone had trudged down to the fishing hole or up to the cemetery tucked higher along the rough trail.

As he climbed, Cal's eyes wandered toward the changing view below. The warm afternoon sun had already dissolved into the fog stealing over the marshlands. It blurred the lines of the landscape, like some fancy French painting. He could hardly hear the sounds shushing up from the water—the croak of frogs burrowing into the mud, the buzz of dragonfly nymphs, the stir of bulrushes. Even as his feet adjusted to the path, rising and snaking up the hill, his attention remained fixed on the ghostly fingers of mist drifting over the marsh. He was so focused that he nearly stumbled face-first into the entrance of Oakwood Cemetery.

Stepping back from the gate's sharp points, Cal blinked a few times. Then he leaned forward and peered between the iron bars. Gravestones tipped in every direction, weeds climbed the wrought-iron fence, flowers wilted in the shade and at the top of the wild grassy hill, a cobbled work shed, bearded with ivy and capped with moss, slumped like an old troll.

Cal rolled his tongue in his cheek, turned, and looked back down the path. He could head back home. Pretend he couldn't find the place. But he was already in a shitload of trouble.

Glancing back toward the cemetery, he reached out and poked at the gate like it was a sleeping scorpion. It opened with a low whine, then seemed to sigh as it swept closed behind him.

Guess he was staying.

With measured steps, Cal walked through the graveyard. The blanket of fog crept with him, engulfing the place that already seemed a world away from West Shelby in a soft mist.

Not even sure if he was in the right place, Cal began to look around for someone—anyone—who could explain what he was supposed to do here. He brushed past a row of needle-sharp pines, then glanced up at the oak trees so tall he couldn't see their tops. Colored leaves drifted down, end-over-end like confetti at some sad party where no one had come. It made him want to yell or shout just to hear a sound, and he wondered again what the hell he was supposed to do. Cut the lawn? Rake the leaves? Sure, he could blow off eight or ten hours, but a hundred? Not unless they expected him to polish each gravestone by hand. The corners of his mouth inched upward, then fell. Maybe they did.

As he neared the shed, the fog shifted, spiraling around the stone building like a silk cocoon. Coming up on the long side, Cal cupped his hand against a small window. The dark silhouettes inside revealed nothing. He rounded a corner and found the garage door slumped in its frame and, beside it, a smaller door ajar. Inching it open, he stepped inside. The choking smell of gasoline and motor oil caught in his throat. As his eyes squinted through the poor light, he felt the creepy drape of cobwebs curtaining down, landing on his shoulders. They fell over every surface and grayed the tools along the cluttered walls. Uncertain, Cal shuffled toward an old workbench hoping there'd be a note, something that might give him direction. He tripped over a watering can and a flurry of spiders scattered from beneath it, forcing a burst of dust into the air. Light-headed, he covered his face with his sleeve and coughed just as a voice came booming up from behind.

"Boo!"

Cal jerked around. A tall man with huge bent shoulders

emerged from the dust cloud, his wide yellowy eyeballs glaring like a pair of egg yolks from the bottom of a black skillet.

"Sorry, for comin' up on you like that. Did I frighten you?"

Cal stared at him. "No."

The man muttered something about trying harder next time, then held out his hand. "I'm Stan Heyman, the caretaker here." His handshake took Cal by surprise. Its power seemed to surge through his arm, yet the fingers had a weightless quality about them.

The man hoisted the garage door and fresh air rushed into the workshop. "I can always use volunteers around here, any pair of willin' hands."

Cal hesitated. "Uh, I'm here to work off a hundred hours. Community service—court-ordered."

The man's demeanor grew serious. "Hmm, we better get goin' then. The clock's runnin'. Behind you there you'll find hand tools—hoes, rakes, shovels, spades—a bin for rags and hooks full of extension cords and hoses. Over there are the trimmers. They need greasin' after every use, just like the mulcher. It 'll clog like an old drain if you don't clean it now and again." He held up his hand as if to squelch some silent protest. "I know, I know, obvious stuff, but sometimes the simplest things are the hardest to remember—unfortunately, they're often the most important, too."

The caretaker drew Cal further into the cavernous room, ducking beneath low beams while his hands swatted away cobwebs with an almost rhythmic movement.

"Over there is the workbench with a slew of spare parts—nuts, bolts, gaskets—anything you might need. The loppers and hand pruners are in the far corner and these here are the mowers. I'm afraid you'll be fixin 'em as much as you'll be cuttin' with 'em. That's why we resort to the old-fashioned method most days."

The old man patted the handle of an ancient hand mower, its perennial readiness an obvious winning point. "You any good with engines?"

Cal glanced at the jigsaw of rusted parts lying about. "A little."

"Well, you'll know a whole lot more 'n that when I'm done with you!" The man laughed, ducking his gray scrub brush of a head as he passed another low beam.

Cal followed, his head rising and falling in tandem with the curious caretaker's. His heart sank with every step. He didn't think community service would be like this, stuck with a boss showing him the ropes like he was going to make a career of it. A hundred hours? No wa—

Whack!

Distracted, Cal's head finally caught one of the low cross-beams in a solid hit.

The caretaker glanced back. "I was goin' to warn you about that one, but a good smack to the head is all the remindin' anyone ever needs. You won't forget again."

Cal rubbed his left temple. "Thanks."

"Last thing I got to show you is back here, an old wash basin that you can use to scrub off the mud and grease that's gonna stick to you like glue."

Cal squinted. The wattage from the bare light bulb hanging over the work bench didn't quite reach. But he didn't care, not about pumice soap or paint thinner or whatever else the old man stashed at the shed's back end. He took a breath and coughed. The air tasted like mildew and smelled like rot and he wondered how his life had gotten so screwed up that spending Friday afternoon in a graveyard listening to an old man talk about rusty tools like they were his best friends was "the best of his options".

"Well, enough of the grand tour." The caretaker slapped his thick palms together, turned and headed toward the mouth of the shed. Outside, he surveyed the graveyard as if it was a giant chess board. Watching him, Cal saw an intensity in the large yellowy eyes. Tinges of black still streaked the wooly gray mat of hair on his head and the guy looked strong, like he still hit the gym now and then. When not bent by the confines of the work shed, the caretaker stretched well over six feet.

"Normally, I'd set you right to the grass. With these temperatures, the lawn's been growin' like it was June. But seein' as the trees have figured out its autumn, we'd better get to the leaves first."

Cal looked at his watch. Fifteen minutes down. Ninety-nine hours, forty-five minutes to go.

Ducking into the shed, the caretaker returned with a pair of rakes, then led Cal along a wandering path to a circle of ancient maple trees. "We'll start in the high-rent district." The caretaker grinned. "I like to call it Centerfield."

As Cal walked toward the yard's tallest tombstones, he found himself shuffling knee-deep into the leaves.

"You don't have a leaf blower, huh?" he asked, struggling at times to maintain his balance.

Stan leaned upon the rake's handle, puckered his lips and let his brow wrinkle with concentration. "I recollect we do," he said, popping his lips. "Two, in fact. One needs fixin' though and the other's missin' a part."

For the rest of the afternoon, the steady scrape-crunch rhythm of their rakes filled the autumn air. As they moved out of centerfield and made their way down the yard, the caretaker tried small talk. But Cal wasn't into it. He felt like he'd fallen into some weird time vacuum. He glanced at his phone. It didn't seem right. Maybe there wasn't any service here. A dead-zone—in more ways than one. It felt like he'd been working for hours. It had to be six, maybe seven o'clock. Already, he felt the chill of late afternoon creeping into his chest, his hands blistering around the rake's handle.

Snatching another time check on his phone, he suddenly lost footing and fell backward, hitting the ground hard, smashing his shoulder on a gravestone. He tried to get up, take a breath, but his lungs balked, his feet wobbled. It felt like some underground gravity was weighing him down. Gasping a few times, he detected a drizzle of blood beading up through his torn shirt and was about to check it out when he saw the caretaker's expression.

"What?"

Stan didn't answer. He just stood in the adjoining row glaring at the back of the black glossy tombstone which Cal had fallen against, the yellowy eyes hot enough to sear a hole right through the back of the granite. Then, as the old man turned toward Cal, he let his rake rest against the massive stone. Damn if it didn't seem to sink, shrinking under the rake's slight weight.

But Cal wasn't sure if his mind was right, if anything was right. His chest ached and his shoulder stung. Stan offered him a hand. Cal grabbed it and felt as if a crane was hoisting him off the ground. He sucked in a breath and felt his lungs inflate. After a second, he gave his head a shake.

"Let's have a look at your arm there." The old man fingered aside the flaps of torn flannel. "Hmm, just a brush burn." He turned and picked up his rake again. "It'll heal."

Cal glanced beneath the tear in his upper sleeve, then did a double-take. There was nothing. Nothing. He could have sworn that stone cut him. He'd felt the gash, the blood seeping through his skin.

"Well, seein' as this is your first day, you can wrap things up, if you'd like," the old man said, his voice jovial again. "Don't worry, you'll find your balance." He added, "Not much day light left anyway, and the marsh is no place to be after dark."

Releasing the rake into the caretaker's outstretched hand,

Cal turned and negotiated the downward slope, dodging the mounds of leaves and tombstones as if they were landmines. He was just a few rows from the gate when the sound of a lone rake echoed down through the graveyard. Glancing back, he saw that the place wasn't even half cleared. A dozen piles of leaves littered the yard. They seemed to float upon the smoky mist of late afternoon like little volcanic islands. Unless they self-erupted, Cal knew they'd have to be moved. In an instant, he thought of everything he'd rather be doing then heard himself say, "Want some more help?"

The caretaker looked at each of the piles, then back to the shed some fifty yards away. His lips curled into a thick smile. "You got time?"

Yeah, Cal wanted to say. Ninety-eight more hours.

For the rest of the afternoon, he helped the old man collect and drag the leaves back to an enormous compost heap behind the shed. By dusk, the fog hung so thick he could hardly see Stan on the other side of the old tarp they used for each haul.

"You've been a real help today, son," the caretaker said after the final drop. "Just keep showin' up and I'll track your hours for you." He fingered a pencil stub and a faded yellow piece of paper into his shirt pocket.

Cal nodded, turned, and began to walk down through the yard.

"Watch yer step," the old man called after him. "I'll see you tomorrow."

Cal's sneakers squeaked to a halt. He considered work, rehearsal and homework all at once. "Tomorrow? I can't make it."

"Well, next week then. We can't mow on Sunday. Seein' as tomorrow is Halloween there'll be plenty to do by Monday."

Cal turned and headed toward the marsh once more, the iron gate visible only by its tips poking through the fog like skewers in a crème sauce. He tugged at it. The gate groaned as it swung wide. For a moment, Cal let his hand linger on the damp metal. He peered back through the bars. But there was nothing to see. The shed and the gravestones and the caretaker were gone, swallowed by the pervasive mist and the encroaching veil of nightfall.

CHAPTER
THREE

As Cal wound his way down from the cemetery, he stopped on the bridge to listen to the gentle lap-lap-lap of the water below. Eventually, his gaze shifted toward town, the dusky skyline just bright enough to trace the gothic profile of St. Francis Church. He envied the statues, becoming silhouettes against the sky. Soon they would blend with the darkness and simply become night. He wished he could go and dissolve with them, too.

Closer by, he scanned the shoreline. A forlorn cluster of summer cottages along the North side gave way to the estates on the high bank of the South end. The grandest, by far, belonged to Star's aunt. Hidden by a drape of willows at the property's edge, its chandelier glimmered through the branches, casting golden tiers of light on the cove's marshy waters.

It reminded him of what he saw when he looked at Star, what no one else could see: a vivid ring of energy glistening like a halo. No matter how many times Cal saw the light around her, it never failed to astonish him. But after Star's sister went missing, that amazing field of energy began to falter. Started right after the memorial service. If he had any sense at all, he'd stay out of it, steer clear of the whole family. He knew well enough that beautiful things could be dangerous. Still, he felt compelled—

"This is a hell of a place to hang out."

Cal turned, startled. On the other end of the bridge, Star sat watching him, her legs swinging down from the rail, her lips black and glossy, her eyes checking him out.

"You look like... Where've you been?"

Cal glanced down. Grass stains streaked his jeans, mud splattered his white sneakers. He thought he caught her eyes lingering over the muscles in his upper chest—swimming laps had its advantages.

"At the graveyard. You know, community service."

She shook her head. "So, you're still holding out about the arsonist. And those gorgeous blue eyes look so innocent."

She grinned, a liquid sweetness softening her brown eyes. Only Cal was the one melting. It made him want to tell Star what he knew, how he knew it, why he was convinced Alula wasn't dead. But telling her he saw things no one else could see, that he could watch the fabric of a soul unfold—wouldn't suddenly make him an amazing guy, just a kid with a mental quirk to go along with his physical one.

"Look, sometimes stuff happens and I"— his voice got thick and he realized he was terrified of what Star might think of him—"I just buck up and deal with it."

Star looked at him, her eyebrows scrunched, then the corner of her mouth lifted, a dimple denting her cheek. "I bet Princess Eva's pissed about all the drama, so kudos for that anyway. Still doesn't explain why you took the rap for the fire."

"It's a stupid rumor. I had nothing to do with that arson. Besides, the trespassing charges were dropped. They just

27

nailed me with community service 'cause I wouldn't talk. Thought I knew something."

"Do you?"

Cal shook his head, his bangs waving like golden marsh grass. "Look, it was a mistake. Sort of. Bill didn't mean to—"

"Bill Emerling? You're covering for that idiot?"

Cal sighed. His eyes shot over the darkened waters. "It's—it's complicated."

He heard Star's deep exasperated sigh, then watched as she stretched across the rail, the soft curve of her hips accentuated by the hug of her skinny black jeans.

"Or maybe it just seems that way 'cause you're here, standing over this swamp. Honestly, you've gotta find another place to hang out. All this muddy water, it's messing with your head." Star peered over the rail. "Chemicals. Pollution. Something..." Suddenly she jerked back.

Cal watched her face pale. She bit her lip, craning her neck just far enough to see past the rail. For a moment, she became a statue, gaping at something beneath the surface of the water. After a moment, she leaned back and shook her head.

"What is it?"

Her fingers, blackened with nail polish, pressed over her eyes, stretching the lids in circles. "Just tired. Thought I saw something."

"Like?"

"A reflection but...not mine." Star glanced back toward the water, then turned away. "I swear it's this stinking marsh. Never had trouble when I lived at my father's house. Then I had to move *there*." She pointed toward her aunt's sprawling home perched above the water. "My head hasn't been right since."

Cal glanced back to the McClellan estate still visible in the milky gray twilight. Darkening the corner of one towering window, he saw a silhouette watching from behind a veil of sheer curtains.

"Doesn't look like such a bad place from here."

Star hopped down from the rail, her high-heeled boots striking the planks of the bridge with renewed attitude.

"Yeah, Aunt Zoe's done all right for herself. Homeopath. Best around, I'm told. That is before her health tanked and forced her into retirement." Star glanced back toward the peak of the black cupola rising behind the willows. "She is a sweet-heart, though. Never hassles me. My room's a raging mess. I don't eat the stuff she cooks. Never do the dishes. Pretty much come and go as I please. But every now and then, I break down and have a cup of tea with her." She shrugged in a careless way that he loved. "After all, she's got to be hurting, too."

Star came alongside Cal, propped her foot up against the rail and let her shoulder brush against his. A soft, musky scent wafted toward him. He watched her eyes make a nervous glance toward the water, then blink away. After a moment, she looked up at him and grinned, the sweetness in her eyes playing off the tough edges of her facade. "She doesn't like you much, though."

Cal's brows arched.

"Yeah, I know. She likes everyone else. But when I mention your name, she gets all weird."

Cal was still digesting the idea that Star had brought up his name, that her aunt had any opinion at all about him, when his hands began to tremble. He grit his teeth, placed his hands square on the rail, and pressed them into the rotted wood until they stilled.

"Hey, are you alright?" Star's eyes squinted, so they looked as narrow as the swirl of cinnamon on toast. "You know, you really need to chill somewhere else."

He took a deep breath, then lifted his eyes to the darkening sky, watching as the first stars blinked into view. It offered him a chance to change tacks. "So, which one are you named after?"

Star tilted her chin and scanned the sky. "None of them. My father named me after his favorite flower—" she scrunched her nose, "—*Aster*. But my mother preferred Star, the shape of the flower. It stuck—thank God."

"What about Alula?"

"Cool, right? An actual palindrome. Way better than *Aster*, anyway."

Cal kept gazing at the stars, gathering courage. For the past few weeks, he'd seen a smoky cloud of doom gathering around Star. Just like he'd seen for her sister. He had no idea what the right thing to do or say was, but somehow had to clue her in—without tipping his hand about his own painful truth.

Star seemed to sense his distraction. "Hello?"

He hesitated, then turned toward her, his ponytail brushing the back of his neck. "I was just thinking."

She cocked her head in a way that let a pair of pink strands tumble sensuously over her eyes. Even her blackened lips slipped into a smile, the single dimple in her cheek deepening.

Her voice gave a provocative rise. "About?"

"Your sister."

Cal could hear her breath heave beneath the collection of chains and amulets layered over her chest.

"I think about her, too," she said, her eyes glistening. "About her cute expression, all those freckles—too big and too many for such a little face. How she smiled even when she was sick. Which seemed like all the time." For a moment, Star's whole body seemed to sag under the weight of her thoughts.

"I meant I was wondering…" He didn't know how to say it, how to sound anything other than stark raving crazy. "If she needs help?"

Star looked toward the darkened water invisible at the

other end of the marsh. "Nothing can help her now. She's down there somewhere with the water soldiers…"

"Only if you believe it. If you believe the lie."

Star's boot slipped off the rail and hit the boards with a thud. Even in the near darkness, Cal could see her eyes flare, the flecks of light within them blaze like fire. Her lips rolled into a fierce pout.

"Is that some kinda joke?"

"Star, it's just—things don't add up."

"Like?"

"The drowning."

"Alula couldn't swim. She was four years old. What's so hard to understand about that?"

"What about the memorial service? There was no body."

"They couldn't find it." Star began to pace, her footsteps angry assaults against the boardwalk. "For God's sake, they dredged the marsh three times!"

"Exactly."

"Everyone knows the current on the east side is wild. Especially when it rains hard like…like it did that week. It pours right into the river."

Cal didn't let up. "What about your father?"

"He was misunderstood. No one appreciated his passion for science."

"I mean his suicide."

Star began to back away, nearly tripping over a raised plank. "H-he was with Alula when she fell into the water. Probably felt responsible for what happened."

Cal went on. "Then there's the stuff I saw at her memorial service—"

Star's eyes became razors. "What do you mean?"

Cal reconsidered. "Forget it."

A choking silence fell over them then, broken only by the rustle of dried reeds shifting below the boardwalk. Star's lips began to tremble, but she seemed quick to steel herself against the emotion. For all the fire in her eyes, her expression turned to ice.

"You know, I never pay attention to what people say about you, about how weird you are. We've known each other since forever, but now…" She turned away, tugging the waist of her skintight leather jacket. "…well maybe you *are* crazy."

Cal tried to salvage the train-wreck of a conversation even as Star disappeared down the boardwalk. "Look, I'm just trying to help…."

He stared after her, even when there was only darkness to stare at. He heard the shushing of the marsh water beneath the bridge—*tsk, tsk, tsk*—it seemed to scold him.

Of course, she'd stormed off. Who wouldn't be pissed? He'd just told her that her dead sister wasn't dead, the funeral was a sham and her dad's suicide was suspicious. Evidence? Zero. Because he didn't have the guts to tell Star how he knew what he knew.

The price of clinging to normalcy. When there was nothing about his life that was normal.

CHAPTER
FOUR

Still stinging over his run in with Star, Cal got ready for work the next evening wondering why he couldn't let the Alula-thing go. But then, that was like asking a person why they breathe. When something felt wrong, when something looked wrong—at least to him—there was no letting it go, even if it meant messing up his life beyond repair or turning off people he'd give anything to be with. Like Star.

As he readjusted his black bow tie in the hallway mirror, he could tell Eva was in a snit. She couldn't find her uniform, her favorite hair tie, or some other near-crisis, so he stepped outside for a moment to breathe in the quiet of the night. It didn't last.

"Calvin? Oh, Calvin? Over here."

Reluctantly, he walked over to his neighbor's driveway.

"One of my cats has gone missing. Fitsy and Mr. Tibbs napped all afternoon, but Ellsworth was restless, so I let him out. It's been three hours. I've tried calling his name, even ringing the treat bell, but no sign of him." Her milky eyes scanned the neighborhood as she clutched a pair of tangled leashes in her frail hand. "Thank goodness I kept the kittens inside, what with this fog and all.

Cal glanced across the marsh in the direction of the McClellan estate. Wasn't sure why. It seemed a place where people and things disappeared. "I'm sure he'll show up, Mrs. Kenefick. Probably just checking out the reeds for mice. Sometimes people dump garbage out there."

"No, Calvin," she insisted. "I can *feel* it." Her drooping eyelids fluttered and the tips of her fingers began to undulate like the tentacles of a giant jellyfish. "Ellsworth is in trouble, I *know* it."

"Why don't you take Fitsy and Mr. Tibbs inside? We're headed to my uncle's place tonight, but I can look around when we get back."

The old woman's eyes snapped open and beamed at the restless felines that circled her feet. "Mr. Calvin's going to find your friend. Isn't he wonderful?"

The cats twisted their fluffy heads toward Cal, then purred a decided no.

"You are such a dear, Calvin. Really, I mean it. No matter what people say about you. Wait. Before you go. Come over here. Give me your hand. No, no, it's no trouble. I insist. It's the least I can do for you."

Cal tensed, knowing what was to come. Mrs. Kenefick grasped his hand and gave it a small shake. There was a silent implication that if he couldn't manage to hold it still, she would do it for him. Then she lowered her face over his hand and let her breath, dry as dust, puff over his skin.

"Hmm. Yes, right here. It's good news, Calvin. You're entering a very fortunate period. Good things coming your way. I bet it's started already. Yes? Yes?"

He nearly laughed aloud. Her prediction couldn't have been more wrong. But then, Mrs. Kenefick's divinations were always vague and conveniently retroactive. Like last year, when she told all the neighbors she *knew* the marsh was going to flood—after everyone's basements were already wet.

"Probably noticed the positive change at school this week, hmm?" she continued. "Well, if not, next week for sure." She glanced back down at his palm, her eyes widening as she stroked along a different crease in his skin. "But what's this? An old friend causing trouble? Well Calvin, I'd watch out for that one."

Cal glanced over his shoulder. Eva stood waiting in the driveway, her foot tapping an impatient beat.

The old woman looked past Cal and frowned. "Tart one, isn't she?"

"Gotta go, Mrs. K."

———

Cal jogged past their driveway and joined Eva, who was already walking up the street, her mood as black as the night.

"I can't believe Mom is making us work tonight. There are at least two parties I could have gone to. Instead, I'm here, walking halfway across the neighborhood just to get the car keys so we can go to Uncle Max's place." Cal followed her up the stoop to the Emerlings' front door and waited while she jabbed at their doorbell.

"And for the record? I don't see why Mr. Emerling's little midlife crisis has to complicate *our* lives." A new sense of injustice narrowed her green eyes. "And it definitely shouldn't require Dad to pick up the slack."

"Maybe Mrs. Emerling isn't as cool with the divorce as she pretends," Cal said, sounding speculative.

"She's handling it fine. Besides, if the dishwasher breaks, she needs to learn how to call a repair service. And what about your buddy, Bill? Can't he fix it for his mother? Or is his skill set limited to playing football and being rude?" Eva crossed her arms and leaned against the wrought-iron railing. "Thank God Tori isn't like her brother."

The door rattled open and Mrs. Emerling offered a fleeting smile. "I guess you're looking for Bill and Tori. They're not home. They're—" she struggled to say the words, "—at their father's place in town."

"Actually, we're here to see our dad," Eva explained. "We tried to call. Can we come in?"

"Oh, I don't pick up the phone these days. Too many robo calls."

Cal and Eva stepped past Mrs. Emerling and walked through the house that had been like a second home to them. Brushing by a stack of newspapers and a pile of laundry in the hallway, they found their father in the kitchen, his head lodged inside the mouth of the dishwasher.

"I think I've found it, Dee," he said, his voice echoing out as if he were in the back of a cave. "You're lucky. It won't cost you a dime. It's just a fork." He pulled the culprit out into the open and brandished it. "Caught in the overflow protector." Noticing his children in the kitchen, he smiled. "Great costumes, guys!"

"Dad, they're not—" Eva rolled her eyes. "—forget it. Mom says you have the car keys. Uncle Max's, remember? He'll have an aneurism if we're late."

"Got 'em right here." He motioned with his chin toward his shirt pocket, then leaned in toward the sink and edged aside a few plates and a sticky blender to wash his hands. "Well, Deidre, I think we're done here. I'm going to head out with the kids now. You should be good. Dee? Deidre?"

But Mrs. Emerling didn't seem to hear. She was lost somewhere, a different place, a better time maybe. A shower of gray ashes tumbled from her cigarette. Cal didn't mean to stare. Really. But her energy…God, it was just so broken. Eva caught his too-long glance and gave him a quick jab to the ribs. Cal jumped, knocking into a stack of plastic plates that clattered from the counter and wheeled off across the kitchen floor.

The sound snapped Mrs. Emerling from her daze. As Cal raced to scoop up the runaway plates, she began a desperate slew of bribes—soft drinks, chips, cookies, a mixed drink for their dad—to postpone their departure. Eva, nudging her father to the door, declined for all of them. By the time she and Cal were speeding toward Uncle Max's catering hall, she had more than a few choice words.

"What was with you back there? It's like you're five-years-old or something. Can't you control yourself?"

Cal looked at his sister for a long, disappointed moment, amazed after all these years that she hadn't put at least some of the pieces together, that she didn't have a clue about him. She radiated intuition, had the energy to move mountains, but wasted it sweating over small stuff. Finally, he just shrugged. He knew Eva wanted some kind of confirmation, a pledge he would try and be a better brother, a normal person when, really, he couldn't promise any of those things.

Arriving in the bustling back kitchen of Maxine's Catering, their uncle gave them a big smile, but Cal and Eva quickly learned the price of showing up late for work.

"Figures we get stuck up here in the old banquet hall," Eva muttered as she finished the last of the place settings.

Cal concentrated on folding a limp napkin into a sort of pyramid before it collapsed in a shapeless heap. "The guys in the kitchen said the downstairs room got a buffet."

"Yeah. We get stuck with table service and no carts. We'll have to tray everything."

Cal eyed the musty room crowded with cheap folding chairs, paper streamers, and a mirrored ball that spun lazily above the dance floor. In the corner, a white cake layered with sugared roses teetered beside the bar which would stay open so long as everyone kept their fists in their pockets and the father-of-the-bride kept the tab going.

"Man, this place needs a makeover," Eva said. "Plastic centerpieces? Come on. What about tea lights or candles?"

"You know Uncle Max," Cal smirked. "His insurance premiums would go up and his bottom line would go down. Disaster."

Eva's smile faltered. "I guess the candles *could* be a—fire hazard."

The words set an awkward chill between them. Cal was glad when a voice from the kitchen yelled out, "They're here!"

Cal and Eva waited until the bridal party took their seats. When the best man raised his glass for the toast, they slipped back into the kitchen and found the prep staff in high gear. They filled Cal's tray first and kept it that way all evening. He guessed the time he'd spent joking around with Juan and the rest of the kitchen crew early on hadn't hurt. Eva, on the other hand, had been glued to her phone, whining to her friends about the parties she was missing. This small kink in the overall serving process played out poorly for Eva in the dining room and her tables were quick to notice:

"If we were sitting on *that* side of the room, we'd be halfway through dinner by now," a woman with a high hairdo announced to her friends. "I hope the food isn't cold when it gets here 'cause I'll send it back. I swear, I will."

Cal watched Eva try to make up time. Hoisting a tray of empty salad plates to her shoulder, she wheeled around the room, through the swinging doors and down the steeply angled stairs toward the kitchen, her soft-toed shoes feeling blindly for the edge of each step. Just as she hit the halfway point, her knee buckled. The tray began to tip wildly in her arms, veering toward one wall, then the next. In a single leap, Cal managed to catch her and steady the tray. A pair of glass bowls weren't so lucky, spilling over the side and exploding at his feet.

"You okay?" he asked, stooping beside Eva while balancing the wide tray on the stair above.

"Yeah, it's just my knee—ouch! Don't touch it!"

"Is this from the…"

"Yeah," she said, brushing his hand aside. "I fell at school during the evacuation for the fire. Been bothering me ever since. Kinda like *you*."

The jab didn't even register on Cal. He was preoccupied with the ooze dribbling from the broken scab, the red streaks drizzling away as if the blood beneath her skin was on fire.

"Eva, you should've seen a doctor days ago. This looks like blood poisoning."

"I have to get back to my tables. I'm way behind." She braced her hands against the stairwell to get up but winced and eased back onto the stair.

"Hey, the kitchen's getting backed-up down here. What's going on?" Uncle Max bellowed from the kitchen doorway.

"Just an accident. No big deal, we've got it." Eva reached over to scoop up the glass chards from the stairs then chucked them onto her tray. "Like they were made of gold or something…" she muttered before turning to punch away her brother's arm. "Cal, leave it alone already. My knee is fine. It feels better now. Hey, you all right?"

He wasn't. Touching the wound, transferring his energy, had basically flattened him. But before he could explain, Uncle Max hollered up the stairs again and, without another word, he and Eva were back on their feet, darting in opposite directions.

An hour later, as the whirr of crushed ice announced the reopening of the bar and dance music began to thump through the speakers, the wedding shifted into post-dinner mode. With a reckless clatter, Cal scooped up a fistful of soiled silverware and dumped it onto his tray. It slid against a jumbled stack of dishes that looked as unsteady as a Jenga tower.

He was about to lift the tray when he looked up and caught a glimpse of his sister on the other side of the room watching him, a shit-eating grin plastered across her face. *Bet you can't do it*, she mouthed.

How much? his lips motioned back.

Standing behind the head table, Eva crossed her arms and considered the precarious tray, then lifted five fingers. Cal grabbed two empty glasses from a nearby table, raised them for her inspection, then skillfully added them to the tray's rim. He counter-offered with a flex of ten fingers and a crooked half-smile.

Eva shook her head.

Cal reconsidered his load, forgetting even as the wedding raged around him that he had anything more urgent to do than prove his sister wrong. He piled on two more dinner plates, a coffee cup and wine glass, then looked up. Eva nodded.

Concentrating on the challenge, Cal surveyed the tray and its weight distribution with scientific scrutiny. Shifting a water glass to the left side and a couple of forks to the right, he scanned the tray's equilibrium one more time, then, with a weight-lifter's grunt, hoisted the load over his head. Eva's eyes bulged, but just as her hands moved to applaud the feat, Uncle Max zoomed up from behind Cal.

Uh-oh.

Abruptly, Eva turned away, pulling fresh packets of sugar and tiny buckets of half-and-half from her pocket while Cal suffered an earful, his dish-clearing bravado unappreciated. Finishing the lecture, Uncle Max yanked the tray from Cal's grasp, pointed toward the kitchen and, just like that, Cal was gone.

A couple hours later, Eva hunted him down in the kitchen.

Hoisting herself onto one of the empty serving carts, she asked, "So, what was the verdict?"

"What d'you think?" Cal answered, snapping a dishrag at the sink he was scrubbing. "Sentenced to hard labor."

"At least you weren't stuck out there," she tossed her head toward the banquet room, "dealing with drunken assholes all night."

The first set of kitchen lights clicked off as Uncle Max came hurtling through the swinging doors, his bald head damp with perspiration. "Sorry about the delay. Thought I'd seen every-thing…unbelievable…right in the middle of the last dance—bam! The maid of honor decked the groom. I'm lucky it didn't turn into a wholesale brawl. The furniture…"

He walked around doling out tips, mostly tens and twen-ties, to the crew before they sifted out the back door and into the alleyway. Cal edged his way to the front of the pack.

"Hold up there, Cal! Over here. I'd like a word," Uncle Max called out. "You too, Eva."

Cal let the other workers filter out around him before returning to where Uncle Max stood, a clutch of bills in his hand.

"I'm grateful for your help tonight. You bailed me out in a pinch, and I appreciate it. Short notice, too." He handed a hundred dollar bill to Eva and seventy-five dollars to Cal. "Sorry, kiddo, but you were off your game tonight. Maybe next time."

His words hardly registered. Cal looked toward the window, at the shadows retreating down the alley, then glanced at the clock. "I can bring the car around," he offered, clearing his throat as the twist of urgency tightened his voice. Eva made a face, tossed him the keys, then resumed talking with their uncle. Once outside, Cal felt invigorated by the rush of cool air, especially after an evening in the smoke-filled hall. But the night hadn't been all bad.

Following his stunt in the dining room, Cal had been relegated to the greasy pots-and-pans-only basin, the absolute bottom rung of the kitchen ladder. Miserable job that it was, he found the time passed easily when Addie, an old middle school friend, joined him there. They caught up, sharing stories about their different high schools, their siblings—Eva and Juan, both in the kitchen that night—and mutual friends. Then, out of nowhere, she mentioned Star, how she'd heard the sad news about her sister and father. Then she wondered aloud if the rumors about Star were true. But before she could fill in the details, Uncle Max blustered over and sent her to another corner of the kitchen—apparently Cal hadn't looked miserable enough. Now he hoped to catch up with Addie and finish the conversation.

Outside, Cal found the alleyway empty. Jogging up a few yards, he reached the street, but it was just as quiet. As his eyes adjusted to the darkness, however, he caught sight of some kids hanging out at the corner.

He walked toward them and recognized Juan just beyond the glare of the streetlight. As he grew closer, he noticed Addie, too, standing off to the side, her arms folded, her gaze impatient as she eyed a side street that was more of an alley.

"Addie?" he called out.

She started at the sound of her name, then gaped, as if Cal were the last person on earth she wanted to see. "I…I'm just waiting…I'm not with…I have nothing to do…" Then she turned and skittered away.

Bewildered, Cal stared after her, watching as she retreated through the slanted glare of streetlights, until the darkness at the end of the alley swallowed her whole. For moments afterward, he was oblivious to anything but the heavy pounding of his heart, the disappointment flooding its chambers. But, as always, his senses spun on overdrive and he found himself tuning into a world that he didn't want to hear.

"…come on, mister, that's more than last week."

"Yeah, you told us—"

"Sorry, amigos, but the price is what the price is."

Recognizing the voice, Cal pulled his attention away from the empty side street and toward a couple of neighborhood boys—no more than eleven or twelve years old—cowering in front of Juan's imposing figure.

Another person would leave this alone, he thought. They'd turn away, go home, and the evening would be done. It would be over. But in the zoom-lens way in which his mind worked, he saw things that simply wouldn't allow him to leave—at the moment, Juan's muddy gray energy oozing toward the boys like wet cement. There were other things, too: the plastic bags of crushed leaves and white powder, the large bills, the trembling fingers, the young faces—confused, almost angry—and above it all, Juan's big easy smile.

"You want the stash, I need the cash," he pressed them. "I got other—Cal, buddy! I didn't see you standing there. Sneakin' up on us, eh?" He looked down the street in the direction where Addie had disappeared and deftly played to Cal's weakness. "You like my sister? Well, don't worry about her. She's too shy—I always tell her so. And who's got time to waste on a girl like that? Plenty enough chicas around, right? You and me, we should hang out sometime. I'll show you 'round the neighborhood."

Cal hated what Juan was saying about Addie, hated that they lived under the same roof. And he hated what he was up to right now. He stepped closer and felt the ugliness of Juan's intentions crawling over his skin.

"What's going on?"

"Just a little business transaction." Juan smiled a large phony smile and gestured with his arms. "Tryin' to teach my friends here a little somethin' 'bout *supply and demand*." He glared at the boys, then turned his easy smile back toward Cal.

"So why don't ya give me your number? We'll hang sometime. I'm a little busy right now." A hint of impatience colored his relaxed tone.

"Don't do it, man," Cal said. "C'mon, they're still in grammar school. You don't want to mess up your neighborhood like this. For what, a fast buck? C'mon, you know better."

Juan listened, his plastic smile shriveling to a grimace.

"Not for a buck, for a lotta bucks—*mucho dinero*. I don't have a rich uncle handing me a C-note at the end of a good night. And yeah, it's my neighborhood, but it's filthy and poor. Not many people get outta here unless they're clever enough to claw their way out. So, save your sermons for Sunday, choir boy, and get the hell out of *my* neighborhood."

While he and Juan argued, Cal noticed the boys growing nervous, nearly dashing off when a sedan slowed at the corner. If they ran off now, Cal knew Juan would just find them on another street corner on some other evening.

"Listen," he said, turning to the boys, "I know someone—a friend of mine—who got messed up with drugs, wound up starting a fire a few weeks ago that almost killed a lot of people. You don't want to go there. It's a bad road." He wagged his thumb at Juan. "And you gotta lose this dude, because every time you buy a stash from him, he's laughing at you. He's laughing at how dumb you are, that he's fooled you into buying his crap."

Simultaneously, the boys turned their faces toward Juan, who, with his plastic smile, indeed appeared to be laughing at them.

"And each time you come, this bad-ass gets richer and you get poorer and he laughs harder."

The older boy who had a scar on his cheek spoke up, "Nobody laughs at me!"

"Yeah," his friend echoed. "Nobody." Suddenly, the boys

turned on Juan. "Keep your crap, mister, and—" they struggled to end on a rebellious note, "—shove it!"

Then they turned and dashed down the street, disappearing over a fence like a pair of wild rabbits. Juan watched them, his smile hardening. When he turned toward Cal, his eyes were feral.

"So clever, aren't you?" he jeered. "Think you saved the world, saved this flea-bitten neighborhood from ruin. Well, tomorrow I can sell this shit like that"—he snapped his fingers with a quiet fury—"and to kids even younger than those. So, tell me now, Superman, who ya really saved?"

Cal felt the ever-familiar sense of defeat squirm within him, the ache of good-intentions-gone-flat, another crash-and-burn attempt to make the world a better place. But somehow, he couldn't help himself. Even now, looking up at Juan's taunting expression, he couldn't stop trying.

"How much?"

"What?"

"For the bags."

Juan flashed a dark grin. "More than you got, amigo."

"How much?"

Juan laughed. "Or maybe Superman isn't so high and mighty as he pretends to be. Maybe he wants the goods for himself."

Cal flattened his shaking hand into the back pocket of his trousers and pulled out the seventy-five dollars. He didn't have time to bargain. Eva would be out soon.

"Here," he said, fiercely. "Give me what you've got."

Juan gave a mocking snort. "A man of your habits should know the going price."

Cal stared into the careless, hollow eyes. Like a giant spider. He felt tangled in Juan's sticky web and tried to wrangle free.

"Let's say you give me your little plastic bags right now,

and in exchange, I don't call the cops, rat you out, and make your life a whole lot more difficult than it already is."

Juan's smile faltered.

"I'll bet a dude like you already has a substantial rap sheet. And I doubt that juvie status covers you anymore."

Juan's expression no longer held any trace of a smile.

"So, what do you say, *amigo*? We got a deal?"

Juan squared his jaw but grew uneasy under Cal's arresting stare.

"Ah, what the hell. It's diluted shit anyway. Take it."

In a single movement, he shoved the pair of bulging plastic bags into Cal's gut while snatching the money from his hand. Then he turned and swaggered down the street, avoiding the circles of light beneath the streetlamps as if they were pools of poison.

Cal looked down and puzzled over the fat pouches of leaf and white powder in his hands. Then stooping at the curb, he peeled open the bags and shook their contents between the grates of the street drain, listening while the water gurgled it away.

A few minutes later, Cal started up his father's car and pulled up to where Eva stood waiting at the curb. She didn't get in. She seemed frozen in place, her shoulders fixed in an upward crunch while a cold stream of breath blew from her nostrils. Cal slid over to the passenger side and dropped the window.

"C'mon, let's go. You better drive. I don't have my license with me."

At length, Eva managed her feet around the far side of the vehicle, got behind the steering wheel, punched the car into drive and navigated the streets toward home in utter silence. Cal watched her, puzzled by the fiery plasma of energy radiating from her like an angry sun. Then in some unconscious rewind of the scene at the corner, his mind refocused—not on the money slipping through his fingers or the bags slapping into his gut—but the girl standing back at the curb with the hoop earrings and the black hair and a smile shattering into a million pieces, turning away just a moment too soon.

All the way home, he thought of a dozen ways to lie, to tell the truth, to say something to make her understand or at least see the better part of who he was, even if at times he had trouble recognizing it himself. As the car pulled into the driveway, he managed a few words, but they weren't any of the ones he'd planned.

"Eva," he asked, "why do you always think the worst of me?"

She slammed the shift into park and lifted her scorching gaze just long enough to answer.

"Because you never give me any reason to think otherwise."

CHAPTER
FIVE

C al wished he could turn it off, tune it out. Just live. But lately, he saw more than colors. He had weird vibes, too. For the first time, everything he saw and felt seemed aimed at a single idea: that something bad was coming down for Star. Just like it had for her sister. He had to figure it out before it was too late. Too late for what? He had no idea.

Haunted by his thoughts, Cal climbed the sloping ridge toward Oakwood Cemetery, oblivious to the scent of burning leaves that embalmed the air, the low wail of the black gate as it closed behind him. Once inside, he didn't see the caretaker around, but grabbed a rake propped against a tree. Figuring it didn't matter how he spent his hours, he started raking over a row of flat markers. As the rake's tongs swept the snarls of leaves away, the half-buried gravestones unfolded before him. Like the weathered pages of a lost book, they told their brief stories, one by one:

George Evans, Devoted Husband 1905-2000
Helen and John Staniewski, Loving Parents 1891-1954, 1906-1984

Eleanor Cleary, Cherished Daughter 1991-2017

The names and dates seemed to jump out at him and he couldn't help but do the math: Ninety-five years old. Sixty-three years old. Seventy-eight years old. Eighteen…

Cal's rake scraped to a halt. He stared at the plain stone for a moment, then went on, brushing along the row of flush markers with a quickened snap of his rake. But Eleanor followed him. All the way up the row he wondered about her, what she looked like, her friends, her hobbies. What did she want to be when she grew up? Had she wished for more time… He glanced back at the flat slab of granite. It said nothing. Nothing of the girl who lay beneath it, her smile, her dreams, the places she had gone, the people she'd loved. He scanned the graveyard. But that's how they all were. Names and dates. Nothing else. He shook his head. There should be something more—a favorite podcast or song, some crazy hashtag—a hint of the person's life. But these tombstones were as cold as icebergs, revealing nothing of what lie beneath them.

He was at the end of the row now, raking the ground with an agitated thrust, when a bluesy sort of whistling came up from behind.

"Helloa there, Cal!" the caretaker called out. "I'm afraid you'll have to give that rake a rest for now. We got some other kind of work today." He slapped an old rusty crowbar against the palm of his hand.

Cal eyed the tool. "Uh, what about the grass?"

"Not today. We got something more urgent." Using the crowbar as a pointer, the caretaker indicated several toppled markers. "Halloween. Brings 'em out every year. I honestly don't get it. What do these hoodlums think is goin' to happen? Push over a gravestone and watch a ghost come out?"

Cal shrugged. "Maybe they want to show off to their friends, you know, act tough."

"Wonder how brave they'd look if a ghost *did* pop out and chased 'em home," the old man muttered. "Anyway, there's at least four, probably more, so I'm gonna need every ounce of your strong muscles and young back to make 'em right again."

His large hand slapped Cal on the shoulder, nearly knocking the breath from him. Then he took off, straddling the yard's smaller gravestones, navigating around the taller ones. When Cal caught up, the caretaker was gazing at a crooked monument.

"We'll start with Miss Armstrong," the caretaker said, smiling at the gravestone as if he was smiling at the old woman herself. "She'd liked that. Always in the front row at church, always first in line at the bakery on Saturday mornin'. Well, I suppose when you're youngest of eleven kids, you get tired of bein' last." Stan bent over and slipped the crowbar beneath the pale gray stone. "No waitin' today, Hattie."

"Did you know her?" Cal grunted as his shoulder shoved the stone into place.

"Do I look old enough to know her, to know any of these dead folks?" the caretaker grinned, showing nearly all his teeth.

"Well, you seem to know about them."

"Hazard of the job, I suppose. Say, clean off that loose dirt on that side there, will you?"

Stan balled up a rag and quick pitched it over to Cal who snatched it from the air one-handed.

"Nice catch. You like baseball?"

Cal shrugged, indifferent.

"Triple A fan, myself," the caretaker said. "Ain't no million-aires playin' in Durham or Providence or Buffalo. It's where the game still has heart. No worryin' over endorsement deals or high-flyin' contracts. In the minors, it's just baseball. Pure and simple."

He peered up at Cal from beneath the brim of his cap and

gave a wink. Like so many other scraps of conversation, though, Cal let it die away. Maybe one of these days the care-taker would stop trying to make this fun and realize he just wanted to finish his hours and leave. Cal didn't need small talk or lectures. Just a hundred hours. Nothing more, nothing less.

They spent the rest of the afternoon crisscrossing over the shadowy graveyard floor, prying tombstones into place, righting toppled urns, removing graffiti and talking little. With the damage in check and the low-wattage sun dimming, Stan picked up the pace, grabbing the hodge-podge of tools and chemicals scattered about the yard with an impatient snap of his large hands.

"Get a move on there, Cal. It's time you head home. Marsh is no place to be after dark."

Just a few rows from the caretaker, Cal had stopped between a pair of rose-colored crosses, his sneakers nearly crushing a small white cherub. It lay face-down in the dirt, its folded hands dug into the ground like a tiny trowel. He reached down and scooped up the fallen angel just as the old man came up from behind.

"She'll need some bonding," he said, his voice grave. Pulling a clean rag from his pocket, he tenderly whisked away the mud wedged between the creases of the chalky white elbows and fingers.

To Cal, his grief was as plain as the purple blue haze around him. "Can you fix it?"

"Maybe. Go around again. Check the yard." Stan turned toward the shed. "See if we've missed any others."

Cal drifted through the rows of gravestones, looking for more collateral damage from the Halloween hoodlums. He passed through centerfield, as Stan liked to call it, where the stones of *Quinn, Andrejewski,* and *Smith* commandeered the best real estate in the yard. One a skinny black spire, the next, an obelisk in severe gray, and the last a white heart framed by a pair of ugly marble columns. Again, they revealed nothing of the souls that lie beneath them. Like all the others, they were just names and dates on a slab of cold stone.

Cal reached the lower end of the yard and guessed the vandals had either run out of nerve or time. Everything appeared in place. He was about to turn and hike back up when he noticed an unusual gravestone glinting in the half-hearted sunlight. Walking over to it, he realized it was the stone he'd stumbled against last week and unlike any other in the graveyard. In the monument's high sheen finish, he could see himself as clearly as if he were standing before a mirror. The stone was so glossy, so black that everything around it shone within its dark surface, from the line of small white crosses in the next row, to a distant clutter of cottages slumped on the furthest bend of the marsh. As Cal gazed into the water-smooth surface, he looked past his reflection to the single word etched into the stone: PEACE.

There were no dates or a name. He was just wondering to whom it belonged when Stan walked out from the shed, his yellowy eyes narrowed with concentration. At his direction, Cal came over, lifted a small tube from the old man's shirt pocket and squeezed several dots of the bonding agent onto the top of the monument. Cradling the angel in his massive palms, the caretaker lifted it so gently, the statue seemed to float to the top of the stone.

"There you go, Theresa," Stan murmured, stepping back to admire the repair. "Good as new."

As a sad smile rippled across the old man's lips, Cal couldn't help but ask his question again. "Did you know her?"

And in the stillness of the November afternoon, the entire graveyard seemed to wait for the answer.

"I didn't know them all, Cal." He nodded. "But I knew Theresa. She was my wife."

By the time Cal left Oakwood it was well past sunset. Stan had lost track of the time and when he finally realized the hour, he'd nearly shoved Cal through the gate. But even in near darkness, Cal found beauty in the marsh. Stopping at the top of the marsh bridge, he gazed across the muddy water, watching the distant shore lights as they came up and brightened the water. It was a still night, not even the long, willowy branches of the trees wavered. The fish, the frogs, nothing stirred. It was as if every corner of the marsh was holding its collective breath.

Then he saw something. Amongst the reeds. Something that didn't belong. He knew every plant, animal, and insect that inhabited the place. This looked like none of them. It glistened, almost sparkled among the weeds, gliding toward him through the water, black as the night itself. Jumping down from the bridge and onto the muddy bank below, he went to investigate. As he waded into the reeds, Cal suddenly felt a blast of cold air—like a giant freezer door had just opened—and shivered in a way that had nothing to do with his hands.

Somewhere on the far side of the marsh, a short-eared owl screeched. Glancing up through the shroud of evening mist, he listened as the echo curled around the marsh, running up the hill toward the cemetery, then rolling back down. He listened as it died off slowly, then looked back to the cluster of weeds. But whatever had been lurking there, whatever he had seen or almost seen, was gone.

CHAPTER
SIX

Eva yawned her way into the school newspaper office, her travel mug empty, her patience razor thin. The weekend's events left her tossing much of the night. Now her eyelids felt like window shades that wanted to close. Heading to the back of the room, she ignored the welcoming smile of the paper's faculty advisor, Mr. Cummins, but met the flame-throwing glare of the editor-in-chief with a smirk.

"*Finally*, we can start," Meredith huffed from the front of the room. "So, what do we have?"

Gerry Kominski spoke up first. "Boardwalk safety issues as renovations are postponed—again."

"Who else?"

Samantha Keegan raised her hand. "I have a story on the new class officers." She was one of them.

"We got pics for that?"

"Yep," the photo editor answered. "One for every class."

"You breaking in the new guy?"

A murmur rippled across the room. In just weeks, Orrin Parker had half the girls in the senior class—and a few boys—drooling over him. Eva doubted there was any personality behind those skintight shirts and butt-hugging pants, but when she caught his pale perfect face looking her way during class last week, she had to admit she was more than flattered.

"Yep," the photo editor said. "He's caught on real quick."

"What about ads?" Meredith asked, crossing her legs and letting her stretch skirt inch up her thighs.

"We're a bit short," the business manager answered, his voice low. "Houdini's Grill was a regular, you know."

The topic stilled the room, heads bowed, conversations lowered.

Meredith glanced back at her laptop. "So, who's working on the arson update and the Board's decision to… oh, I've got it here. Already submitted. We'll lead off with it."

The first period bell rang.

"Remember, final copy by 3:00 p.m. today."

The staff grabbed their laptops and began to head to class when Eva spoke up. "Wait. Why are we leading off with the arson story? That happened two weeks ago. It's old news."

The shuffle for the door stopped. Glances were exchanged.

"The fire is still a big story, Eva. Everyone's talking about it."

"Well, maybe everyone should be talking about the crumbling boardwalk—the one that half the student body uses to get to school every day. If you're half the editor you pretend to be, you'll put Gerry's story, the one that matters most to students, up front."

Meredith didn't flinch. "The arson story stays."

"It's ridiculous."

"It's relevant."

"It's redundant."

"Sorry, Eva, I'm not burying the story on the back page because your brother's square in the middle of it."

Eva glowered at Meredith, her voice bristling. "You're not an editor. You're a two-bit yellow hack."

"Enough! Everyone to class. Now!" Mr. Cummins clapped his hands to disperse the group. "I'm not writing out late passes. Meredith, we'll talk at deadline this afternoon. Eva, I'd like a word with you now."

Eva slumped against a desk, her fingers tapping in a heavy roll. But Mr. Cummins didn't notice. His creepy gaze hovered over the hem of Meredith's skirt as it shimmied out the door. When he finally turned toward Eva, his nostrils flared. "So, what was all that about?"

"Just a healthy editorial debate."

"In the future, let's not let our personal feelings cloud our judgment, hmm?"

Eva's throat burned. It was hard enough to suffer through these meetings knowing Cummins had reneged on his promise to appoint her editor-in-chief, but swallowing Meredith's incompetence with a smile? She couldn't—she wouldn't —do it.

"This is not about me or my brother. Meredith's burying an important story because it's more fun to sling mud."

"It's her editorial opinion."

"And mine? This newspaper is sinking fast. If we don't start reporting stories that mean something around here, the school district is headed straight down with it."

———

At lunch, with the burn of the morning's standoff still fresh, Eva zeroed in on the far side of the cafeteria and scowled. There he was. Fooling around with his friends. Clueless. What was wrong with that kid? Cal should be miserable. The whole school was talking about him and if Meredith had her way, he'd be the unlucky cover boy for the next edition of the school paper.

He looked up, saw her, and smiled; his mouth bent like a

crooked piece of wire. Eva tore her eyes away, furious. She hated when he did that—that—that look! Like he could see inside her head.

But there'd always been something about her brother, something not quite right. It was as obvious as that fractured smile playing across his face. Oh, he was a clever chameleon, blending in, covering up, flying below the radar. Still, in the casual coincidences and constant excuses that littered his life, there was something…

Like that day, two weeks ago. It started like nothing. Cal headed, as usual, to the corner table where a strange puree of the most unpopular kids hovered over their lunches like a bunch of spooked squirrels. The moment his tray landed, though, they seemed to transform. Smiles flickered; backs straightened. She could almost hear their collective sigh.

But that day, Cal seemed distracted. She remembered his eyes scanning the room. Looking for crazy Kevin or maybe burned-out Joe. Or even Bill, who was more likely hawking answer keys in the bathroom or shaking down some rando freshman for money than eating lunch. When it came to friends, Cal set the bar ridiculously low. With his lunch untouched that afternoon, she watched him get up, amble toward the exit then bolt out through the glass doors. Even now, she could recall the unsettling malaise that crept over her. Something had felt wrong, weird in a universal sort of way, as if the earth had just slipped off its axis and no one had noticed the blip but her.

That feeling took root in the pit of her stomach and didn't let go. Minutes later, when the fire alarm rang during English class, a quiet panic rose from her gut. Wide-eyed, Eva followed her classmates down the corridor, but just as they reached the emergency exit, she remembered her cell phone—back in the classroom, square in the middle of her desk, in plain sight.

Cummins got a hard on every time he confiscated one and he'd love to have hers.

Eva ducked out of line and dashed back to get her phone, the wail of the alarm shredding the stillness of the corridors. She ran to the classroom and back and was just steps from the emergency door when it slammed in her face. Pressing against the wide handlebar, Eva found it wouldn't budge. She remembered feeling as if she were the only one left in the building, the blasts of approaching fire trucks dousing any last-minute hope that this might be just a drill, after all. With her heart pounding, she threw her full weight against the door.

"Open the door!" The palm of her hand hammered out the syllables. "Op—en—up—and—let—me—out! Someone… Anyone…"

Then the door gave way. Eva toppled onto the pavement like an upended doll. Her knee smashed to the ground, blood drizzling down her leg as the skin tore away. She looked around. Firemen, students and teachers spilled into every corner of the schoolyard. But no one was looking at the school. It wasn't even on fire. The building across the street, on the other hand, was toast. Its charred remains sending ghostly streamers of smoke into the air.

Eva looked down at her knee, then back at the school, wondering why the emergency door had malfunctioned. Then she saw the girl with the pink streaks of hair falling over her face and a gotcha smirk pasted over her pierced lips, the point of her boot propped beside the door. She should have gone after Star, given her a nasty stop-drop-and-roll right there, but the chicken shit made off as soon as Eva got to her feet.

Eva remembered scanning the schoolyard, kids and teachers alike gaping at the fiery spectacle on the other side of the road. No sign of Cal. Then she heard someone laugh aloud about that "weird Hughes kid" and looked across the street. Clearly on the wrong side of the caution tape, Cal stood staring into the dying embers. A fireman tugged at his sleeve. No response. Then a policeman came up and motioned for him to move along. When he resisted, they shoved him into a squad car. And just like that, Cal was gone.

Focusing back to the lunch table, Eva fingered her throbbing temple and forced herself to tune into her friends as they debated weekend plans.

"…It won't be like that, Tori," Lin insisted. "I mean, sure, there'll be a lotta kids from the soccer and cross country teams, but… Whatever. How about you, Eva? Smitty's parties are always a blast."

"I have to work this weekend. Another wedding. Apparently, my uncle's catering hall is double-booked since Houdini's got fried. My parents volunteered my services—again. Daughter…more like indentured servant…"

Tori looked up from her phone. "I love weddings! They're so romantic." She glanced at Hank, a heavy boy sitting alone at the end of their table, his tray brimming with soda and ice cream sandwiches. He ventured a nervous grin, but Tori quickly looked back down to her phone.

"Whatever. Text me if you change your minds." Lin stuffed the remainder of her lunch into her backpack and jogged off.

"You know, I'm working Saturday, too," Tori said, flipping through a fashion app on her phone. "Babysitting. Maybe we could do something when you're done at your uncle's place."

The bell rang. Eva got to her feet, her expression on the unlikely side of maybe.

"What about tonight, then?" Tori prodded, the urgency rising in her voice. "We could catch a movie at the Playbill or get some coffee or—"

"Homework—tons of it—and a stupid Cummins essay to boot."

"Please." Tori grabbed Eva's wrist. "I was stuck at my father's apartment all weekend. Dismal doesn't begin to describe it. I need to get out."

"Um, okay. The Last Drop? Say seven o'clock—hey, watch it!" Eva whirled around. The cattle rush from the lunchroom had sent a binder stabbing into her side.

"My bad," a silvery voice apologized. "It's crazy in here. You'd think the place was on fire."

Eva stood speechless, unsure whether it was Orrin Parker's phrasing or his too-white smile throwing her off guard. She watched him glance at the mad dash that had shoved him into her path, his smile deepening.

"You know, if everyone had physics after lunch like us, there'd probably never be a stampede out of here."

Us. The word spun through Eva's head in a heart-fluttering loop. It was that unfortunate state of consciousness, she later realized, that kept her from noticing a couple of losers from Cal's grade closing in and taking aim.

"Hey, Eva! Tell your idiot brother to get a new hobby."

"Yeah, kinda old to be playing with matches, don't ya think?"

As laughter reverberated across the room in ever-widening waves, Eva felt her face flush a hot, fiery red. At some point, Orrin slipped from her side. She couldn't blame him. Thanks to Cal, she'd suddenly become a magnet for every moron with a crack about a botched prank or a lit match. And who needed to hang around with a girl like that?

CHAPTER
SEVEN

That evening, Eva was in no mood for talking. Felt less like listening. Listening required opening your heart, and if she listened too hard, she was afraid of what she might hear rising from her own troubled soul. But she had to admit, if a person needed a shoulder to cry on, there was no better place than The Last Drop. Beneath the quiver of votive candles, the room soothed in shades of cocoa and cream with tables thinner than English tea biscuits and chairs plump as marshmallows. From somewhere along the curved walls a cappuccino machine roared, competing with the sound system through which a trio of musicians played songs no one heard before to people who didn't care. The place percolated with conversation, the nods of attentive companions, and people who seemed desperate to drown their troubles beneath the caffeine, the music, and the candlelight.

Eva glanced across the table, waited for Tori to open up, then offered a no-brainer. "Worked on any college apps this weekend?"

Tori lifted her round face from her teacup with an agonized glare. "My father's apartment is so small I can barely breathe in it. It was all football, all weekend. He and Billy kept the TV so loud, I felt like I was sitting on the fifty-yard line. I couldn't have concentrated if I tried—and I didn't. What's worse, between games I got to listen to my father justify my parents' breakup, blaming it all on my mother even though that 'figment of her imagination' calls him every half hour on the hour. And in a few weeks, I get to do it all over again. Thanksgiving. *His* turn."

"What about your mom? What's she going to do?"

Tori shrugged, trying to flag down a waitress.

"I saw her Saturday night." Eva tugged at the dangle of her turquoise earring. "Maybe she needs something new. I talked to my uncle and—"

"What she needs is her husband back."

"Any prospect of that actually happening?"

The arrival of a fresh pot of tea headed off the conversation's dangerous path. Tori promptly redirected the dialogue.

"Cool place, huh?" Her eyes zeroed in on a cozy booth at the back of the coffeehouse. "Don't look now, but guess who is in the corner making out with a guy that's gotta be *at least* twenty-two, maybe twenty-three?" She shook her head and Eva wasn't sure if the gesture indicated reproach or envy. "I'll bet Kelly Hanson brings one of her college boyfriends to the Marsh Madness Dance and breaks half the hearts on the varsity football team." She stared a moment longer, then leaned forward. "So, who do you want to go with?"

Eva scrunched her nose. "It's months away. I've hardly thought about it."

"Don't be cool with me, Eva Hughes. You've been thinking about it since the first week of school, just like every other girl in the senior class. What's more, I *know* who you want to go with."

"Really? Well, fill me in 'cause I haven't a clue," Eva drawled.

"That dreamy looking thing that *bumped* into you after lunch today. I saw your face and, I swear, you were melting right in front of Orrin's eyes."

Eva sipped her mocha, glanced around, then gave Tori an excruciating wince. "Was I really that obvious?"

"Incredibly. But so what? At least he knows you're interested."

From the small platform stage, the band announced a break. As they dissolved into the crowd, the dynamics in the cup-shaped room stirred. People began to move about, mingling and sidling up to the counter for refills.

"Hey, Carol Zempke's up at the coffee bar now. You want to go say hi? They say her father's been having a hard time. Doctors thought it was just smoke inhalation but now they think he's got pneumonia." Tori grinned. "Heard she's got a crush on your brother."

"She obviously doesn't know him very well."

"Hey, and isn't that Smitty next to her? Too bad Lin isn't here."

"You go ahead. I'm not up to socializing tonight."

Tori stepped into the crowd and left Eva brooding at the table, absorbed in images that couldn't be blinked away. Until a few days ago, she'd hoped she was wrong about her brother, that her suspicions were unfounded. But then Saturday evening happened, and it all came together, every suspicion, every worried ache in her stomach. Still, knowing she'd been right gave her no sense of victory. She was just beginning to wish her coffee mug was filled with something a little stronger when Tori came back to the table, her eyes bulging.

"Eva, you should have come with me! I was at the bar standing next to this incredibly hot guy—way out of my league—when I noticed him ordering some mineral water from the barista. And I started thinking, *cool, he's in a coffeehouse and doesn't care he's probably the only person not drinking something caffeinated.* So, he notices that I noticed, and he starts asking me stuff like, do I come here often and what kind of music do I like and what do I think of his band—Eva, *his* band. At this point I started freaking out because you *know* I have a thing for musicians. Anyway, we started talking about our favorite artists and he asked me if I want to go check out some local bands with him some time." Tori closed her eyes and pretended to scream.

Intrigued, Eva strained to see the coffee bar, but the crowd, coagulating like clumps of clotted cream, obscured her view.

"Holy crap!" Tori grabbed Eva's arm. "He's coming this way."

Eva looked up and immediately frowned. The lead singer was weaving his way toward them between the tight cluster of tables. He had a slight build and wore his brown hair long enough to curl below his ears, a rakish goatee setting off his dark complexion and eyes. His clothes had a bohemian air about them—worn but carefully chosen. A frayed scarf looped low around his neck not quite matching the flat woolen cap propped on his head.

"Hey, Tori," he said in a strong, husky voice, "you gotta get a better table next time. I'll try and get you moved up." She was still bathing in his words when he opened up on Eva.

"So, what's with your brother? It's like the dude's checked out."

Eva shrugged. "I don't know. Why don't you ask him, Turk?"

"I would if he showed up at rehearsal."

"Guess he—forgot." Eva tipped her palms upward, then grabbed her mug and took a long dreg. "Anyway, he's got bigger concerns these days."

"I don't care about his community service gig," Turk said. "The music is the music. The band is the band. We all got crosses, man. Deal with them."

Tori listened, a dreamy cast twinkling over her gray eyes, oblivious to the tension rippling across the table.

"Ya know how we got this gig tonight?" he asked with a quiet fury. "We got it last minute 'cause some other group couldn't get their act together. That can't happen to us. I won't let it. Cal shoulda been here tonight."

Eva yawned. "And this concerns me—how?"

The singer's voice, which sounded musical even when he spoke, softened. "If anyone can reach him, you can."

"You overestimate my powers of persuasion," she replied in an arctic tone, "as well as my concern with anything related to my brother."

Turk regarded Eva with a ferocious yet helpless stare. Stroking his goatee, he seemed to consider a number of responses, then settled on the one which required the least number of words.

"If you would be so cool—" he pressed a folded sheet of composition paper against the table and slid it toward her—"I need chords for these lyrics. Soon. We got a big gig next month."

Unmoved, Eva's expression remained glacial. "I'm not his keeper. Why don't you give it to him yourself?"

"He's a tough guy to reach. Paul tried him Friday."

"Community service."

"Saturday night?"

"At work."

"This afternoon?"

"Who knows? Listen, Turk, did it ever occur to you that Cal's just not *into* the band anymore?"

The singer flinched at her words. Utter blasphemy.

"Maybe he's simply outgrown you boys. Or maybe," she paused for effect, "he's gotten himself into—something else."

Turk brushed back his long hair, regarding Eva mistrustfully now. "Just give Cal the message. He either breaks this funk or...or..."

Then, with a fleeting wink at Tori, he went back to the stage, strapped on a battered electric guitar and began tuning up for the second set. Tori, whose gaze hadn't left the stage since Turk mounted it, edged her chair away from the table to get a better view.

"Your brother is in *this* band?"

"Yeah."

"And you know John Turkel?"

"Sort of. He's just this jerk my brother hangs out with—no offense."

When the music began a moment later, Eva recognized the tune, White Rainbow. She'd heard her brother practice the melody dozens of times and just as quickly recognized that something in it was missing—his part.

The second set had an entirely different feel, rock-based fusion with a hint of jazz. Eva noticed the tepid crowd warming up to the band's original compositions, applauding more loudly with each piece. Tori listened in rapt awe to every lyric, half-mouthing the words she was quick to memorize.

"Are you going to tell Cal?" she asked between songs. "Turk sounded pretty serious."

Eva stared at her coffee mug, her finger tracing mindless circles around the rim. "Probably not."

"But it could ruin everything for your brother."

"That's what I'm counting on."

Tori's eyes finally shot away from the band, her expression mystified. "Eva, why do you want to hurt Cal like this? Isn't his life a big enough mess right now?"

Eva leaned over the little spool of a table and lowered her voice. "For years I've watched my brother. He's always at the wrong place at the wrong time, constantly at the fringe of trouble. Well, this past weekend my suspicions—at least some of them—were confirmed."

"What do you mean?"

"Saw the cash-for-stash exchange with my own eyes. Right outside my uncle's place after work."

"I don't believe it."

"It's true."

"Okay, but what's that got to do with Cal and Turk?"

"Everything. That band means the world to my brother. You should have seen how upset he got last week when I forgot to tell him about rehearsal. Anyway, unless Cal hits rock bottom, he'll never turn his life around. Getting kicked out of the band might be the trigger he needs to set himself on the right road again. After all, the sooner his world falls apart, the sooner he'll have to pick himself up and pull it back together again." Eva glanced back toward the stage. "So, what's wrong with giving the process a little push?"

CHAPTER
EIGHT

Grabbing his guitar and jacket, Cal walked out the kitchen door to meet up with Paul and Phil, clearing out before Eva could pick a fight for which she seemed more than ready. Turning the corner onto Bittersweet Road, he noticed a car, lights dimmed, crawling over the Crossover Street Bridge. He guessed it was Paul's sedan. The car blew out headlights more often than it leaked oil, but it was the most reliable car among them, so they went with it.

Heading down the street, guitar over his shoulder, he let his eyes drift up to the early evening sky where only a few stars had twinkled into existence. Aiming a half-hearted plea toward the brightest one, he wished for a way to make things right with Star again. Maybe for a day. Maybe for just an hour. But how? One day, Star answered his texts, the next three days, she'd ignore them. At school, she swung from sullen to combative in a blink. She cut classes, got detention for everything from mouthing off to vaping and freaked out classmates with boasts about herbal spells and curses.

Cal slowed his pace and let his eyes drift downward. He needed to reach her. But how?

The slam of a car door shook him from his daydream. He looked up with anticipation, then frowned.

Lieutenant Gavin.

Rounding the front end of a police cruiser, the officer swaggered over, knocking back the brim of his hat and sniffing the air in Cal's direction. "Sometimes, you can just smell it." He sniffed again. "Trouble."

"I'm waiting for my friends."

"You mean *loitering.* And I suppose *that's* a guitar?"

"Yeah, matter of fact, it is."

"Bring it here," he commanded. "That's far enough. Now back off."

Then, without explanation, the officer grabbed the case, slammed it onto the hood of the patrol car and began rummaging through its compartments, working it over like he was frisking a felon. He yanked out spare sets of strings and electrical cords, sent a capo, slide, and phase shifter careening to the ground and rough-housed the guitar in the process.

Cal stood by wincing. Every clunk of equipment a punch to his gut. Under any circumstance the search would be infuriating, but it was worse because Cal knew why. He could see it in Gavin's energy, shriveling now into wormy strands of ruddy brown. It was the same anger-fueled cloud he'd carried for years, ever since that time at camp when Cal refused to lie and vouch for his son, Tom. Thing was, Cal *had* tried to help Tom, tried to stop him from breaking curfew—got a punch to the gut for his efforts. That same night, Tom snuck out and sunk all the canoes, his revenge for having lost a friendly race that afternoon. Then there was the lab incident at school. Again, it was Tom. Messing with chlorine dioxide, causing an explosion. He was expelled that time and Gavin tried to deflect the blame.

"That Hughes kid is always around when there's trouble and my Tom always gets the blame."

And Cal always *was* around, but only because he was

trying to save Tom—and everyone else—from the chaos he created, the chaos Cal *saw* coming. For this and who knew how many other imagined infractions, Dick Gavin held a grudge against him. In his energy field, it showed as clearly as if the word *revenge* were tattooed across his forehead.

Cal remembered a time when he didn't understand what he saw around people—the waves of color. Over the years, though, he started making connections between the different shades, their movement and patterns. A haze of bright red energy meant anger, fury. A yellow cloud, a sure sign of self-ishness. Green was all about envy and any shade of purple or indigo was a sign of intuition, thoughtfulness. Darker colors—brown, gray, dull green—indicated a darker side of personality, negative thoughts, even dangerous intentions like Juan's. Sometimes there were streamers, too, that stretched between energy fields. He wasn't surprised that people could sometimes sense they were being watched. If the energy was strong enough, it could be felt. One thing years of observation had taught him: before a person acted upon an idea or a feeling, it swirled in their energy field first. People literally did things emotionally before they did them physically.

The thought made him refocus on Gavin, whose energy field was darkening dangerously, its addled swirls swallowing what little light it held. Even from behind the policeman's back, the sense of malice was so overwhelming, Cal hardly noticed the man's hand slipping into the pocket of his uniform. He had no idea what the guy was doing, but he saw the intention and that was enough.

"Don't even think about it," Cal said in a low, careful voice.

Gavin froze. For a moment, neither of them breathed.

"Just put it away," Cal continued, talking as if he were guiding someone down from a ledge. "It was a long time ago, Lieutenant. Let it go. You can't hold the grudge. It's"—he looked into the pulsating plume of red energy—"eating you alive."

The policeman seemed to shuffle with something small, fingering it back into the pocket of his uniform. Then he rounded on Cal with a fury his energy field had already betrayed.

"Just give me half a reason, Hughes—any reason—and I'll haul your ass in and make your life as miserable as you've made Tom's!" He finished through clenched teeth. "And next time you cause trouble, I promise, you won't community-service your way out of it." With a sweep of his arm, he sent the guitar flying off the hood of the car and crashing to the ground.

If he was lucky, Cal thought, it would have ended there, with him picking up the scattered pieces of his gear and Gavin peeling off in his cruiser. But luck didn't find him very often and just as the lieutenant got back to his car, Paul's old, rusted Dodge came flying around the corner, radio blasting, muffler missing, the inspection sticker so expired it was peeling off the windshield. He spied the patrol car, but too late.

For the next few minutes, Paul and Phil endured the lieutenant's demoralizing scrutiny. He circled the car, savoring the vehicle's every infraction—inventing a few along the way—while Cal gathered his gear and slid into the back seat. When Gavin finished, he shoved a stack of tickets at the bewildered driver, then leaned into his window and took a sniff.

"By the way, your car stinks." He sniffed again. "And I think it's coming from the back seat."

When the cop car was out of sight, Paul turned around.

"What the hell was that?"

"Long story." Cal rubbed his aching eyes. "Let's just get out of here. Turk's gotta be waiting."

And he was. They could hear the notes of his guitar tripling into the night air as they pulled up for rehearsal. They found

Turk sitting on a bag of grass seed inside an old garage that Phil's grandfather let them use. Leaning over a vintage Les Paul, he seemed oblivious to the stench of fertilizer and the space heater that droned like a tenor stuck on a low note. He didn't acknowledge them. The rhythmic tap of his foot, however, gave them a sense he'd been waiting. A quick warmup ensued—frenetic scales, stuttering drum rolls, growling bass lines. The moment Turk looked up from his guitar, however, they stopped. Utter silence.

"I've learned through reliable sources that our Battle-of-the-Bands gig is stirring up a redoubtable buzz."

Phil hit one of his cymbals. "C'mon, in Buffalo?"

Turk shrugged. "Last year's winner opened for Dave Matthews. Stole the show. Created a hum. Dudes from mainstream and indie labels have been calling for tickets. It's sold out."

Paul, Phil, and Cal exchanged wide-eyed glances.

"I know guys from Chicago to Cleveland trying to get on the bill just for a chance to play in front of these cats." He clicked on the microphone. "But no worries. Our spot's locked in."

For the next several hours, rehearsal was intense. As always, Cal was amazed that, around these guys, his unpredictable hands moved only as the notes and music required. It was a peace he rarely knew. As midnight passed and the session wrapped, Paul and Phil let off steam, clowning with a bunch of fertilizer bags in a mock contest of weight and wits. Wiping down the neck of his guitar, Cal egged them on. He didn't see Turk come up.

"You got chords for those lyrics?"

Cal blinked at Turk whose foot tapped restlessly on the top of his amp. "What lyrics?"

Everything got a little quieter in the garage.

"The ones I gave Eva. She was supposed to give them to—"

Turk's eyes looked away, his expression hot enough to sear a hole through the bags of seed stacked along the wall. "Forget it," he grumbled. "From now on, everyone makes every practice." He turned to the others. "We're going to step it up. We only have a couple of weeks."

Cal resumed wiping down the neck of his guitar, but Turk's sharp eyes hadn't missed the slight hesitation in his hands.

"Problem, Cal?"

"No. It's cool. Just need to move a few things around."

Turk stared, stroking his goatee.

"Really, it's no problem," Cal insisted.

Turk's eyes narrowed as if searching for an ingenuous crack. Then pressing his thumb against his lips, he asked, "Everyone else cool with the schedule?" He looked from one musician to the next, his eyes resting longest on Cal. Accepting each nod like a signed contract, he grabbed his guitar and headed for the door.

"You need a ride, man?" Paul called out, coiling an extension cord around his arm. "I'm almost done here."

With a slight shake of his head, Turk declined the offer. Then, tossing the ragged tail of his scarf over his shoulder and his guitar onto his back, he drifted out the door and receded into the night. Cal exchanged curious glances with his band mates. None of them knew much about Turk. He didn't go to school and, as far as they knew, didn't have a day job. They weren't sure where he sacked out, either. They had a sneaking suspicion, however, that Turk didn't sleep at all but spent his hours fleshing out melodies that only his voice could birth.

CHAPTER
NINE

he band. Cal needed to show he was all in. But he wasn't sure if he could get his hours at Oakwood rolled back. The next afternoon, however, he found the caretaker surprisingly cool about it.

"Well, music is a good thing," the old man said, standing beside a pile of moldering compost. "What's that they say? Music, a balm for the soul. No problem, son. Do what you have to do. I know you'll make up the time. Just make sure you're here tomorrow."

Cal picked up a shovel and helped Stan stir a mountainous pile of grass clippings and wilted flowers into the compost heap. The motion lifted a warm green stench into the still air and the caretaker began to whistle. Every now and then he'd stop and ask, "Your band know that one?" But each time, Cal met the hopeful question with a shake of his head. Eventually, the old man felt compelled to defend his repertoire.

"Well, they're classics, Cal. Wouldn't hurt for you boys to learn a few standards, you know. Please the older folks in the crowd. You never know, I might come down and see you fellas some time."

Cal fought back the grin threatening to erupt on his lips. "I'll see what we can do."

"Well then, best you wash up now. Gettin' late. Marsh is no place to be after dark."

The next afternoon, as Cal headed over the boardwalk, he consciously fought off thoughts about Star. He didn't know how to fix what had happened between them these last few weeks and was tired of trying to figure it out.

Once inside the graveyard's gate, though, the solitude of the place seeped in and eased the mental storm pounding in his head. Ducking beneath the work shed's low doorframe, he let his eyes adjust to the room's spare light, his lungs to the reek of motor oil. He guessed at the afternoon's chores—a stint on the compost pile or a few futile hours reviving an old mower. Cal looked around the low-ceilinged room. Stan was nowhere in sight. He felt uneasy in a way he hadn't since the first time he'd come to Oakwood. He spied a note on the workbench:

Cal, Veteran's Day is Wednesday. Florist should deliver wreaths by early afternoon. Place them on the veterans' graves. List attached.
Stan

Cal flipped the page. A list of almost two dozen names written in Stan's scrawl ran down the greased-stained paper. Row locations were not included. But why would they be? The man knew the place like his own backyard. Cal could almost hear his deep laugh: "Take your time and look around. They ain't goin' nowhere."

Behind the shed, he found a large cardboard box filled with fresh greens decked out in red, white, and blue ribbons. Looping a half dozen wreaths around his forearm, he scanned the list for names he might recognize. He read: *Thomas Smith. Joseph Andrejewski.* Glad to have a starting point, he turned for the circle of old trees that marked the centerfield area. Then he stopped short. At the lower end of the cemetery, he saw a woman, sharp-looking in an elegant gray coat and hat, saun-tering her way up from the marsh trail and through the gate. Cal realized that in all the weeks he'd been at Oakwood, he'd never seen a single visitor. For a moment, he wondered whether they were allowed. But people came to cemeteries, right? That's what they were for. So, he returned to his list and the scavenger hunt at hand.

Slipping the first wreath off his arm, Cal stepped over the soft grassy mound of the Smith grave and eased the memorial wreath against the heart-shaped base. Instantly, it softened the harshness of the cold white stone. But at the next monument, the wreath had the opposite effect, looking insignificant, a pinky ring around the long finger of granite that belonged to Andrejewski. The search got tougher after that. The next five gravesites took more than half an hour to find. By the time he neared the end of the list and the bottom of the box, his fingers were numb.

With his arm weighted with wreaths for a final time, Cal headed back into the yard. On a hunch, he walked down the damp, grassy slope toward a new grave:

Hallie Lowe 1995 – 2019

Brushing away a clutch of leaves, he sunk the wire wreath stand into the earth beside the young veteran's stone, strug-gling over a lump in his throat. He leaned back on his heels. The rectangle of dirt looked like a flesh wound against the lawny skin of the cemetery. Maybe he could plant some grass seed or get Stan to buy some sod. Then it wouldn't look so fresh…so raw…

"Did you know her?"

Cal turned abruptly, falling back off his heels. The woman

in the gray coat. She looked more intimidating up close, especially because he now recognized her. Pulling out the crinkled piece of paper, he rose to his feet and tried to explain himself to Zoe McClellan.

"No, I just work here. I'm supposed to find the stones of these veterans."

She surveyed him with a tender look, her lips drawn into a perfect line of pink.

"Ah," she sighed heavily. "You're fortunate, young man, if you need a list to find who you're looking for here, if the names on these gravestones are *just* names to you."

Standing on a patch of sunken ground, Cal had to look up several inches just to meet her gaze. He fumbled with condolences. "Uh, I'm sorry about your—"

She cut him off. "Apologies are for accidents. No doubt this place is full of people who've suffered that fate. My brother, however, was not among them. One can feel only so sorry for those who willingly choose death over life. I, for one, would not."

Despite Star's glowing praises and the universally high regard Miss Zoe McClellan held in the community, Cal was on guard. To him, she was a puzzle he couldn't quite solve. The woman should have brilliant energy, bright colors of warm intentions and charitable deeds. All he saw, though, was the thinnest of energy fields around her. Dull, muted colors— except for that day at Alula's funeral. He couldn't explain it. Nothing fit. And he wasn't sure what to make of it.

The wreaths started slipping down his arm, and Cal made a small hoisting motion to keep them from dropping to the ground.

"Are those for sale?" she asked, opening her handbag.

"Uh, no."

She snapped her purse shut and turned away, striding across several graves before pausing at the black stone with the deep mirror finish. She stared at it. "Did you know my brother?"

"Not personally," Cal said, following her. "But I know about him. Dr. McClellan was a brilliant scientist. Respected for his work all around the country."

"Is that what *she* told you?" The pink lips faltered. "I must warn you, my niece is full of false tales. A coping mechanism, no doubt, but don't be drawn in by it. My brother was an astute doctor and a daring scientist, but ultimately a failure. Oh, he had early success, but as his personal life struggled, so did his grasp on reality. His work suffered for it."

Cal knew the story that was all but legend around town—the bold doctor, his groundbreaking biogenetics work, then rumors of rogue research, followed by a string of personal tragedies.

"After his wife's death, I helped him refocus. Urged him forward. That's when he did some of him most impressive research. But alas, the grief, the encroaching madness undid him and he deserted everything. I'm afraid it's all been too much for my niece. Since her father's passing, she's grown—" Star's aunt paused as if considering polite words, then seemed to pick the most unkind. "Dysfunctional."

There wasn't a trace of kindness or sympathy in her voice. Again, Cal wondered at the place of honor Zoe McClellan held in the community and in Star's own life. Even now, her gaze was as cold and flat as the grave markers in the yard.

"Star's lost so much in a short time," he said.

"Yes, but sometimes—"

Again, the hesitation that feigned a search for kind words.

"—I fear she's inherited a bit of *his* madness."

Cal's eyes followed her hand, which pointed accusingly toward the grave he now guessed belonged to James McClellan.

"Lately, I think she has the same fear." She paused a

moment, then smiled, the expression forced, unnatural. "Poor girl. Needs to find peace."

"Is that what it means?" Cal asked, his gaze turning toward the inscription on the glimmering black stone.

"How would I know?" the woman snapped. For the first time, her expression grew steely and her features seemed better suited for it. "This is what my brother asked for in the note he left behind. This tombstone, this plot, in this cemetery, that's all. Nothing more."

"No names?"

"What are names anyway?" she huffed. "My brother took the most prestigious name in West Shelby and sullied it. Still, I had them added."

Stooping down, Cal brushed aside the grass at the stone's base and saw the McClellan inscription, but was keenly aware of the penetrating glare behind him, surveying his muddy jeans and worn Rolling Stones tee-shirt.

"You'd do well to stay away from my niece," she cautioned, her voice equal parts threat and challenge. "She's a deeply disturbed young woman and has a habit of drawing trouble toward herself and her companions. Stubborn, too, like her father and you can see where that got him."

With a heartless expression, she cast her eyes across the cemetery, the wind buffeting her stiff gray hair around her stiffer gray hat. Though she seemed beyond the indignity of shedding tears, Cal thought something painful was tearing at her expression.

"Here," she commanded, pulling a hundred dollar bill from her pocketbook. "Take this and go to the florist. Purchase something nice for my brother and keep the change for yourself." She looked down and breathed an exasperated sigh. "After all, family is family, no matter how terribly they disappoint you."

But Cal hardly heard her. Those hands...he knew them,

knew them in some terrible way. For a moment he could do nothing more than stare at the crisp bill clasped in the outstretched fingers. At length, he managed to reach over and grasp it.

As she hobbled away, some part of his brain strained through a decade of foggy visions and then stopped and focused on one with shocking clarity. Those hands. They belonged to the person who'd been out on the marsh with him all those years ago, the day his life had been ruined forever. And now Star was within their poisonous grasp.

CHAPTER
TEN

Bumping through the crowded hallways between classes, Cal found it easier than usual to ignore the whispers that trailed behind him like a long, mangled chain:

"… pyrohead…freakazoid…gravedigger…"

All he could think about was Zoe McClellan and her weird request. Yesterday, he'd been convinced she was the one out on the marsh with him that fateful day ten years ago. But today he was filled with doubt. Could he really be sure what he did or didn't see as a five-year-old kid? Or was he so desperate to make sense of something that made no sense at all he kept seeing connections where there were none? He considered telling Star his suspicions but decided against it. Their relationship was already on the skids. Any trash talk about Aunt Zoe would probably finish them off for good. Besides, there was really nothing to tell. All he had was a hunch, some cloudy memories, his damn trembling hands and more questions than answers. For the time being, he let it go.

Then there was the problem of his Telecaster. Ever since Gavin roughed up the guitar, it hadn't sounded right. Turk had noticed it, too. Probably the pickups or the heads but replacing them would cost. He considered squeezing in a night or two at the catering hall to earn a few bucks, but with extra rehearsals and community service looming—"

"Yo, Cal! Chem homework. You got it?"

Before Cal could blink, Bill was in his face, corking open a pen and grabbing some looseleaf papers from his unsteady hand. He leaned up against a row of lockers, began copying the answers, then stopped.

"Damn! This is going to take at least ten minutes. The bell's going to ring any second."

"Would have taken a lot longer if you actually did it."

"Dude, no time. The swim meet ran late last night."

The words sliced Cal fast and deep. He was surprised how much they hurt.

"How'd you guys do?" he asked, recovering.

Bill's mouth twisted into a sour frown. "Lost again. But what d'ya expect with Thornley using freshmen swimmers on the varsity squad? They're dragging the whole team down. So, I complained and, get this, he tells me to worry about my own lane of the pool."

Bill stopped writing, shook his pen a few times, licked the tip, then reached over and yanked one from the spiral of Cal's notebook, ignoring the fourth period warning bell as it rang overhead.

"So, I told Thornley to go suck it."

Cal's eyes widened.

"Not really, but he knew I was thinking it."

As the hush of the emptied corridor closed in around them, Bill looked up and stopped writing. "Hey, I've got an idea. Put my name on your homework and I'll put yours on mine."

"Yeah, right." Cal laughed, then saw Bill's sober expression.

"Look, if I miss another homework deadline in Finn's class,

I'm headed for Saturday detention. We have a meet this weekend."

"But then I'll get—"

"Dude, you're already off the team. You got nothin' to lose, right?"

Cal gazed at him, stone-faced. Even Bill, oblivious to nonverbal cues, seemed to get it. He looked over Cal's shoulder, down the corridor, toward the echo of classroom doors closing. A dark light bulb seemed to go off.

"Screw it." He shoved the loose-leaf papers into Cal's gut, then pasted himself up against the lockers, ducking past the classroom window before dashing toward the bathrooms and phones at the end of the hallway.

Cal stared after him, shook his head and turned toward class. Across the hallway, he saw Eva and Star talking—no, facing off. There was some kind of exchange before Eva stormed off leaving Star with an especially wicked smile on her face. To him, she looked like some hot movie villain with her black makeup, tight leggings and scatter of piercings. All of it outrageous because of the contrast he saw, the strand of platinum energy shimmering around her like a rare dazzling ribbon.

"Cal!" she exclaimed, over-smiling and poking her finger toward the bell rattling overhead. "Uh-oh, you're late. Late. Late-late."

Cal shrugged. "I've got nothing to lose."

She laughed—too much, too loud. Seemed to sway. "Now *there's* attitude."

"What are you up to?"

"Cutting class." Then, with great animation, she leaned in and whispered, "But we'll all be outta here before you know it. Shhh! Mute it."

"Huh?" Cal looked more closely at Star. "Wait. Are you —high?"

Star sniggered. "No, are you?"

He ignored the question. "So, what was all that with Eva?"

Star scrunched her brow, confused, then slapped her thigh. "Oh, that! Your sister's hairbrush fell out of her backpack. *I* was decent enough to return it to her."

"And?"

"And I just cleaned out the brush before I handed it over." Star pulled out a ball of matted black hair from the pocket of her tunic and rolled it between her forefinger and thumb. "No sense wasting it, I told her." She offered a depraved sort of grin. "Useful for all sorts of remedies…"

"I doubt that went over."

"Nothing goes over with your sister. She's too busy judging everyone from atop that f---ing throne of hers."

"Yeah, well Eva is Eva. Anyway, what do you mean by remedies?"

"My dear aunt. So smart. So many ways to feel better than people know. We're all blind, really. She's opened my eyes."

Cal looked into Star's eyes, so narrow they hardly seemed her own. No trace of that sweet cinnamon color. She blinked hard. Then blinked again. Her fingernails, darkened with black polish, reached for her eyes, missed, then found their target and rubbed in circles.

"Look, about your aunt—"

The hall monitor walked by, shot them a look, but didn't ask for passes. Cal waited until she was out of earshot. "Let's go somewhere and talk."

"Here's good," Star said obstinately. She folded her arms and leaned against the tile wall, a water fountain inches from her shoulder.

Unnerved, Cal brushed back the hair from his forehead. The movement distracted Star, and she reached over and stroked the ponytail loosely gathered at the back of Cal's neck.

"Cute, but what about a man-bun? Might work."

"Too pretentious." Cal nudged Star's hand away. "Look, don't be so quick to buy into your aunt's ideas. I'd think twice about taking any of her advice."

"Really? Well, Aunt Zoe is the only reason I've survived the past few months."

"Yeah, well, she might not be what she seems."

Star's smile faded. "Are any of us, Cal, really?"

Cal shook his head, tired of hinting at things, struggling to reach her, trying to make her understand. "It's just that at Alula's service, she looked—off."

"What, was she wearing the wrong shade of black?" Star tossed her head, fury rising in her voice. "Who the hell are you to judge?"

"It…it wasn't her clothes. It was—"

Cal stopped. Star's gaze had fallen toward the water fountain, where a splash of water was pooling in the clogged drain. She stared, then gaped, glaring as if a ghost were swirling in the circling water. She glanced away, seemed to forget Cal for a second, then clutched an amulet over her chest. When she found her voice, all the animation in it was gone. "Leave me alone, Cal."

"But—"

"I don't need this. Just…just go away. Leave me alone."

———

When Eva slipped into class, her face was so red, Tori knew she was a ten out of ten on the mad-as-hell scale.

"Star ought to be kicked out of school," she offered in commiseration. "Why does your brother even bother with her? She's nothing but trouble."

"Maybe that's what he's looking for," Eva mumbled, barely able to speak.

As they sat down, Mr. Schlenz approached the podium in

full safari gear, a pouch of archeological tools hanging from his belt. Even as he began class with a drawling British accent, Eva continued to stew over the episode in the hallway. Her brother might be stupid enough to humor a degenerate like Star, but she wasn't going to get sucked in by that crazy. Next time she tried to tangle with her… Tangle. And what the hell was Star going to do with those strands of hair? Eva had a sudden urge to shave her head clean.

Her ears perked up as Mr. Schlenz called on Tori who'd fallen speechless, as starry-eyed as the time their teacher donned a swaggering toga and posed as a Roman senator. Smirking, Eva lifted her hand to her mouth and mumbled a few words of salvation in her friend's direction.

"Um, DNA analysis and carbon dating?"

The teacher's monocled eye narrowed at Eva. "Correct, Tori. What else? Come on, chaps, it was all on page 215. Smitty, enlighten us with two more methods by which an artifact's age is determined, if you please."

The boy glanced down at his blank notebook and pretended to sift through its pages.

"Perhaps your textbook might prove more informative."

Smitty's head shrunk lower. He hadn't brought it to class. Removing the monocle from his eye, Mr. Schlenz drew a large white handkerchief from his breast pocket and proceeded to rub the glass vigorously.

"Class, regardless of which archeological dig one finds his or herself upon, without the proper tools, there's no sense leaving base camp. Simply showing up won't do. Now, my good man, if you can name the last two methods, you may continue to participate in this expedition. Otherwise, you'll report here at 2:30 p.m. where we'll discuss mission preparation in detail."

Eva figured that either Smitty's friends had slipped him the answer or the primordial fear of spending even an hour more in school than necessary jogged the big soccer player's memory, because with little hesitation, he blurted, "Satellite imagery and chemicals tests."

Mr. Schlenz was about to continue the lesson when the public address system crackled to life:

"Teachers, your attention please. Attention all teachers. Please escort your classes to the nearest exit. Again, teachers please escort all students to the nearest exit. Classes are canceled for the remainder of the day. Buses are on route."

Mr. Schlenz remained calm and in character. "Nothing to be concerned about," he assured. "Just a parliamentary matter, I'm sure."

But the announcement unsettled Eva and fueled her ever-growing sense that even normal things, like going to school—or owning a hairbrush—were becoming hazardous in West Shelby.

———

For Cal, early dismissal meant a chance to slip in a few extra hours at Oakwood, a chance to forget about his crash-and-burn talk with Star. Besides, with the gig coming up, he figured it might be a while before he found time to get back to the cemetery. When Cal reached the top of the yard, he found Stan wrestling a couple of young trees into a battered wheelbarrow.

"Hang on," Cal called over. "I'll get them." He found it no small struggle to shoulder the weighty saplings into the bin.

"Well, thanks for your muscle there, Cal. They may be small, but them root balls weigh like iron." He looked at the twiggy trees, smiling as if they were little children. "Maybe it's 'cause they got all that growin' stored up inside of 'em."

"Kinda late for planting, isn't it?" Cal asked, the question streaming from his mouth in a long shivery pant.

"Actually, it's the best time. You see, the trees are what you call dormant now. When they wake in the spring, they'll never know they were moved. Same branches, same trunk, just a different place to wiggle their roots, is all." He started down the yard. "We're runnin' out of time, though. First killin' frost hit this mornin'."

Cal strained to level the runaway wheelbarrow. "What about using the trailer? We could hook it behind one of the ride-on mowers. Might work better."

"It surely would. But the bearings on the trailer are shot, so we have to do things the old fashioned way today. I see you got the wreaths in place."

"Yeah," Cal grunted, swerving and just missing the Armstrong marker. "Took a while longer than I thought."

"Well, an A-to-Z list would've been easier, but since folks don't die alphabetically, it's kinda hard to bury 'em that way," he laughed.

And maybe it was the futility of steering a wheelbarrow with a mind-of-its-own or working in a place where nothing worked, but Cal found himself grinning and joking back. "What really would have helped was having the guy who knows all these dead people like next-of-kin, here with me."

Stan shrugged. "It was Tuesday, m' day off. I get one, you know."

Cal nodded, but somehow the idea seemed absurd. It wasn't that the old guy didn't deserve a break—hell, Stan was three times older and did five times the work—but he couldn't imagine the caretaker anywhere else but here, rambling around the workshop or graveyard with a rake or hoe in his hands. Even now, before the wheelbarrow skid to a stop, he was grabbing the shovels and reaching in for the first tree. Cal gave him a hand, but suddenly it didn't matter. Somewhere between the shed and the bottom of the cemetery, the laws of gravity had changed. Going into the wheelbarrow, those saplings felt as heavy as a stack of guitar amps but coming out —with help from the old man—they barely had weight at all.

"A little deeper there, Cal," Stan directed as they worked the ground with their shovels. "The whole ball needs to go beneath the ground. If we go too shallow, they'll topple over in the first windstorm." His toothy smile returned. "Deep roots make for a sturdy foundation, you know."

As Cal's shovel continued to split and scoop the soft earth, his eyes caught sight of the McClellan tombstone just a few rows away. He considered mentioning the encounter with Star's aunt but decided against it. The sight of the monument's reflective surface, however, nudged up a question nagging at the back of his mind.

"Why don't they say something?"

Stan looked up. "How's that?"

"The tombstones. Why don't they say more than just a name and a date?"

The caretaker stopped digging. "Why, Cal, if a person lives his life right, he leaves his mark when he's living, among the living—not on stone." His shovel patted the dirt over the roots of the last tree. "Nothin' left to say once a person gets here."

CHAPTER
ELEVEN

The next morning, curiosity over early dismissal and the bomb scare that prompted it consumed all homeroom conversations. Except for the Weir boys. Less concerned with yesterday's pranks than today's torments, they passed the time sharpening their crude wit and verbal munitions. When Cal walked headlong into their crosshairs, he knew they'd be ready.

"Hey, it's the crypt keeper," Jardo started up.

"L-looks more like the walking dead," his cousin, Ted, joined in. "Smells like it, too."

"Graveyard goon," one of their cronies added. "Watch out or he'll, uh, he'll…"

Cal could almost hear the halting gears grinding in their brains. Ignoring their laughter, he headed for the corner of the room where his friends' poker game was underway. He used to join in but couldn't block the energy swirling around the players. He always knew when someone was bluffing or if their cards were hot. Took out all the fun, so after a while, he just sat out and watched.

Today, Pete was in trouble. Kevin, too. Bill was trying to be cool, but his cards sucked. Unless one of them pulled an awesome bluff, Cal predicted the new guy, Gerry, was going to clean up.

"Doesn't have much to say, does he?" a voice gruffed out behind him.

"Maybe they cut out his tongue," Ted snorted, drawing a fresh round of heckles from his crew. "Or turned him into a zombie."

More rough laughter. Cal glanced over. They were passing around a caricature of him sleeping in a coffin with a can of gasoline and matches. He turned back toward the poker game. It wasn't so much a question of sticking up for himself—like Bill always nagged him to do—it was a matter of energy. The Weirs fed on humiliation. They waited for someone to land on their sticky web of insults, then taunted them, sucking their energy dry. No way he'd give them the satisfaction.

"I'm out," Kevin called, tossing down his cards.

Bill glanced eagerly at the bills crumpled in a heap on their adjoining desks.

"Got nothing," Pete admitted, showing a miserable hand.

Gerry began timidly, "Well—"

"Three of a kind!" Bill interrupted, showing off his cards. "C'mon, Ger. We don't have all day. The bell's going to ring. What d'ya got?"

"Well, I'm not sure," he faltered, "you guys ran through the rules pretty fast, but didn't Kevin say if your cards ran in sequence, you know, one after the other like this, it was good?"

Kevin and Pete laughed aloud while Cal smiled at the newbie's dumb luck.

"Tomorrow we're playing up to speed," Bill sulked, shoving the clutter of bills away. Then he turned on Cal. "I'd be ten bucks richer right now if you woulda kept playing."

"Emerling, you're just a lousy bluffer," Kevin said. "It's got nothin' to do with the players or the cards."

"Double or nothing tomorrow, pal!" Bill said, pointing his finger like a dagger.

As the teacher called attendance, Cal changed the subject. "Lucky break yesterday, huh?"

Still in a huff over the poker game, Bill didn't answer.

"We got dismissed before Mr. Finn collected the homework. He never knew you didn't do it."

Bill shrugged his stocky shoulders. "I wouldn't need luck if you hadn't been such a prick and gave me your homework."

Cal ignored the peeved tone. "Did you get it done? You had all afternoon."

"Sort of," Bill said, a mischievous smile darkening his face. "I made my sister do it. Hey, she took chemistry last year, so why sweat through it? Besides, I told Tori I'd pound her if she didn't."

Primal zombie grunts began to drift over from the direction of the Weirs along with hands knocking in a mock tremble against their desks. Cal blocked it out, but then he heard a sound worse than any the bad-boy cousins could belch out.

"Stop being so annoying, Jared. Can't you just leave Cal alone? If your parents knew…"

Cal winced. In a careless second, Carol Zempke's whiney voice had tossed her right into the Weirs' sticky trap. It set off a semiautomatic hailstorm of insults that ripped apart everything from her big nose to her baggy clothes to her not-so-secret crush on Cal. He closed his eyes to block out the storm of color the scene brought on. When they reopened, he found Bill glaring at him.

"You're gonna let them get away with that?" he said in a gruff whisper. He glanced at Cal's trembling hands. "I mean, your *situation* is bad enough."

Even as Bill sat there grinding his fist into the palm of his hand, Cal knew he was all talk. The guy had a yellow streak a mile wide. Still, being left alone was a privilege Cal rarely knew. He sometimes fantasized about being anonymous, moving through crowded hallways and classrooms with the placid immunity of a ghost. Keep it cool, he told himself every morning. Take each day, one hour, one minute at a time. Amazing how often that simple mantra failed him.

The sensation of little wet splats ticking off the back of his head alerted Cal that Jardo and his larger ape cousin were entertaining their halfwit cronies with target practice. Cal lifted his unsteady hand and flicked out several wads of paper lodged in his collar.

He leaned toward Bill. "C'mon, do you really think anything would change if I said something? Look at them."

Bill strained his body around to see the group of overgrown juniors, amusing themselves at his friend's expense.

"When they graduate—if they graduate—what's the best they can hope for? Third shift? Parole? You can only imagine what 'back home' is like." And maybe Bill couldn't see it, but Cal could. In the rough pitted waves of energy around them —hopelessness.

Bill grumbled, shaking his head at the Weirs' antics. "They're jerks and they're making you look stupid."

"Ted's drooling and the rest of 'em are moaning like zombies. Who looks stupid?"

The classroom phone rang, and the teacher answered it without much notice from the students. When she hung up the receiver, she turned to the class and in her roll-call voice, said: "Calvin Hughes, the principal would like to see you in his office—immediately."

Heads whipped around, eyes widened. Again, the wish for invisibility washed over Cal, but realizing that the quicker he left the room, the sooner he'd be out of the glaring spotlight, he got up, slid his books off the desk, and with a trembling hand took the corridor pass from the teacher's outstretched arm.

He walked toward the door, eyes lowered, trying to tune out the whispers around him. But he couldn't avoid absorbing the emotions that followed his egress—curiosity, condemnation, Bill's disgust, Carol's pity, the Weirs' twisted admiration. As the door closed behind him, he heard Jardo's odd salute:

"You have to admit, the dude's got balls—8:05, and he's already in trouble."

———

Cal shifted uneasily in the hard chair. Beside him, Star met his questioning glance with a careless shrug. On the other side of the massive brown desk, the principal tapped his fingers, one hand against the other.

"So then, Calvin. Let's have it."

"Have what?"

"Yesterday, the bomb scare?"

Cal brushed his hair back off his shoulders and answered more obstinately than he'd meant to. "What about it?"

"The hall monitor reported that you and Ms. McClellan were on the second floor near the payphone where we've traced the threatening call between third and fourth periods."

"What? That payphone actually works?"

Despite her edgy voice, Cal sensed a different Star today. Dressed in a soft black sweater and jeans, she slumped in the chair, her eyes wide but sleepy, her hair an uncombed tangle of pink and red.

"Not all of our students can afford cell phones, Ms. McClellan. Some don't come from privileged homes."

Cal looked at Star. He could see her energy spike red at the implication. He spoke up, as much to defend himself as to save Star from what she might say—and regret.

"I had nothing to do with that phone call."

"So, you were nowhere near the phone or that corridor yesterday?" the principal clarified.

"Well, I didn't say I wasn't near it," Cal stammered, recalling the pre-class homework panic with Bill, their position against the lockers in ready sight of the payphone and lavatories.

"Look, I went to chemistry class and didn't make any phone call. End of story."

The telephone rang on the principal's desk. He glowered at each of them before answering it. Star's hand reached over Cal's armrest and began to scribble on his binder.

"So, you'll cover for some people some of the time, but not everyone all of the time," she taunted in a sultry whisper. "You're an enigma, Calvin Hughes."

As she leaned toward him, Cal could feel her charismatic energy. It vibrated like a powerful electric current. He turned to hold her gaze for a few seconds. Unsettled, she blinked hard and turned away. A moment later, her low raspy voice swam into his ear. "What did you mean yesterday when you said my aunt looked *off* at Alula's service?"

Cal knew this wasn't the place. He had so much to tell her. The principal was wrapping up his phone call. He only had a second to explain. "Her energy," he began in a hushed whisper, "all wrong."

Leaning back, Cal caught Star's skeptical smirk. It said: *What the hell are you talking about?*

The principal hung up the phone and turned to Cal. "That was Mr. Finn. He said you were indeed in class yesterday." Cal began to breathe easier. "But you were late."

"Maybe," Cal admitted, "but I didn't make that bomb threat and I don't know anyone who would even want…"

But his words died upon the awful realization that he did know someone who not only could've made that call but benefited from it.

"That brings us to you, Ms. McClellan. Mr. Finn said you never showed to class and we have two witnesses who place you near the phone at about the time of the incident."

Her voice rose, "You got security footage?"

"We, uh, don't have cameras there. They were, uh, cut from last year's budget."

Star tossed her head, yawned, then fingered the studs on her leather wristband. "Hearsay is not evidence."

Frustrated, the principal stood up, indicating the meeting's conclusion. "A day's in-house suspension, Ms. McClellan, for skipping class."

Star rose from her chair, the stud quivering in her nose, her mouth pouty, impatient. "What about Cal? Letting him off easy?"

"Uh, we'll make that a final warning for you, Calvin."

Cal waited 'til he and Star were in the hallway beyond the straining antennae of the office staff before opening up. "What was *that* about? You could have gotten me suspended."

Star's eyes made a guilty start, her voice, however, was flippant. "What can I say? Misery loves company."

"You don't think I'm miserable enough?"

She bit her studded lip. "Maybe I just wanted to piss you off, see what'd you do. See if you'd get mad enough to leave me alone, stop bothering me."

"I never want to bother you, Star." He swallowed hard and looked beyond her at something only he could see. "I just want to help. Amazing how hard that can be."

For a rare minute, there was nothing between them but silence. Cal watched a shiver tremble over Star's black lips, her sleepy brown eyes fill with sadness. For a second, she looked at him in a way he'd been hoping for all fall. He dropped his gaze, stared at his sneakers, and kicked at the mosaic floor. There was no other way to explain it, to explain what he saw, explain his fears. The truth. It was time. Finally.

"Sometimes, I see stuff..." He rolled his tongue in his cheek. "That other people don't see."

"Like ghosts?"

"No. That would be easier. I see energy. Human energy. In colors."

Cal looked up into Star's sugary brown eyes, waiting for her to laugh, to swear, to walk away. He'd just revealed the biggest secret of his life. He expected *something*. For a minute, he wondered if she was even listening.

He went on. "The colors tend to mean things."

"What does this have to do with my sister's memorial service?"

"Look, everyone at the service had the kind of energy I'd expect. Sad blue clouds of emotion filtered through shades of pink—love they felt for Alula." He swallowed. "Except for Aunt Zoe. Her energy was red. *Only* red. Fury."

Star eyes narrowed to a skeptical sliver, her brows rising. "So? Maybe she was pissed that my father didn't take better care of Alula. Or pissed at God. Or life in general. There are a million reasons why she might have been *red*." Her fingers made big quotation marks.

"There's more. The day of the fire, I felt something radiating from the old marsh paths that run behind Houdini's place. Alula's vibe. I could tell she'd been there recently. The heat from the fire ramped up the energy trail she'd left behind. I stood there absorbing it, hoping for a clue. Couldn't tear myself away. Probably why they nailed me for it."

Star shook her head. "You know, you're making your life friggin' miserable. Why don't you ignore all the crazy shit you see or *think* you see? That's what I do—I mean, *would* do if I was as messed up as you."

As she blustered away, Cal looked after her, immune to the drama. No amount of attitude could change how he felt about her or what he saw around her. Still, he needed to make her see that there was something about sweet Aunt Zoe that was darker than the marsh waters on a moonless night.

CHAPTER
TWELVE

That night, Star lay awake against the soft ticking of a bedside clock. She felt a subtle expectancy in the quiet moments that led up to midnight. Like something was about to happen, something other-worldly that only this hour could host—the witching hour. She closed her eyelids, black and runny from the day's smear of makeup and waited for it, for the mystery she felt teetering here at the brink of twelve and the answers she hoped were behind it. Yet with the hour came her nightly struggle, not so much against sleep, but the visions that interrupted it. Eventually, she fell into a fitful slumber and the reflections or, as she had come to see them, the hauntings began…

Alone. Tumbling. Even as she struggled to breathe, to stop herself from falling end-over-end, to fight the invisible thing dragging her to her death, she knew it was too late. As the frantic sound of her heart thumped more and more slowly in her ears, her spirit began to drizzle away. Silently, she surrendered. All at once Cal appeared, his blue eyes piercing through the watery blur like brilliant beacons. Without uttering a word, his strong hands encircled her waist and thrust her toward safety...then the murky ripples of the reflection began to change...again, hard to breathe. Lying on the ground. A crowd, grim, hovering too close. A man with a concealed face, a girl sobbing into a bouquet of wilted flowers and broken stems. And Cal? Gone. She knew without any doubt, it was her fault. Then the masked man laughed, his eyes flaring like the last embers in a fire...

Star rolled over, but kept her eyes sealed. From the distant tower of St. Francis, she listened as twelve low chimes marked the moment when deepest night yawned into earliest morning. She listened hard, then harder still. But there was nothing more, just the tick-tocking of her bedside clock and, further away through her open window, the sound of a hailstorm rolling up from the marsh. Her eyes fluttered open and filtered over the familiar outlines of her room: a toss of clothing, a stack of books, a teapot still warm on the side table. She scanned them for a clue, a shadow, anything that might explain this foreboding vision. But her room, like her life, was miserably unchanged.

She thought about the ending. How it always filled her with dread, with the sense this was no ordinary dream, but a warning—a promise.

Unless she did something to stop it.

She fought back an urge to dismiss it. What had she told Cal? *Ignore all the crazy shit you see.* If only it was that easy. After all, hadn't those reflections—wavering in everything from marsh puddles to water fountains—come true? Bomb scares, fires, even that one about Alula. She should've recognized what they were sooner...

But Cal was wrong about Aunt Zoe. She'd always been there for her. A rock to hold onto. Especially now. Besides, she wasn't even sure if she understood what Cal had been talking about. When those sapphire blue eyes dazzled her way, she couldn't think straight. Gazing back at them was like falling into a serene mountain lake, drowning but not caring…

Star lay awake for another hour, the rattle of ice tapping like nervous fingernails against her window. With the weight of Cal's well-being crushing her conscience, she knew it was time to stop waiting for answers to materialize in the dark. Every minute she spent with Cal put him in danger. Despite the blurry reflections, that much was crystal clear to her.

Lately she'd tried—really tried—to keep distance between them, even that failed attempt to piss him off in the principal's office yesterday. Nothing worked. And telling him about her dreamy reflection would only make matters worse. If he thought there was any truth in it, any chance that she was in harm's way, he'd never leave her alone.

No, it was time for drastic measures. The longer he spent any time at all with her, the more likely the fatal vision would take hold. So, no matter the price, she *would* save Cal. Even if it meant losing what she wanted most in the world—his affection.

CHAPTER
THIRTEEN

O f all the nights for a storm. Cal peered through the car window framed in ice. The road beyond it shone slick and black as a seal's skin. Revving the engine, he braced his arm against the headrest and backed down the driveway. His foot leaned heavy on the gas, then over-compensated with the brakes and sent the car into a wild skid. As the back tires smacked into the curb on the other side of the street, the car jolted to a stop. Cal held his breath, then glanced over his shoulder. Guitar, amp, speaker, stand. All in place. No damage. Turk would have extras of everything. Still, this was not the night to take chances.

He turned onto Alder Lane, the half-slush, half-ice pavement a steady driving challenge. It made Eva's parting message echo at the back of his mind: "First winter behind the wheel? Good luck. At least one accident—guaranteed." The conditions were nothing he couldn't handle, he told himself. Just a slower drive is all. He was hours ahead of schedule. No problem.

As he drove, the car's headlights roved over the marshy landscape, a vast black hole except for the shadowy glow of the McClellan estate. Looking through the tangle of willow branches, Cal wondered about Star, how he'd asked her to come tonight, how she'd said no. But then, a few hours ago, she texted him, asked what time the band would hit the stage. Maybe she changed her mind. The corners of his mouth inched upward. It would make his night to have her there.

He felt the tires begin to slip against the icy road and edged off the gas. Another turn—a careful one—and his tires began a steady click-clack over the steel grates of the Crossover Street Bridge. Smoothing onto the better paved, better plowed roads of the South side, his foot eased onto the gas pedal. It was only eight-thirty. Plenty of time. He could blow a tire, get lost, even grab a bite and still be in Buffalo in time for set-up. No worries.

Still, the calm he struggled to preserve was constantly tested. Every few minutes, new worries fluttered up from his nerve-racked stomach like skittish bats from a cave, each trying to convince him that his watch was wrong or that he'd forgotten something at home. He glanced toward the full gas gauge, then looked back up to the road.

Through the blur of rain, Cal could see the lights of Main Street come into view. He blinked, scrutinizing the sidewalks and storefronts of the business district for time bandits, anything that might hint at delay. Somehow, everything appeared cool. This is too easy, he thought. Then he glanced into the rearview mirror. His breath froze. A white car had crept into his lane and appeared to tail him. Of course. Lieutenant Gavin. If he knew how much this evening meant… At the next corner, however, the car's headlights swept west disappearing from Cal's mirror. He took a deep breath. Another worry drifted out from his stomach.

Up ahead, through the smear of windshield wipers, he saw the watery outline of his former teammates approaching The Last Drop. They were crouched against the rain, their gym bags slung high over their shoulders. Bill was an easy stand-out, his flimsy wave of energy unmistakable, its streamers branching out, siphoning off the vitality of those around him.

Reaching the outskirts of town, he turned the car onto Route 33—a two lane drag that would take him most of the way to Buffalo. The rain was slacking off, slowing the frantic scrape of the windshield wipers, and he began to breathe a little easier. He passed cattle fences and dairy farms, country bars with red neon beer signs, even an old barn where a star had been newly traced in Christmas lights across the hayloft door. Looking down, he checked the dash. Fuel tank, engine temp, oil level—all good. Another trio of bats fluttered out, and a trickle of relief began to seep through his veins. He was just thirty miles from Buffalo and still had more than an hour to spare.

Accelerating, he turned onto a wider bend of road where the country churches and feed stores fell away to chain stores and fast-food joints. All at once, Cal realized he was starving. Until now, hunger seemed too small a detail. Or maybe his stomach, so full of worries, didn't feel empty. Looking ahead, he saw a bright sign with a blue neon hot dog dancing arm-in-arm with a toasted bun: *Manny's World Famous Charbroil.*

Yeah, that would do it. Take the edge off. It would be hours—maybe morning—before he'd have a chance to eat again. He signaled and crossed into the right lane just as his phone went off. Keeping one hand on the wheel and both eyes on the road, he fumbled through his pockets. He glanced down. Paul's number flashed on the screen. When he pressed the phone to his ear, Cal wasn't surprised to hear Turk's voice.

"You almost here?"

"Yeah, less than half an hour," Cal said. He turned off his signal and watched the wiggling hot dog slip past his window. "What about Phil and Paul?"

"Here," Turk said, using words as sparingly as if he were paying for each one. "Any problems?"

"No. Everything's cool. I'm on my way."

There was a pause. For a moment, Cal thought the signal dropped. Then Turk's husky voice sounded out, a notch above a whisper.

"We need you, man. For once, let everything else go. Tonight, just be *here*. Don't stop."

Click.

Cal tossed the phone onto the seat. What was that about? Sure, his track record wasn't perfect. He'd missed a rehearsal here and there, but how could Turk even think he'd mess this up? Still, the call ushered in a thousand new worries. They gathered in the pit of his stomach, and almost made him forget how hungry he was—*almost*.

The rain shifted to a sort of misty snow. Between the intermittent swipe of the windshield wipers, Cal could see the outskirts of the city coming into view. Up ahead, his headlights roamed over a sign: *Buffalo next three exits.*

It was 9:30 p.m. He had time. Maybe just a drive thru. How long could it take?

Brushing his bangs out of his eyes, he realized almost instantly he'd gotten off at the wrong exit—15 not 15a. It was okay though, just a little longer on side roads. Not as direct a route, but it would still get him there. He coasted up to the end of the ramp, to the traffic signal, cracked open a window and waited at the red light. Drumming his fingers over the steering wheel, he glanced around the neighborhood and suddenly froze mid-tap. On the other side of the road waiting, it seemed, just for him was Burger King. He barely held on for the light to turn green before gunning his car over the roadway and into the parking lot.

There were small things in those first few minutes, details that hardly registered, things that meant nothing at the time, but eventually everything. The brown station wagon idling in the lot, the rusty hinge on the glass door, the girl with pink barrettes. But when he first walked into the half-empty restaurant, Cal was only aware of the hollow aching in his stomach and the open counter that let him walk straight up and order: "A burger, chocolate shake, and fries—make that a large order of fries."

A few minutes later he was smiling down into a paper bag, inhaling the greasy aroma of the burger, grabbing three and four fries at a time, hardly conscious of walking toward his car or of anyone passing him in the lot.

Suddenly he stopped, his sneakers skid a little against the wet pavement. He glanced over one shoulder, then the other. Nothing. But he felt the brush of something against his arm. Unmistakable. A sensation, sharp as a razor's slash yet as intangible as the wet flakes swirling in the night air. He searched for the object. Maybe a plastic fork tossed from a passing car, or an empty can thrown his way. But even as his eyes scanned the ground, he knew he wouldn't find anything. It wasn't that simple. Never was.

Cal looked over his shoulder. On the near side of the parking lot, the station wagon guy was trudging toward the restaurant, a confusion of frizzy hair half-tucked beneath his cap, glaring at Cal as if to warn him away. There was more, but Cal didn't want to see it. Still, it was there—the energy throbbing in a rhythm so menacing that even in mere passing he'd felt the man's dark intent.

Cal took a few halting steps toward his car. A voice inside his head—which sounded less like his conscience than Turk—pleaded with him:

Get in…drive away…just get in the car and go…

How easy it should be to do that, do the thing he was meant to do tonight, the thing *he* wanted to do. Even as the drum beating within his chest begged him to turn around, Cal tried to deny his senses. Clutching the warm greasy bag of food in the palm of his hand, he convinced himself it was nerves, hunger. Yeah, that was it. Embracing the fragile lie, he reached for more fries, unlocked his car and slipped behind the wheel.

Then he heard a sound. A sound that didn't belong. Not here, not anywhere. Unless, maybe, you were playing a video game—or at a shooting range.

And in that second, the night was no longer his own.

Jumping from the car, Cal dashed through the parking lot, running on fuel embedded so deep in his core he hardly knew it was there. With the bag of fast food still clutched in his hand, he raced back up the driveway, bounded over the curb, and tugged open the door, its rusty hinge announcing his arrival with brutal clarity. He had less than a second to take it all in— the bulging eyes, the forgotten meals, the frightened customers, the nervous bandit—a still-life painting of terror. And now he was in the middle of it.

"Hit the deck!" the man screeched.

Then, without waiting for Cal to do so, the robber fired his pistol. The bullet struck the glass door behind Cal in a spectacular crash and he dove for the floor, sliding belly-first into a pool of broken glass. Blood spurted across his temple and Cal felt his eyes roll toward unconsciousness, but then he caught sight of the unsteady hands aiming a gun barrel at him and his eyes sobered wide open.

"Go 'head, try me!" the man barked, taking Cal's unshakable blue stare as a challenge. "Go 'head, like Pops over there." He waved his pistol toward an elderly couple still quaking beside a newly burnt hole in their upholstered booth. "See where it gits y—"

The man stopped. His head lifted with a sort of animalistic jerk, as if he'd heard something no one else could hear.

"Hurry up!" he screamed at the girl behind the counter.

Using the barrel of the gun like an extension of his fingers, he directed her from one cash drawer to the next where she stuffed fistfuls of bills into a paper sack. When it was full, he snatched it away.

"Gimmee that," he bellowed, his bravado caving with the shudder in his voice. He turned and hesitated.

And now the awkward moment of escape. Cal could see the man's confusion, a singular ribbon of light wrestling against the darkness of his energy. After all, it had been almost easy busting into the place, threatening the life out of everyone, demanding cash. But now, with the loot in hand, he had to try and slither away, avoid any ambush attempts, then drive off before the cops showed up and chased him down like a wild dog.

Backing away from the counter, the thief swung the gun in a semicircle of protection, aiming it at the diners.

"Stay back," he warned. "No heroes. I said, stay back!"

The half dozen or so patrons exchanged bewildered looks. No one had dared move.

"Don't screw this up or so help me God…"

His eyes ricocheted wildly around the room. His movements became erratic. At first, he sidled toward one exit, but seeing the mess of glass and Cal's sprawled body partially blocking the doorway, he jerked away and made a break for the opposite door, lurching in quick backward steps while shouting at the employees.

"Back away from the counter—back away! And if even one a' ya reach for a phone, I'll pump this place so fulla bullets, they'll need a bulldozer to find your bodies."

At this, a fresh wail arose from a booth near the door, from a mother hugging her children in a wide protective embrace. Throughout the stick-up, Cal noticed her struggling to keep her composure, her lips moving silently, as if in prayer. Until now, it seemed to be the glue holding her together.

"Shut-up!" the robber screamed. "Shut-up!"

But the louder he yelled, the harder she cried. Cal could see she was beyond herself. She buried her head into the small shoulders of her children and wept hysterically.

"Shut-up! Shut-up!" he bellowed, pointing the gun at her, his mad glare bouncing from table to table. "I mean it! Don't push me!"

Until this last outburst, Cal felt it would be okay, that with the registers empty, the money in hand, and everybody quiet, there would be a peaceful end. But now the man's energy field began to change, swirling faster and darker like a tornado about to touch down, his nerves spiraling out of control. All at once, he lunged at the sobbing woman and grabbed one of her children from beneath her arms.

"Shut-up or she gits it!" he spat, pressing the gun just below the girl's pink barrettes.

Cal felt his heart pound against the glass splinters. This wasn't what the guy wanted. It was going all wrong, the deed raging beyond him. He looked as scared as the little girl whose eyes were bulging above his restraining arm.

"For the love of God!" the mother cried, half-swooning into the aisle. Other sobs joined her own.

Somewhere back in the kitchen, an untimely pot clanged to the floor.

Cal's jaw tightened. The place was falling apart. Time was running out. Without warning, the old man in the corner booth stood up. "Taking money is one thing, but someone's little girl—"

Before he could finish his brave speech, the robber fired a shot, just missing the old man's leg. His wife screamed, then she started crying, too. Across the room, people began gasping and sobbing in new tones of hysteria. Cal knew there were only seconds before the whole thing turned into a bloodbath. The guy was losing it. The reddish-brown lesions, invisible to everyone else, were bleeding anger, frustration, confusion. Clutching both the bag of money and the terrified little girl, he seemed unsure of what to do next. He dragged her toward the door.

"Wait!" Cal shouted.

For a second everyone stopped breathing, stopped whatever terrified sound they were making and looked at the crazy boy with the bloody temple who was setting himself up for a gunshot to the head. Even the bandit froze, amazed at Cal's audacity.

"Take me," Cal said, the glass crunching as he got to his feet, his trembling hands raised above his head.

The man's steely eyes surveyed Cal and his courage with pure loathing.

"I don't need baggage," he said, gritting his teeth.

"Exactly. So, leave the girl."

"She's insurance."

The man tightened his grip.

"I can drive," Cal blurted, his face flush, his blood racing so fast and hot that it hurt. "Wherever you need to go."

The thief seemed to relish the quaver in Cal's voice, the tremor of his hands which he misread as fear. For a moment he just waited, then with a cock of his head, he moved the gun away from the little girl, closed one of his eyes and aimed it directly at Cal's head.

————

The downtown streets were a minefield of potholes and black ice over which the old wagon's loose steering and spongy brakes couldn't manage. Cal's foot eased off the gas.

"Whatta you slowin' down for?" the man barked at his side. "Keep drivin'."

"Where?" Cal asked, adjusting the rearview mirror downward. It offered a better view of the pair of small, frightened eyes watching him from the back seat.

"Anywhere a ways from here."

Anywhere and nowhere. Cal focused on the road. But around every corner he saw Turk's face, heard the echo of his voice. Maybe he could still make the show…

Each time the bald tires slid over a patch of ice, Cal had to pump the brakes and fumble with the steering. At one point, he tugged at the temperature switch, but when the heat kicked in, the smell of body odor and urine rushed through the car.

"Where's the bag?" the thief suddenly demanded.

Cal's eyes turned from the pitted roadway just long enough to glance at the sack of money stashed between the man's knees.

"Not *my* bag!" the man snapped.

Cal looked around doubtfully. But there it was. Stuffed into the seat beside him. Somehow, in all the confusion, he'd managed to hang onto his meal.

The man saw the bag at the same time, snatched at it, and began woofing down the cold fries before tearing off the wrapper around the burger.

Once or twice during the early minutes, Cal hazarded a glance at the thief. In the half-light of passing bar signs, he noticed the ruddy face, the frizzy mess of hair, the soft sadness in his eyes dueling with the gruff scowl bent into his unshaven chin. When he was eating, though, the guy looked like a wild animal, his boxy hands tearing clumsily at whatever he wanted—at the moment, fries at the bottom of the bag. Then Cal saw it, the thing that made the man look so bestial: his left hand was missing a thumb.

It had been a moment's distraction, a glance, but long enough that the loose steering took over. The wheel slipped through Cal's fingers. Without warning, the car skid over a patch of black ice and into the path of an oncoming delivery van. Cal wrenched at the wheel, the van swerved, their side mirrors scraped. The driver laid on his horn and flipped Cal off.

"Ya tryin' to kill us?!"

Cal exhaled heavily and steered back into the right lane. He glanced through the rearview mirror again. "Got any seat belts in this thing?"

The thief laughed. "Don't even have a radio. Sometimes no heater. It's only for gittin' places." His voice dimmed. "An' sleepin' sometimes..."

"'S okay. My mama's car don't have none of that neither."

The small voice curled up unexpectedly from the back seat, sweetening the dank air like a song. Cal could see the whites of the girl's eyes rolling in the rearview mirror as her voice hop-scotched along.

"She says we don't need no seat belts. So long as me and my brothers hold on to each other."

Her words seemed to unsettle the frizzy-haired felon. Wiping his mouth with his sleeve, he let the bag of fast-food drop between his boots to the floor. With a long, lonely sigh, he leaned his head against the side window.

Cal drove on, his eyes trained on the road, but his mind fixed on the mess of a person beside him. But there was light. A sliver, thinner than a crescent moon. And where there was light there was hope. After a while, he braved a question.

"What are you going to do with the money?"

"Huh?"

"You know, what are you going to buy?"

The man spat back, "Nunna your damn business."

"'Cause I know if I suddenly came into some extra cash, there's a bunch of stuff I'd go for."

The man said nothing—a silent permission slip, Cal thought.

"Mostly, I'd use it for my guitar. This cop busted it up a few

112

weeks ago, and it needs work. Now, my sister, she'd blow all the money on earrings. Probably some gummy bears, too."

"Oh, I love those things," the girl in the back seat cooed.

Cal adjusted the rearview mirror again, caught her eye and aimed a smile in her direction.

"Now, my mom," Cal continued, "would go for something simple, like new towels for the bathroom." The man turned and made a face. "No, really, she's like that. A million dollars and she'd splurge on some fancy soap or candles, weird house stuff like that."

There was a pause, a moment that went by quietly but uncomfortably.

"It's not a million dollars, though," the man said in a small voice. He glanced down at the paper bag between his knees. "It's probably not even a hundred." The realization seemed to absolutely defeat him. "I'll git cigarettes, some booze…"

"Nothing for the family?" Cal risked.

"Girlfriend left me after I lost…" his voice trailed off.

They drove on. Another slippery turn, another unfamiliar street, another wrench at the steering wheel. The sad rhythm seemed to play on all night. And then Cal heard it—a sound so small, so soft, he'd almost missed it—a crack. The hard-boiled surface of the man whose life had cooked him until he was not only done but undone, had just begun to split.

"Where do you want to go?" Cal asked, his tone gentle.

"I dunno. Just drive."

And Cal did, though he was so lost by now he hadn't a clue as to where he was. Buildings, warehouses, abandoned lots, even a police station and a city mission began to look familiar and he despaired at the futile path he was tracing through streets and neighborhoods that raged like war zones. He knew hours had passed. Somewhere his band was taking the stage…

The tiny voice chirped up from the back seat again, "Um, you got any of them fries left? I'm *starving.*"

Cal heard the bag rustle at the man's feet. "No," he snapped. Glancing back down, the thief pulled out the straw and the milkshake poking up from the bag. Stretching his arm over the seat, he nudged the frosty cup into the girl's hands. "Don't spill it."

They drove on as before, with the addition of slurping sounds coming from the back seat, and the man grew thoughtful.

"Y' from around here?"

"No," Cal answered. "West Shelby, about an hour away."

"On the marsh?"

"You heard of it?"

"Heard of it? Me and my grandpa used to go fishin' down there. Place called Ackley's Bend."

"Great fishing hole. Not too many people go there anymore," Cal said.

"Haven't been up that way since my grandpa passed on."

Then they were awkward again, not in the way they'd been when the gun was pointed at Cal's head, but in a way that men are when emotions are raw and bubbling too near the surface. At length, the frizzy-haired man broke the silence.

"I wurnt always like this," he began, his voice a bare mumble. "I had a trade, made money. I mean, was never rich or anything, but I did okay. Had a place, a pickup truck, a few bucks put away."

"Yeah?"

"I was a carpenter," he declared, proud as if he'd said President. "Did custom work and side jobs I picked up on my own. Made a good livin' and I was good at it."

From the corner of his eye, Cal could see the colors in the man's energy field begin to lift and dance around him. His voice strengthened.

"They called me in when they wanted to update the woodwork at the Rath Building. Picked me for lead carpenter on the Clement mansion restoration…"

Cal drove on, listening to the melancholy tale accompanied by the slow rhythmic breathing of the little girl, asleep now in the back seat. Occasionally, the blare of oncoming headlights would flash through the windshield and illuminate the thief's expression, his weathered cheeks and weary eyes brightening as he recalled better times.

"But since I wurnt injured on the job, I couldn't git workman's comp. Gave up on physical therapy." His voice faltered. "Started drinkin'. Then drugs. Flo left me. I lost the apartment." He shook his head in new disgust. "Funny, how long it takes to piece a good life together. How fast it all falls apart…"

The man's head lowered, his scruffy chin sinking into his chest. Cal knew this might be his only chance. He slowed down, pulled the car to the curb and shifted into park.

The thief's head jerked upright. "What are ya doin'? Start drivin'!"

"Listen, it's not too late. You can turn things around, pull your life back together."

"Git this car back on the road! Now!" He picked up the pistol, nearly forgotten in his lap, and started waving it in Cal's direction.

"Put that thing down. Look at the gauge." Cal's finger thumped the dash. "We're running out of gas and you're running out of time."

The thief snorted. "I got more time than I got anything else."

"Yeah, well, you're wasting it. You don't have to be like this."

The man glared at Cal. "Yeah? Then how come I am?"

"Because…well…I don't know. Sometimes, I guess, we get tested."

"Why?"

"I don't know!" Cal shot back. "We just do. Maybe it's to see—to see what we're made of. I can tell you this much, though, you're a lot better person than you pretend to be."

The man opened his mouth, a curse on his lips, then stopped. "How d'ya know?"

Cal fumbled for an explanation. He couldn't tell the guy how he knew because he couldn't tell him what he'd seen, that even during the heat of the holdup there was always some light reflecting out from his soul—though it was as fleeting as the glimmer of a marsh firefly.

"Because you could have killed a lot of people back there and you didn't," Cal explained. "Because you know the difference between right and wrong."

The thief moaned, his deformed hand clamping over his face in anguish. "I do! But it's too late. I tried to change. The only thing I'm good at anymore is bein' bad."

"You're wrong," Cal said as he watched new light drizzling through his energy field. "You have no idea how wrong you are."

The man stared brazenly into Cal's eyes, then seemed to humble. "What I gotta do?" he whispered.

"One thing. Just one small, good thing. That's all it takes. That's how you start."

"What's that goin' do?" the man scoffed.

"Try it, you'll see. It can change everything."

"One good thing, huh?" A dark grin wrinkled over the stubble of the man's chin. "Ya don't get it, do ya? I'm a convicted felon in a hot car with a bag fulla stolen money, a stash a' weed under the seat, a kid in the back seat that don't belong and a gun. Where's a dude like that goin' to start doin' some good, huh?"

"Start here," Cal said unshaken. "Start now." He nodded over his shoulder. "Let her go."

Maybe it was the sight of the sleeping kid curled on the

back seat, her arm wrapped around the empty milkshake container like it was a favorite doll. Or maybe it was the calm blue insistence in Cal's eyes, but all at once the rest of the hard-boiled shell cracked off. The man reached over the back seat and gently nudged the girl.

"Hey, kid, can you git home from here?"

She sat up, blinked, seemed to recognize a dilapidated playground. "This ain't far from Mama's." A moment later, he was opening the car door and lifting her onto the curb. She walked sleepily up the block toward a huddle of rundown apartment buildings. Cal stepped on the gas and sped off before anyone could see them.

They drove on, the car so light mere fumes seemed to fuel it. Once again, the man didn't seem to care where they were going, but this time Cal knew exactly where he was headed. Ten minutes later, he pulled to the curb, parked the car, and turned off the engine without any protest from the thief. For a moment, Cal watched him struggling with himself, the scowling lower end of his face seeming to do battle with the lighter upper end. When he finally spoke up, his voice was fierce.

"I wanna do it again."

Already Cal could see the fissures in his energy field healing, years of angst mending.

"I need to know there's more a' that in me, more than *just* one good thing. Help me," he pleaded. "What else can I do?"

With a steady finger, Cal pointed up the block to a place he'd noticed hours ago, to one of only two buildings on the street still open. The man's head lifted hopefully. But looking through the rain-spattered windshield, all the anticipation drained from his face.

"The cop station? That's where ya think I should go?" He looked down, rubbing the long end of the pistol with the stub of his thumb. "Well, I can't. I can't turn myself in. Prison ain't gonna fix me. I been there. It don't heal you. It makes ya grow hard." He breathed a defeated sigh. "I thought maybe ya had some other good idea. Like the last one."

"That's not what I was pointing at," Cal answered softly. "Across the street."

The man's head sprung up and his weary eyes glared at a white cinder block building. Above the doorway a hand-painted sign wavered beneath a shivery yellow light: *City Mission*.

"Listen, you can't do any good if you're tired and hungry." Cal hesitated. "And a warm shower wouldn't hurt either. The people over there can help you get the basics in order, then maybe you can see about getting back to physical therapy. Your brain still has the skills. You just need to retrain your hands to use them."

The man glanced back and forth from the pistol in his hands to the shabby little mission up the street. "Shit. I dunno. I never been to a place like that before."

"Yeah, well, you've been to prison and you know what that's like."

They sat awhile longer, the man stroking his gun, the traffic light blinking directions to an empty street. Somewhere, a few blocks away, a church bell tolled twelve long times and Cal dared to let his mind wander off to another part of the city, to the place where he was supposed to be, to the people he was supposed to be with. By now, the show would be over. He could almost feel the frantic shudder of his cell phone vibrating across the seat of his car, begging him to answer...

All at once, the car door creaked open.

"Wait, where are you—"

"I dunno," the man said, slamming the door behind him.

"What about the car?"

"Dump it."

Then he started up the street, throwing furtive glances over his shoulder like he was going to make a break for it. Once or twice, where the sidewalk broke off into a side ally, Cal was sure the man had ducked into the shadows, but then he would reemerge on the other side of the gap walking steadily toward some fate, Cal wasn't sure which.

Just before the man reached the point where the police station and mission seemed to stand at a crossroads, he stopped. There seemed a great confusion about him, but Cal's attention had to cut away.

Inching up along the left flank of the car, a police cruiser seemed to be checking Cal out, zeroing in on the expired registration. Cal dropped his head, his breath as still as his heart was frantic. He pretended to fumble with the seatbelt. The police car, however, passed without incident, parking ahead in a space reserved for officers who worked at the station. With a heaving sigh, Cal looked up, focusing on the far end of the street again. But there was nothing to see. The thief was gone.

CHAPTER
FOURTEEN

The return to West Shelby was quiet, uneventful. Cal drove beneath the dark, starless sky, thinking little and feeling less. He did not look at the gas gauge or notice the time. Could not have said whether his seatbelt was fastened. The radio was silent, his gear still. He drove on, unaware as the city ghetto became an entrance ramp, a highway, and then a country road lined with feed stores and white clapboard churches. Only when he saw the barn with the thread of Christmas lights stretched across the hayloft door did he feel the slightest pang. It was here, he remembered, the evening held so much promise.

After that, the rest of the trip seemed difficult, winding through scenery that appeared the same but no longer felt the way it had a few hours ago. Not because it was different, but because he was. All the long way home he found himself wondering about the thief, how his life had gotten so low, so hopeless, that pressing a gun against a little girl's skull actually presented itself as a viable idea. Maybe next time the guy would stop and think. Maybe there wouldn't have to be a next time...

Cal let these thoughts play out while avoiding others. But every now and then, a rogue thought broke loose and he'd anguish over the people he did not help that evening—people he'd screwed big time.

…For once, let everything else go. Tonight, just be here…

It was as if Turk had known.

As the minutes dragged on, it got harder to keep his eyes open. By the time Cal drove past the marsh and over the Crossover Street Bridge, he was barely awake. With his home just blocks away, the crushing weight of exhaustion fell upon him. He turned—more like swerved—onto Bittersweet Road, then Alder and Watercress lanes, and finally Creeping Cress Court. His eyelids flickered, closing and opening every few moments so that the last seconds of the trip seemed like a slide show…streetlight…stop sign…Bill's house…Mrs. Kenefick's… police car…his own house…

Cal pulled into his driveway half-asleep, his head bowed so low that his forehead almost touched the rim of—wait. Rewind. Police car? He bolted upright. Impossible. But the spastic uptick of his pulse seemed to verify what his semiconscious mind had already processed: a police car was parked in front of his home, its strobe lights illuminating the darkened neighborhood with blinding flashes of red and blue.

Great. Someone had obviously seen him get out of the stolen car. They must have followed him to his own vehicle, then reported it to the police. But what did he expect? How did he ever think this evening wasn't going to catch up with him?

Cal got out of the car, careful not to slam the door. He wasn't sure why. Half the neighborhood had to be awake by now. Even Mrs. Kenefick's place looked unnaturally bright for the hour. He headed up the driveway, debating the best explanation for an impossible story. But was grateful for one thing: the thief, whom he'd chauffeured around for the better part of an evening, had never told him his name.

Cal opened the side door, shuffled up the steps, and entered the kitchen. His mother zeroed in on the gash of dried blood crusting over his eye and gasped. He brushed aside her probing hand, turning just as Eva swished out of the room in her night robe.

"Well, well, look who's come slinking back home," Lieutenant Gavin drawled, tipping back and forth on one of the kitchen chairs like a sheriff in some old Western.

"Look, I can explain everything," Cal began, his voice steady. "This is just a misunderstanding. I didn't steal that car and I wasn't part of the holdup. Someone might have seen me driving it, I mean, I was driving it but I didn't...have anything...to do with...the...rob—"

His words froze upon the air, suspended like dark bubbles he instantly wanted to pop. Glancing around the room, he saw his father's bespectacled eyes wince, the policeman leaning against the refrigerator stiffen, and Gavin's mouth grow wide like a lizard that'd just swallowed an especially juicy insect. It was that look, in particular, which had stopped Cal mid-sentence.

"Uh, that's why you're here—isn't it?"

Gavin dropped his chair to all four legs with a bang. "I think we've heard enough, Al, don't you? Somewhere in all that crap, there's got to be a confession."

"Wait!" his mother cried out. "There must be some mistake, Dick. Those weren't the accusations. That caller said nothing about a car—or a robbery."

As his mother pleaded, Cal saw the pleasure in Gavin's eyes. Colors swirled, arced and jagged all over the place, but he didn't have time to figure them out. The officer who'd been standing in the corner was crossing the kitchen now, his fingers working to free a pair of handcuffs from his belt.

"Calvin Hughes, you're under arrest for illegal possession

of bomb-making materials with the intent to detonate a device on school grounds. You have the right…"

The words came as his arms were yanked behind his back. The cuffs snapped onto his wrists like jaws. Cal's mind raced to find some connection between the events of the last few hours and the accusations being thrown at him now. There was nothing.

"What the hell are you talking about?" Cal protested. "The school cleared me…the principal…I told him…" He calmed his voice. "You got this wrong. It was just a prank, some phone call. It wasn't real. I had nothing to do with—wait, bombmaking stuff?"

"Your little chemistry set in the garage," Gavin said. "Blueprints, too."

"I don't have anything in the garage," Cal said, his voice cracking.

"Yeah? Anonymous tipster told us different. They were right. Jackpot." Gavin patted a Toshiba notebook tucked under his arm. "Now, we'll see what's in here."

"Hey, that's my—"

"Not anymore," the lizard grinned. "It's evidence now."

Hours later, maybe two or three, Cal found himself in the back seat of his parent's car, exhaustion, shock, and dumb grief crushing them into silence. Bail had been expensive—he suspected Uncle Max helped out. As the car wound through the vacant streets of West Shelby, he waited for the inevitable inquisition and lecture, the *what-were-you-thinking* tirade. The grand finale? A punishment that would dwarf all others.

Down Main Street and through the deserted town, he waited. Over the cold marsh and up the driveway, he waited. Into the kitchen—place of all airings—he waited. He watched his mother slide open the hall closet and hang up her coat, his father open the refrigerator, look inside but take nothing. Then his parents climbed the stairs and closed their bedroom door.

But as Cal stood alone in the dark kitchen, he didn't feel like he'd escaped anything. A much starker notion settled into his brain: this time it had gone too far. Mr. and Mrs. Hughes had officially given up their son.

CHAPTER
FIFTEEN

Eva stared at the veggie wrap wilting in the middle of her lunch tray, stinging with every congratulatory word tossed her way.

"The school paper never looked better," Lin said, flipping through the latest edition. "The Hot Downloads feature is a great idea and that YouTube pick-of-the-week feature? Brilliant."

"Everyone's buzzing about the Marinating section. What a way to hook up!" Tori saluted Eva with her plastic knife.

"Yeah, well, I'm just acting editor-in-chief until Meredith feels better."

"C'mon, Eva, even if Meredith comes back tomorrow, Mr. Cummins wouldn't dare demote you, not after this." Tori pulled a copy of the paper from beneath her lunch bag and slid it across the table where it lodged beneath Eva's tray. Her eyes fell over the headline.

Student Suspended Following Bomb Scare
Had Been a Suspect in Earlier Arson

Eva's stomach tightened. It was harder than she'd expected

to see it in black and white. Even the unflattering photo of Cal felt like a betrayal. Brushing the paper aside, she let her gaze drift across the cafeteria to her brother's table where the usual characters sat mining through each other's leftovers like a herd of goats. They were, as always, a pathetic bunch, but seemed more so because Cal wasn't there giving them that intangible something that somehow made them all seem a little better, a little brighter.

"I know what your next front page story should be," Tori went on, clueless to Eva's mood, "an investigative piece about why the administration opened next semester's internships to juniors. Those spots should be for seniors only."

"It's true," Lin said, licking the last of a protein drink from her lips. "I heard about it in AP Bio. Smitty's ticked off. He didn't get either of the internships at the medical center."

"Who did?" Tori asked.

"Star McClellan, for one," Lin answered. "I mean, she does have the highest GPA since Einstein, but I'm sure it doesn't hurt that the Biogenetics wing there is named after her father."

"Wait, wasn't her aunt the one who donated all the money..."

But Eva wasn't listening. To her the cafeteria suddenly felt hot, claustrophobic. The tables too close, the air too thick. Big Hank, who seemed less big by the day, was dragging over some metal chairs so his new friends could sit at the table, while somewhere the rusty wheels of the janitor's bucket squealed like an angry pig. Beside her, Tori continued to mince her lunch into a pile of cubes while her mood steadily unraveled.

"...so, it's going to be really tough this Christmas. I used to buy my parents a joint gift, like a restaurant certificate or theater tickets. But this year...well, I don't know..."

"Maybe we could go shopping tonight and help you out," Lin said, kicking Eva beneath the table. "Right, Eva?"

"Yeah. Sure…" But Eva hardly heard Lin or the urgency behind her suggestion. All at once, it felt like ants were crawling over her, pulsing up her arms, marching down her neck. She shivered beneath her blouse. Around her, the room seemed to ooze with whispers of her family's name.

Suddenly, she'd had all she could handle. Grabbing her books, Eva bolted to her feet and shoved back her chair, unaware that the janitor's bucket was parked right behind it. Instantly, dirty water sloshed across the floor. Laughter reverberated around her. Even as her friends lifted their soaked feet from the pool of brown water and shot her dirty looks, she dashed from the table and raced out of the room.

Reaching the relative calm of the corridor, Eva slumped against a row of lockers and pressed her forehead into the cool metal doors. She squeezed her eyes shut and took several heaving breaths, glad that the bell hadn't rung, that the floodgates of the cafeteria were still closed, that she could find some peace. It didn't last.

"You got a minute?"

The voice came from somewhere close behind her—a sound like sandpaper tearing against silk—the last person in the world she wanted to talk to.

"It's about your brother."

Eva's eyelids rose, slow and heavy, like steel doors. She pushed away from the lockers to face the girl whose every feature was painted, outlined and brushed in the same haunting hue.

"It's not a good time, Star," Eva said between her teeth.

"Look, *princess*, I said it would only take a minute. I need you to give Cal a message. He's not answering my calls—or texts."

Eva's mind raced for words fierce enough to ward off this, this *thing* that felt like a plague. She opened her mouth without knowing what she was going to say and was surprised when the next words she heard were not her own.

"She *said* it wasn't a good time."

Turning at the sound, Eva nearly melted. At six-foot-two, Orrin Parker looked savage when addressing Star, but when he turned toward Eva, his sculpted cheekbones and plump lips offered a warm smile. She felt herself clinging to it and to this unexpected but very welcome intrusion.

"This...is...none of...your business, Parker," Star sputtered, her voice betraying her nerves, and Eva thought it surprising, for a change, that it was Star who looked spooked.

"It's everyone's business," he said, his voice liquid and smooth. "Feeling good is what we should all be about, not making each other *crazy,* annoying someone who's already had a bad day when all they really want is to be left alone."

Eva sighed. It was as if Orrin were reading her thoughts, his voice massaging her. She could feel every tensed muscle in her body release. His presence, however, seemed to have the opposite effect on Star.

"Shut up, Parker!" Star spat. "No one asked you to come over. Get lost, we have stuff to—"

"Now, Star," and though Orrin's hand had been a mere feather landing on the sleeve of Star's leather jacket, Eva saw her jump, "tomorrow's another day. I'm sure Eva would be happy to talk with you then."

He paused and looked at Eva who indicated no such willingness, then turned back to Star. But she'd already dashed off, retreating down the corridor, hissing away like a frightened snake. Eva watched the ferocious intensity in Orrin's eyes as they followed Star's egress, but when they returned to her, they were kind and consoling.

"Some people don't know when to quit, I guess."

The bell rang and the corridor around them filled with the

clatter of lockers and conversation. Yet Orrin made Eva feel as if they were alone. His dark eyes were mesmerizing, penetrating, kind of like Cal's, but they didn't make her feel uneasy. She struggled to gather her thoughts.

"Uh, those photos you took for the paper today were great. Really...uh...made the front page..." Eva felt sick again at the thought of the story.

"How *is* your brother?" Orrin asked with a tenderness that made Eva feel all at once broken. She realized that between the buzz about the arrest and the praise over her first issue, no one —not even her best friends—had ventured to ask how Cal was doing.

"I honestly don't know," she said. "This whole thing is such a mess."

"You know," he began in a hushed voice, "maybe it's not all Cal's fault."

Eva's heart leapt at the suggestion, the first positive note she'd heard on her brother's behalf all day.

"Maybe it's got less to do with him"—his gaze lifted over Eva's shoulder down the corridor to where Star had stormed off—"and more to do with *others*."

The warning bell rang and Eva felt a sense of panic, not for getting to class, but having to leave this guy with the glassy voice and hypnotic vibe.

"Tell him to hang in there," Orrin crooned, and Eva liked how his smile suddenly made everything better again. "Hey, any chance you're free tonight? I know it's last minute, but I heard there's a good trio playing at the Last Drop."

Somewhere inside the tips of her pointy leather boots, Eva could feel her toes curl with delight. Her face flushed as Orrin's hopeful smile beamed down at her. Then she remembered a shopping trip, Lin kicking her under the table, Tori's voice tipping and bobbing like an unsteady toy.

"I can't," she said.

Orrin sighed, the arc of his smile eclipsed by Eva's response. "Maybe some other time."

Then he was gone and with him the blanket of serenity he'd wrapped around her.

CHAPTER
SIXTEEN

After his arrest and suspension from school, Cal found he'd lost all control over his life. He wasn't sure what was worse, the long hours of indentured servitude in Uncle Max's steamy kitchen or the even longer evenings catching up on schoolwork at home where his parents' glares were only outdone by Eva's stone-cold stink eye.

One windy morning, he'd had enough, grabbed his heavy winter jacket and stole away for a few hours. With his skull cap low over his eyes and his trembling hands deep in his pockets, he ducked his chin into his jacket and pounded a quick pace over the boardwalk. He stopped only once, at the top of the bridge where one of the planks had rotted full through and fallen into the muddy water below. It wasn't a huge hazard, he thought. The older kids could hop over the gap easy enough, but the little kids might have a problem.

He giant-stepped over the missing board and continued across the bridge, the wind buzzing in his ears. But nothing could block out the storm raging in his head, those two simple words that had bounced against his brain for weeks now:

Anonymous tipster.

Each time he heard it, his heart responded with its own haunting echo:

How could she?

The gale force winds followed him along the dirt path and up to the wrought-iron gate. But once beyond it, he found utter calm. Maybe it was the high secluded geography of the graveyard or maybe it was his imagination. Whatever the reason, it made the cemetery feel like a place of rest for the dead *and* the living. To him, it'd never felt more welcoming.

As he made his way up the sloping yard, familiar markers seemed to jump out and greet him: Quinn, Andrejewski, Smith, Mrs. Heyman's angel, the PEACE stone, and the monuments he could never pass without a pang of grief—five small white crosses inscribed with a singular date of birth and death. Stan called them "the young ones".

At the top of the hill, Cal wrestled open the shed door and stepped inside. Instantly, he felt as if he'd entered another world. The low-ceiling room felt warm beyond reason and reeked of earthy scents like sawdust, worn leather, and dried leaves. There was something old-fashioned and timeless about it. A place where nothing worked but where everything was being worked upon. Even now Stan sat, bent over his workbench, rubbing a piece of steel wool over a rusted ball hitch until it gave off an unnatural sheen.

"Why, Cal," he smiled, glancing up with big yellowy eyes, "I'd hoped you'd be comin' by when your schedule eased some."

Cal closed the door and avoided the real reason for his absence. "I didn't think there was much to do this time of year."

"Oh, always things to do. But better and faster with a pair of helpin' hands."

Cal pulled off his cap, slipped his jacket over a nail above the mowers, and was glad the caretaker put him straight to work. There were hoses to clean, weed whackers to string, and the messy chore of winterizing the mowers. And sometime during the mid-afternoon, when Cal's fingers shone slick from linseed oil, Stan dusted off the workbench, waved him over and pulled out an old metal lunch pail with a couple of bologna sandwiches wrapped in wax paper, a picnic thermos of hot black tea and cookies, somehow oven-warm. They talked about nothing and everything: the crumbling board-walk, marsh weeds, baseball, B. B. King. But not once did the old man ask why Cal was there in the middle of a school day or why, when dusk began to yawn over the marsh and the little window became a bruised blue, he seemed so reluctant to leave. And for that, Cal found himself endlessly grateful. Even-tually, though, it was time to clean up.

"Use the pumice soap. Over there, between the faucets. But I warn you. Water's gonna be cold—ice cold." The toothy smile beamed as if the frigid plumbing offered unshakable proof of the caretaker's own steely mettle.

After scrubbing his hands under water that felt cold as melted snow, Cal noticed a box of scrap wood under an old coffin stand at the back of the shed. He asked if he could grab a few pieces for the boardwalk, then headed for the door. Lifting his jacket from the nail, Cal glanced back. Maybe he should sweep up or check the mowers again. But with a click of the switch, the caretaker let the place go dark and Cal knew their day was done.

As they made their way down through the yard, he could hear the rush of the wind thundering beyond Oakwood's boundaries. The caretaker didn't seem conscious of it. He walked through the cemetery with a calm and easy eye, scan-ning the landscape of tombstones, nodding now and then as if to acknowledge some invisible acquaintance.

Desperate to stall, to stay in a place so serene even the wind couldn't work its way in, Cal forced conversation. "Are you working through the winter? I'll get here whenever I can. Just let me know."

But the yolk-colored eyes seemed to run from the topic, slipping skyward toward a row of fat clouds looming over the marsh.

"We'll see how the weather plays out. Ice formin' on the north side."

The caretaker leaned against the black gate. It opened with a whine. Reluctantly, Cal walked out into the tempest that seemed to be shredding the marsh from its foundation. Hearing the clank of the latch behind him and the thud of damp work boots fading away, Cal turned back.

"Hey, aren't you going home?"

"Eventually," Stan answered as he tracked back up through the graveyard. "Just need to make sure the place is secure, is all. Get yourself home now. Marsh is no place to be after dark."

Cal buried his chin into his jacket and resumed his downward trek, less concerned about the hour than the notion that Oakwood needed to be secured against anything.

———

The next day, with a couple of hours before another shift in his uncle's kitchen, Cal slipped into his winter jacket, grabbed a hammer and headed out the door. Walking toward the marsh, he watched the snow fall across the streets of the north side— flakes so tiny, so cold, they had no shape or color at all. In the pale sunlight, they covered everything—the streets, the naked trees, even the old marsh bridge—with a sparkling finish.

He passed Mrs. Emerling out in her snowy driveway and offered to help shovel. But she just half-smiled and waved him away with a lighthearted turn of her mitten. Cal wasn't fooled. She shouldered an energy field as thin and pale as spring ice. Even as he watched, it broke and splintered with her thoughts in colors too sad for a Crayola box. He'd never seen anything so tragic.

Crossing the boardwalk, he felt the boards wobble beneath his feet, every footstep offering up a new creak. About halfway across the bridge, he reached the gap he'd noticed yesterday. Squatting down, he worked to fit the piece of wood he'd brought from the graveyard into place, securing it with a tap-tap-tap of the hammer. The rhythm echoed across the marsh like a deep-throated woodpecker. Once or twice, he paused to follow the echo, letting his gaze wander toward the shoulder of the marsh where Oakwood was tucked away, invisible except to those standing in front of the gate. He thought about heading up, clocking in a few hours, but with winter closing in there was less to do around the graveyard. Lately, his chores had become more and more trivial. Cal didn't care, though. He was glad for something to do and for someone to do it with.

Standing up, he tested the board with a heavy stomp of his sneaker.

"Looks reliable," a voice said.

Cal spun around. With the sun as a backlight, he saw the silhouette of a lanky man watching him from the opposite side of the bridge, his foot braced back against one of the stanchions. Cal squinted against the cold white sunlight shading his eyes with his hand, but all he could make out was the ragged ends of a scarf waving with the hand of the winter breeze. It was then, he realized, the words he'd just heard were anything but a compliment. In fact, they were quite the opposite.

"Listen, Turk, I've tried to call but—"

"I know. No cell. Not a fan."

"I tried Phil and Paul, too, a bunch of times, on their cell, at home…" Cal swallowed the words dribbling from his mouth like weak soup. He couldn't finish them.

"Yeah. They're pissed."

Suddenly, Cal felt so stupid, so screwed-up. His cheeks burned with something way colder than the temperature. He squinted into the sun. But maybe it was easier not to see Turk's face.

"I just wanted to say, I'm sorry, man. *Really* sorry. I wanted to—I mean, I really meant to make the gig that night, but I stumbled into this robbery…there was a guy…this little girl…a gun…"

Cal's excuses puffed into the frosty air, begging for forgiveness, a reprieve—something. He figured even a guy who believed most words weren't worth saying had to have something he wanted to get off his chest. But Turk offered nothing. He just stood there on the bridge, the small flecks of snow refracting sunlight around him like shards from some shattered rainbow. After a minute, he reached into the worn pocket of his jacket and pulled out a box.

"Here. Your phase shifter, some pics, a tuner. Got mixed up with our stuff."

Cal walked forward on iron legs. He reached out, but as soon as the box landed in the palm of his hand, he felt like hurtling it over the side of the bridge. It was useless to him now, had been useless to him that night.

"I told you not to stop," Turk finally said, a note of sadness sinking into his husky voice.

Cal recalled the ill-fated conversation with haunting clarity. He hesitated. "Did you guys place?"

A pair of long, thin clouds streamed from Turk's nostrils. It seemed minutes before he answered.

"Second."

The answer knocked the breath from Cal. They'd been so close. How they must have hated him that night! Probably still did.

He heard the thunk of Turk's boot slide down from the rail and grew sad. He didn't want Turk to leave. Maybe he needed the company, or maybe he was hoping for a second chance with the band. More likely, though, he wanted Turk to stay until he could make him understand—but then, as always, that would be impossible.

"What about the—"

"We found a new guy," Turk said ambivalently. "Good vocals, tight playing. Can't match your chops, though." He turned and headed for the Southside, for what might as well be oblivion. Cal knew he'd never see him again. He suddenly hated himself for letting this happen, for his weird vision that came thick with consequences but without the slightest hint of instruction.

All the way back home over the icy marsh, the small cardboard box smoldered in Cal's tremulous hand. He didn't need it. Didn't want it. At some point or other, they all wound up with each other's gear, but it never mattered because it was all about the music, the band. Under that credo, ownership seemed trivial.

"…*mixed up with our stuff…*"

It forced Cal to acknowledge what he'd suspected for weeks now: the band was through with him.

Lumbering up Creeping Cress Court, he saw his home in the snowy distance. It brought no relief. Mrs. Kenefick stood at the end of her driveway, waiting. He waved but knew it wouldn't be enough. Never was.

"Calvin, over here! Quite the chill, isn't it? Oh, but I love it! Clears my head, my lungs." She took a deep breath to demonstrate and settled into a coughing fit that lasted several seconds. "Now the dears," she continued, her voice thick with phlegm, "won't set a paw into it."

Cal listened without listening, dreaming ludicrous thoughts about running away, starting over, changing his name…

"Of course, I had a feeling—you know how I am—but if I

hadn't been at the medical center today, I'd never have been certain about it."

He could start his own band, give guitar lessons, get by on tutoring until things took off...

"But I see it all coming. The triumphs, the tragedies. Of course, in this town it seems more tragedies than anything, lately. Look at that whole arson thing. Back to haunt us again, eh, Calvin?" Her eyes twinkled and zeroed in on Cal's expression. "If the fire wasn't awful enough, now more bad news. Such a pity. I'm sure no one meant for it to end like this."

"Like how, Mrs. K.?" Cal asked, tired of the game.

"Like Peter Zempke, Carol's father. You know the girl, don't you? Sweet thing, a bit gangly. Anyway, early this afternoon, Peter—God rest his soul—passed on. The doctors were taken aback but, of course, I saw it coming."

CHAPTER
SEVENTEEN

Cal got to the church early. Standing-room-only. He was able to grab a spot in the last pew, but all through the service he felt cold waves of energy washing back his way. He tried to distract himself, his gaze wandering over the pine trees towering in the vestibule, the altar bright with poinsettias, the empty crèche ready for the evening's Christmas Eve mass. But they were no match for the draped coffin in the center aisle or the sobs that echoed under the domed ceiling. With just a few minutes left in Mr. Zempke's service, he snuck out the back door to wait for his sister.

Daylight. It'd never felt so good. Cal stood at the top of the steep rise of stairs, absorbing the sun's heatless rays, fighting off the gloom gathering within him, the sense of powerlessness overtaking his life.

Then he felt something. Energy. *Her* energy, so intense, it felt as if she were standing beside him breathing warmly into his ear. Cal squinted into the low December sun. On the opposite side of the street Star stood waiting, her arms folded, her long dark coat and wide silky pants whipping in the wind. To Cal, she seemed frozen. A goddess in black.

He guessed why she was there, wasn't sure if he wanted to hear her excuses. Something in her stance, though, seemed less defiant than usual. She wavered on the edge of the curb, uncertain. Just as she stepped down to cross the street, Eva's footsteps came skittering up from behind Cal.

"C'mon, Cal. We gotta go. They're on the final blessing. Uncle Max'll have a stroke. We should have been there ten minutes ago. Cal? Now!"

He followed Eva down the stairs, his gaze distracted for no longer than a second. When he looked back across the street, Star had vanished, her retreating footprints visible in the thin layer of snow.

———

By three o'clock, the first floor of Maxine's was crammed with luncheon guests from the Zempke funeral. Cal and Eva divided the dining room. At six tables each, it would take some hustle to serve the crowd. After the blessing, they rolled out platters of greasy sausages, home fries, bowls of colorful fruit and pasta salads followed by cold cut and condiment trays.

Unlike the funeral mass, the tone at lunch was upbeat and Cal found serving hassle-free. His side of the room asked for nothing but what they'd been served. So, after his initial run, he hurried back to the kitchen, brewed some coffee then rushed back out. By now, he figured, someone would want more bread, another slab of bacon or a bottle of ketchup. But no one needed so much as a packet of sugar. Easy crowd.

He stepped back and took a breather, watching the dining floor from the kitchen doorway—watching as the people at his tables suddenly needed everything. They dogged his sister for extra butter, rolls, pickles, coleslaw, another coke. He grabbed a tray and hustled out, but as soon as he was in the dining room, the turned heads fell, the outstretched hands recoiled, the raised voices quieted. Despite circling his section of the room several times, no one needed anything at all—until he left.

Eva brushed past him, "What, did you slip something into their coffee? Your tables don't seem to know or care who their server is."

Cal mumbled, "Oh, they care."

The injustice of carrying the whole room, of serving people who wanted nothing to do with Cal, didn't seem to bother Eva, though. He watched as she poured coffee, cleared spills and joked with the guests, floating upon a ribbon of congeniality he guessed had something to do with the pair of earrings tinseling down from her earlobes. They'd arrived that morning with a note that left her grinning all day.

An hour later, he and Eva began clearing the dining area, scooping up centerpieces, stray napkins and flatware even as guests lingered near the coatroom. Yanking a linen cloth from one table, Cal spotted a handbag lying on a chair and was about to head over and ask the last group if they knew its owner, when someone snatched the bag from his shaking hands.

"A thief, too? What's next for your resume? Murder? But then, you've already accomplished that, haven't you?"

Mrs. Zempke's reddened eyes glared at him before a sob broke her resolve and she stormed away. Cal stared after her, a dozen unspoken apologies dying on his lips. It took a minute for him to notice Carol. She stood waiting for him in her usual nondescript way, pale and thin, her blonde hair harnessed raggedly behind her ears, her shoulders maybe a little more hunched. Her eyes—always an indefinite color—began to well, and he saw there *was* something different about her, about the loyal classmate who defended him even when he didn't want to be defended, about the girl who believed he was the best thing ever to happen to West Shelby High School. *That* girl was suddenly and starkly gone. And as the tears spilled over her chaffed cheeks, she seemed to be crying for the boy she thought she knew but was certain now she didn't. Her energy confirmed it, the last trace of pink evaporating as she walked away, stooped and sobbing.

Back in the kitchen, Cal grabbed his coat and blazed into the snow-swirled alley, sick to his core. Eva caught up to him, humming *Jingle Bell Rock,* her long earrings swinging with the beat. But he hardly noticed. All along the seedy block, whispers seemed to follow him. They came from behind shrubs, at the back of driveways, along shadowy yards, urging him toward the darkness as if it was where he belonged. With the distant chime of church bells stirring the snow-softened air, he stopped short and began to walk in the opposite direction of their car.

"Cal?"

"Tell Mom and Dad I'll be late," he said, agitation creeping into his voice. "I have stuff to do."

Eva's smile widened, and she shook her head. "You think you're going to get your Christmas shopping done now?" She waved her hand in a hopeless motion. "Well, good luck."

He looked back over his shoulder. "I need to stop up at Oakwood for a few minutes."

The amused wrinkle of Eva's nose tightened and she changed in other ways Cal wished he couldn't see but did. It was as if the mere mention of the graveyard reminded her that her brother was a hopeless reprobate, an incurable loser.

"Whatever. Just don't be too late. I'm not suffering through Midnight Mass alone."

Cal took off through the sketchy neighborhood, pounding his frustration into the snowy sidewalk. He loosened his tie, turned up his collar, and punched his cold hands deep into his pockets. How long would his sister—would everyone—hang onto this miserable view of him?

Veering off toward the marsh, he passed a bodega, closing for the night. He noticed a girl with a black ponytail who looked like Addie in the window.

He gave a half-hearted wave, but the girl disappeared behind a pulled shade. A second later, the storefront went dark. Sure. Why shouldn't she see him in the same wretched light as everyone else? People talked. Bad news spreads fast.

Burying his chin in his jacket, Cal hurried over the marsh bridge. Even the reeds crinkling in the bitter wind seemed full of rebuke. He hiked up the dark overgrown trail, feeling his way along the twisted path until he saw an unsteady glow pouring through Oakwood's gate up ahead. He followed it and thought, for a second, of the Wise Men who chased a light that led them somewhere and to someone they hadn't expected to find. As he came to a standstill outside the wrought-iron gate, Cal knew this was definitely *not* what he'd expected to find. Candles, hundreds of them, glowed upon every grave, illuminating even the darkest corners of the yard. They flickered from within small, perforated sacks so that each one gave off multiple flecks of light.

He slipped through the gate and up the snowy path, stunned at the radiance. In the soft, shimmering light, the old gravestones looked like polished pieces of sculpture. It felt more sacred than any place he'd ever been. An outdoor cathedral.

"Helloa there, Cal!" the caretaker called, his hearty stride crossing the cemetery. "And Merry Christmas! What do you think?"

"It's—it's amazing," Cal said, turning full circle. "What are they?"

"Luminaries. Paper lanterns. It's a Mexican custom." The unsteady light flickered in the caretaker's eyes and reflected off his dark, weathered skin. "Some say they bring good luck; others say they ward off evil. Either way, the Rotary Club pays for it, so I just set 'em up and let 'em go!" He double-clicked the lighter in his hands.

Cal eyed the lanterns. "What about the flames and the paper—you know, when the wicks get low?"

"Oh, no worry there. Sand—at least two cups in every bag —anchors the luminary and fireproofs it at the same time." His face bent into a wide smile that pulled all the leathery skin high into his cheeks. "It's Christmas Eve, Cal. I got us covered. Don't worry!"

But worry was all Cal felt. It suffused his body as much as the candlelight drenched the yard.

"What's the matter?" the caretaker finally asked. "You look as if you've been to a funeral."

"I was."

Stan frowned. "Headin' to the Serenity Mausoleum, no doubt. Imagine spendin' eternity stuffed in a filin' drawer!" He slapped Cal on the back with a breath-robbing jolt. "Well, enough shop talk. Let's get up to the shed and warm up a degree or two before I send you home."

Once inside, Cal found the workshop, like the graveyard, had undergone a metamorphosis. The place looked spotless. No spare parts scattered over the workbench, no disembodied lawnmowers strewn across the floor. Everything was hung or tucked away where it belonged. Even the usual cobwebs that draped the window like a spooky curtain had been wiped aside. A fresh pine branch lolled across the space heater filling the room with a forestry scent while above the workbench, an old transistor radio crackled out a Nat King Cole tune.

"You've been busy."

"Yeah, gettin' ready to close for the season." Stan wrenched the door shut and shook the snow from his heavy checkered coat, too busy to notice Cal's unsettled expression. "Not much to do here in winter, 'cept wait for spring," he added.

"Oh." Cal could hear the disappointment crackle in his

own voice. The caretaker, though, had become preoccupied, fidgeting over a small lockbox parked in the center of the work bench. He shoved it off to the corner then reconsidered and whisked the box up to the highest shelf, edging it back as far as the space allowed.

Watching him, Cal felt stung by his every move. In the window beside the shelf, he saw the reflection of a dozen accusing expressions—Eva, Turk, Mrs. Zempke, even people he didn't know but who seemed to know everything about him—glaring like he was a depraved criminal. And now Stan, too.

"There," the caretaker said, exhaling with relief that seemed disproportionate to the chore. "How 'bout some hot chocolate?"

Cal just stared, his eyes a wounded blue, his throat too thick to speak. He swallowed hard and buried his cold hands, colder suddenly, into the deepest corners of his pockets.

"I'm not a thug," he said, pausing to steady his voice. "You've probably heard a lot of things about me lately. They're not true. Well, not all of them. Anyway, you don't have to worry about whatever's in that box or anything else around here."

Stan pulled the tin box from the shelf, opened the latch, and tilted it so that Cal could see its contents. Sheets of loose-leaf papers filled the box, one bright yellow sheet folded on top, the rest scraps as faded and full of dust as the shelf upon which the box sat.

"I'm not worried," the caretaker said. "Besides, you're not the first to get tongues waggin' in this town." He replaced the box on the shelf, pulled over an extra stool and drew out the old picnic thermos. "Won't be the last, either."

Cal's gaze wandered up to the radio where an old Christmas hymn was now playing through the mesh speaker. It cast a spell of unearthly peacefulness about the room. Along with the dark rich cocoa pouring from the thermos, it urged him on.

"I don't even know how it all started. I was trying to help a friend and it just snowballed outta control. Then I tried to help this messed-up guy"—Cal closed his eyes, wincing at the wounds still so fresh—"and wound-up screwing over my band mates. Now I'm just walking around wondering why the hell I do this stuff."

"Don't dwell on mistakes. Learn from 'em and move on."

"I know. But there are reminders everywhere—in school, at home, on the street. You wouldn't believe the way people change when they see me coming. I can tell just by looking—"

But Cal wasn't ready to go there, not with Stan, not with anyone.

"—at their expressions. I've been kicked out of school, my band, the swim team. I can't wait to see what happens next."

"Well, helpin' people is a funny thing," Stan said, his finger tracing the crevices in his chapped lips. "I mean, why the heck do we mess in other people's business anyway?"

Cal shifted uneasily on the stool, slurping more hot chocolate before answering.

"I don't know. Maybe it just seems like the right thing to do, at least as I see it."

"The right thing…" The caretaker sighed and his face seemed older and longer without the toothy grin lifting it. "I remember one time at my old job when the *right thing* wasn't so easy to figure out.

"I worked with the rescue squad out of West Shelby, fire station #45. One night, when the marsh was kickin' up fog and spittin' out sleet, we got a call around midnight. Multi-car crash outside of town." He licked his lips. "Wasn't good. First vehicle—a car full of kids drinkin'—taken away, all in critical condition. The other car, flipped over. We found a woman in the back seat. Banged up and bloody, but in good shape. The driver—her brother—was in a bad way, though. Internal injuries. Punctured lung. Then we found his daughter, under the shattered windshield. Malfunctioned car seat. Dead.

"My partner was drivin' the ambulance that night I was in the back with the injured man and his sister. His breathin' was bad, labored. As I was reachin' for an oxygen mask, he suddenly grabbed my hand. Lord, that grip! He pulled toward him and with words that scarcely had sound said, 'Let me go.'"

"What did you do?"

"Well, I wanted to do the *right thing*, Cal. And time was short. Bein' close like that, you can smell it. Death. Waitin'. Hangin' on every breath. Anyway, the man kept lookin' at me. As fierce a gaze as I ever saw. And with what little spirit he had left, he repeated, 'Let me go…with my daughter…. help me'."

Cal watched the caretaker's eyes drift through the window and into the candlelit graveyard. It was a moment or two before he could go on.

"So, I helped him. I put the oxygen mask back on the rack, stopped tendin' his injuries, and simply held his hand. He slipped into one of the most peaceful-lookin' comas I'd ever seen. Later that mornin', he was pronounced dead at the medical center."

The old man's large hand swept over his mouth as if to wipe away the words. He reached for the thermos top and screwed it back on. Cal was surprised when the story continued.

"A few weeks later I was sued—"

Cal started.

"—for negligence. Lost my job to boot."

"But how could anyone know that the man didn't just—"

"His sister, remember? In the ambulance."

"But you only did what the guy asked, you know, helped him out."

"Well, like I said, helpin' people is a funny thing. Doesn't always turn out the way we expect." He shook his head. "In the end, though, we all tip the balance. One way or the other."

Cal nodded. He knew that good intentions could implode. He had more fails than he cared to count.

"That's why people say, 'mind your own business', I guess."

With the caretaker's mug empty and the tale finished, he stood up. Cal didn't move from his stool. He wanted more stories, more advice, more of everything this place had to offer. But with the hot chocolate gone, the portable heater losing strength and a different song—a silly modern Christmas tune—on the radio, there seemed nothing left to do but leave. As Stan reached up to turn off the radio, his large hand knocked down a package wrapped in brown-paper.

"Well, thank goodness for unsteady hands," he declared. "I almost forgot. Merry Christmas."

Cal looked up at the smiling caretaker, then down at the parcel. His fingers loosened the twine, then folded back the paper. Inside, he found a pair of tan leather work gloves. Cal slipped them over his hands, unusually still at the moment. The soft lining exuded the same deep warmth as the work shed.

"They're just what I need. How d'you know?"

"Lucky guess." The caretaker smiled. He reached over to unplug the heater and click off the suspended light bulb. His voice continued through the darkness. "Don't forget to bring 'em along when you come back in the Spring. "

Cal stood there, gazing at the caretaker even though he could see no more than his silhouette in the dark. Hadn't he said there would always be things to do at Oakwood? Now, all at once there wasn't. Was the old man tired or just tired of having a troubled kid around?

Outside, they walked through the splintered glow of candlelight and past the frosted tombstones in silence. All at once the graveyard seemed a place for whispers only and they didn't speak until Stan's arm was leaning on the gate, swinging it wide.

"How will I know when to come back?" Cal asked, his head still buzzing with the idea he wouldn't be in Oakwood for months.

"You'll know," the old man said, looking over the snow-covered marsh. "When the snow melts and the mud begins to thaw, it'll be time. Go home now. Almost Midnight. Marsh is no place to be at this hour."

All the long winding way down from the graveyard, Cal tried to convince himself that the time off was great, that he could use the extra hours. But just as quickly he thought, *Yeah, right, to do what?* As he walked further away from the cemetery and darkness enveloped the path, he found himself grieving over the loss of Oakwood, the refuge it'd become for him, and the good company of the caretaker.

Approaching the marsh, he stopped to look at the distant glow of Christmas lights glimmering off the water from shore-line homes. In town, he could hear the faraway chime of church bells. Midnight. It seemed impossible. But then at Oakwood, time had a weird way of passing. Sometimes it seemed to stand still, other times it seemed to race.

He slumped against the boardwalk rail. Right now, his parents were waiting for him, fuming. Eva, no doubt, fueling their anger. But what did it matter? He was already the family outcast, the town loser.

Staring into the dark water, Cal closed his eyes and let out a sigh so deep it drained his body cold. His hands began to tremble, racking him with unusually vicious quakes. He heard a rustle, opened his eyes, stared for a few seconds, then squeezed them closed. He waited a second then slowly blinked them open again.

But it wasn't a dream. There, not a foot from the muddy shoreline, tangled among a trio of reeds, floated a wayward water soldier, well beyond its season. It seemed to bob toward him, gliding on a wide plate of leaves. Cal didn't know what to make of it. It should've been frozen. The velvety petals were black but not withered, luminous in the dark.

Stumbling down the bank to get a better glimpse, he stooped at the water's murky edge, his trembling fingers straining to reach the exotic flower. As his hand brushed its petals the water around it began to quiver and glow, fanning out in concentric waves of shimmering light. Stunned, his fingers slipped off the plant and dunked into the radiant water. Instantly, a jolt shot through his veins. Cal fell back on his heels, dazed. He shook his head, took a deep breath, and looked around. The water was dark again, the water lily had drifted beyond his vision and everything was as it had been before—except for him.

He felt—different. Better. Whole. He got to his feet and bounded back up to the boardwalk, moving with a surge of energy he couldn't explain. As he reached the bridge, it suddenly dawned on him: his tremors were gone. And not just in a pause-mode or semi-controlled state that never quite kept them at bay. They were gone. Gone, gone. He could feel it. His arms free of the tension and twitches that had racked him for years.

Free. It was a high he'd never known. As he ran all the way to town, he wondered if maybe his strange vision was gone, too.

CHAPTER
EIGHTEEN

t was stupid. Beyond stupid. She never meant to hurt Cal. Who knew the whole damn thing would blow up like this? She could feel the guilt fester like a black knot at the back of her brain, bothering a conscience that rarely rumbled. She knew what she had to do. No way around it. It was time to set things right with Cal.

With winter break over, Star made for the boardwalk early, half-asleep and dead dog-tired, cursing the hour as much as the cold. She reached the far end of the bridge, ducked beneath it and hid among the withered alders. After all, he couldn't avoid her if he didn't see her coming.

Shivering in place, she gave an extra turn to the fuzzy scarf around her neck and scrunched her shoulders beneath a bulky wool wrap. Still, the wind found her, tugging at her hood, whipping her hair, biting at her cheeks. Snowflakes mixed and swirled in arctic-born gusts that made everything around her look frozen. Or dead. Kinda like her relationship with Cal. Unanswered calls, ignored texts. Like he'd evaporated. She never figured she'd miss him this much.

In the gray ice beneath her boots, she spotted a worm suspended in a frozen twist. She chipped at the ice with her heel and shook her head. Stupid worm. It could have saved itself. All it had to do was go deeper, where the ice sealed in the pond's warmth. Getting far enough below the ice meant survival, getting too close meant death. She heard the first rumble of footsteps pounding overhead and realized survival was an instinct just as vital above the surface as below.

Crouching further into the dried weeds, she eavesdropped on conversations that dangled through the slats of the boardwalk: tales of binge-drinking, rave parties, and New Year's Eve romps. She waited and listened, but none were the voice she wanted to hear.

Minutes passed. As the traffic thinned overhead, Star leaned out, spat into the weeds and offered one last squint across the white landscape. Where the hell was he? She was about to bail when her eyes focused on a figure rounding the bend before the bridge. *Cal*? Something—no, everything about him looked different today. His careless glance, his cocky swagger, his eyes. She started to climb the bank to meet up with him but, hearing other voices, ducked back down, whacking her head on a cross board.

"...I'm glad break is over. I was sooo bored. Winter's just too depressing..."

It was that Emerling girl—Tori the Tormented—bitching about nothing, as usual.

"Not me. I could have used another week..."

And Her Royal Majesty, Princess Pain-in-the-Ass, fouling the air next. Other voices followed, including a bunch of punks who sounded like groupies:

"Hughes, you're the man!"

"Dude, way to go! Stick it to 'em!"

"Show 'em whose boss, Cal!"

Star blinked away the slivers of snow and ice shaking down from the underside of the bridge as the last-minute school rush rattled above. She tried to get a fix on Cal, but Bill-the-Blowhard opened up next.

"Hey, man, they actually missed you. Who'd a thought? Try not to screw it up this time. Maybe they'll let you stay awhile."

She could hear him slapping Cal on the back as Tori's moan fest continued.

"Are you going to be late this afternoon, Eva? I'd wait for you, but I'm sort of meeting someone."

"I don't know what I'm doing. I might be busy at the news-paper. Meredith's coming back today."

As their voices disappeared from the boardwalk and shifted toward the streets of the South side, Star clamored up the embankment, stumbling on the frayed edge of her long denim skirt. Once topside, she looked around. Damn it. Now she'd have to wait 'til after school. On the plus side, Cal might ditch his entourage of losers by then and the two of them could actually talk.

———

On the way to Mr. Cummins' office at the end of the day, Eva saw Fred the janitor, teetering at the top of a ladder struggling to change a light fixture. She overheard kids busting his chops, muttering about his IQ. She gave him a friendly shout-out, but he didn't look down, his thinly bearded chin set in a grimace. Word around school was he got chewed out for dumping the wrong amount of chemicals into the pool and the district had to close it until the PH balance got fixed.

But the janitor wasn't the only one who seemed messed up today. Things seemed off-kilter everywhere Eva looked. For starters, she'd found out Tori was seeing Turk, a guy sure to break her heart. The real mind-blower, though, was watching the hero's welcome her brother got at school. She caught a couple of kids bowing as he walked toward homeroom that morning, then saw him being waved over to one of the popular lunch tables—the ones Bill was always trying to edge his way into. Last night when they got the news about the suspension being lifted, she'd wondered first, who cleared Cal's name, then how much abuse he was going to take when he got back to school.

Now, all her brother had to do was stay out of trouble so she could keep his name out of the school paper. But as Eva walked into Mr. Cummins' room, she realized it was no longer up to her anyway.

"I've been looking for you," Meredith began, stepping from the newspaper office.

Here we go, Eva thought. Surely the next words from her mouth would be, stay-the-hell-out-of-my-way. Eva preempted her speech. "Don't worry. I brought all the stuff with me: updates, Board of Ed schedule, club briefs—"

"I don't want them," Meredith said, her voice hard.

Eva's brows arched. "Fine. Whatever." She dumped the stack of folders and a flash drive on a nearby desk and parked herself behind one of the laptops in the classroom. She dove into the internet, scouring websites for a piece she was doing on eating disorders. The district's health curriculum hardly touched on the epidemic. She hoped to sidebar the article with an anonymous survey among the school's population. The research was so engrossing, she didn't notice Mr. Cummins pull up a chair beside her.

"Hello, Eva. So, we're all set for tomorrow, 6:45 sharp?"

Eva's mouth gaped. "The staff meetings are starting earlier?"

Mr. Cummins stared back, his brow wrinkling like a withered onion skin. "Didn't Meredith tell you?"

Eva looked over to the newspaper office, now empty and dark. She could almost hear the whistle of a bomb falling.

"Tell me what?"

"I'd like you to take over the editor-in-chief post—permanently. You did a fabulous job in her absence. I know you'll fill Meredith's shoes nicely—and then some." He patted her shoulder and smiled. "We'll talk more in the morning. Now, if you don't mind, I need to lock up. After school faculty meeting."

Eva shuffled into the corridor, dazed. Just like that, Meredith was out. She wasn't sure if she should feel victorious or used. Did Cummins force Meredith out, or did she quit? Was Eva at the top by default or by design?

At dinner that evening, she aired her angst about the unsettling day but got zero sympathy.

"So Tori's hanging out with Turk, what's the problem?" Cal asked. "He's a great guy. Why can't you just let her be happy?"

"Because I don't trust Turk or his motives. The same way I don't trust Lois Lane just up and dumping the newspaper on me."

"Meredith doesn't owe you an explanation."

"But she should've at least told the staff, given me a head's-up."

"Why?" Cal persisted, a tangle of spaghetti hanging from his mouth. "So, you could tear apart her reason for bailing out?"

Eva slammed down her fork. "Since when did you become the defender of every loser in West Shelby?"

"Eva…" her mother warned.

"No, I mean it. He's been swaggering around school all day, like he's some kind of god or something."

Cal glanced up, shrugged, then guzzled the rest of the soda.

"Well, I'm not going to sit here without knowing why—"

"And then what, Eva?" Cal countered. "You'll find out she was tired of it or bored or maybe she's got better things to do and, in the end, what's the point of it all? It doesn't matter. Stop wasting time. Mind your own business."

Eva looked across the table with a steely glare, hating her brother for being outspoken and maybe just a little bit right.

Their father tried to tamper the acidic tone in the room by shifting the topic. "I saw some of the kids from your school at the medical center today. Intern orientation. Zoe's niece was there. Eva's friend, too. Orrin something or other."

Eva smiled helplessly into her dinner plate.

"They got the opening day tour but probably won't get into anything interesting until sometime next week." He paused. "I saw Deidre over there, too."

It was a casual add-on, but Eva saw her mother start.

"With one of the gastro specialists."

Her mother set down her coffee and frowned. "Eva, clear the table, please. Cal, take the trash to the curb, will you?"

While Eva pulled the dishes off the table and emptied them into the sink, Cal got up and glanced out the kitchen window where Mrs. Kenefick was struggling to drag a bag of garbage down her snowy driveway

"I'll take it out later," Cal said, turning from the window. "I have to catch up on some stuff—now that my laptop is back."

"Messages from your *new* friends?" Eva huffed.

"You didn't like the old ones."

"People with a clear conscience don't have to worry about minding their own bus—"

Eva's words dissolved as the side door suddenly blustered open. Cold air rushed into the kitchen, flattening the curtains over the sink and rustling a magazine on the counter. A second later, Tori appeared, shivering up the side stairs, a pair of mukluk boots on her feet, her father's old football jacket slung over her shoulders. She blinked several times, as if she wasn't quite sure what to say.

"Mrs. Hughes? Mr. Hughes? Would you m-mind coming home with me? I don't know what's wrong with my mother. Um… I-I can't get her to wake up."

CHAPTER
NINETEEN

J ust two days in, and Star knew her internship was a complete bust. The research program boasted hands-on technical training and one-on-one doctor contact. Yeah, right. One look at her and those promises got snuffed-out like germs in antiseptic.

She glanced in the mirror above the lab sink, fuchsia hair, facial piercings, an inked serpent coiled below her left ear. Okay, so maybe she wasn't much for first impressions, but this was supposed to be about young smart students getting in touch with older smart professionals, learning from their experiences. Bullshit. They were all hypocrites.

Tugging off her lab coat, Star shut the lights and let the door lock behind her. The real insult was getting stuck here in the hinterland of the facility. Oh, it sounded all high tech and juicy, but they kept her away from anything that mattered. She knew Parker was pissed off, too. When the director announced that he would be working in the medical center instead of the research facility next door, it looked like his head would blow clean off his long lizard neck. Apparently, the officials screwed up or, more likely, switched their assignments because Orrin *looked* like the kind of guy the doctors would want to have around. Star grinned. If the mix-up gave him any measure of misery, maybe it was worth it. Served him right for relying on his pretty face.

She slipped into the emergency stairwell to avoid staffers who seemed just as glad to avoid her, then exited at street level. Even from a few blocks away, she could feel the damp and cold of the marsh filter under her skin. Pulling up the collar of her thrift store trench, she walked down the slope toward town. As the steeple of St. Francis rose into view, the chimes began to sound, echoing warm and full over the snowy sidewalks of Main Street. Approaching the pharmacy, she saw Mr. Driscoll fumble with his keys, closing up for the night. He glanced up from the darkened doorway, startled by the clank of her chains and amulets. With a nervous cough, he double checked the dead-bolt and hurried away.

Star kept walking. Poor sap. That lock wasn't going to make any difference tonight. Yet even as the thought occurred to her, she had no idea how she knew such a thing. Then she looked down. Rippling in the icy puddle, the reflection unfolded before her eyes. Two men in masks, glass shattering, a bag full of pills and syringes…

She blinked it away, her heart pounding, and reached into her pocket. Fingering out a pinch of crushed black leaves, she smeared it under her tongue. Uck. One of Aunt Zoe's God-awful remedies. Tasted like charcoal but it helped—sometimes. Star hadn't actually fessed up about the reflections. But she'd mentioned tossing at night, having trouble concentrating at school and her aunt came up with this remedy. Ground grasshopper, dandelion root, or some shit like that.

On the other side of the street, she noticed a huddle of classmates shivering in line for the 7:00 movie. She watched, envious of their smiles, the strong arms that reached around smaller waists, the frozen fingers entwined, the heat they seemed to radiate in spite of the cold breath streaming from their mouths.

On the sidewalk ahead, another crowd, fresh out of The Last Drop, hit the pavement, honking like wild geese. She checked her pace.

"Let's go to Joe's house," one of the girls proposed. "We always have a good time there."

"That's cool. My mom's out-of-town and Dad's working late again. Ya know, I think he's trying to avoid me."

"Can you blame him?"

Giggles.

Close enough now to see more than their collective breath puffing into the night air, Star caught sight of Cal, his hair wound into a straggly man-bun, his arm wrapped around Kelly Hanson. She whispered playfully into his ear and he leaned into her, turning his head just enough to catch Star's searing stare. Instantly, his smile faltered. Cal pulled back his arm and began to herd the group across the street. Star saw the discomfort in his eyes and pounced on it.

"Not so fast, Hughes."

Her voice fell like a hammer upon the group's light banter, shattering it into broken silence.

"It's, uh, not a good time, Star," Cal said. The sound of derisive laughter rippled around him.

Star's jaw tightened. "Maybe if you'd hadn't blown me off a thousand times or blocked my number, I wouldn't have to chase you down like—"

"Guys, I'll catch up in a minute," he said, growing uneasy. "This shouldn't take long. Go ahead."

As the group moved on, Star could feel their side-long glances thrown at her like poison darts. She waited until they were out of earshot before squaring off with Cal.

"Spoiling your fun?" Her voice was brittle.

"They think so. What's up?"

"Why've you been avoiding me?"

"I've been kinda busy lately."

"Too busy to return a text?"

His gaze wandered up the street toward the retreating party. Star noticed, with a stab of envy, how he seemed less with her than with them.

He turned to face her, impatient. "Maybe. So, what is it?"

"I...I just wanted to tell you that..." And suddenly Star didn't know how to say the thing she'd spent the better part of the last week chasing him down for "...that I'm the one who cleared your name."

"What?"

"I'm the one who called the police and told them you had nothing to do with the all that bomb-making shit and those blueprints in your garage."

"And they believed you?"

"Yeah. Because I put it there. Told them I was just messing with you." She forced a laugh. "Almost got nailed with criminal mischief charges myself but Aunt Zoe smoothed things over. The blueprints were actually hers from a Board of Ed meeting. Anyway..." Star grew flustered and later, in trying to remember where the whole conversation went to hell, she would pinpoint this moment. "I was trying to...I wanted... damn, I just wanted you to leave me alone so I figured if I could piss you off—"

"Mission accomplished," Cal said coldly.

"No, Cal, it's not like that. It's...I don't know. Call it a bad joke, a brain fart." She fumbled trying to explain herself without really explaining herself, her motivation. "But I never called the cops—maybe Gavin has radar on you or something. Anyway, that's what I've been trying to tell you" —She could hear the desperation rising in her voice—"and seeing how things got all f—ed up, I just wanted you to know that I was the one who set it straight again."

"So, you hunted me down just to tell me you're the reason I got kicked out of school and almost thrown into jail and now I'm supposed to be all grateful because you cleared my name for something I never did in the first place. Is that right?"

"And to tell you I'm sorry."

Cal blinked a few times. "Does that require a separate thank you or should I just roll it all into one?"

Star hated the sound of sarcasm in his voice. It was all wrong. It didn't belong to him anymore than those icy blue eyes glaring at her now with a coldness she'd never seen in them before.

"Listen, asshole," she began, so hurt her eyes stung with tears, "I just thought you'd like to know the truth."

"Well, thanks, Star, and I promise I won't be in your way anymore. I guess you could say I'm taking a page out of your book and telling *you* to stay away from *me*."

"But—"

"Just mind your own business. It'll work out better for the both of us."

She stood there on the snowy sidewalk, staring at Cal's receding figure like it was a ghost. And it must be a ghost, a shell, for somehow the heart and soul of Calvin Hughes had been chiseled out, eviscerated. Just when she needed him most.

CHAPTER
TWENTY

"Y ou're not yourself tonight, Aster. What's the matter?"

Star slumped against the long mahogany table, picking at the linen and lace tablecloth. "Damn tired, is all."

Aunt Zoe raised an eyebrow. "Language, dear." She reached for a tea pot trimmed in goldleaf and filled a pair of bone China cups to the brim. "I trust the internship at the hospital is going well? You know, I called in more than a few favors for that one." She added, "But I was glad to do it. For you."

Aunt Zoe slid a cup beneath Star's downcast face. Instantly, the steam rose into her nostrils. She inhaled deeply, could almost feel the spicy green aroma curl around her brain, easing the pain that seemed evermore at home there. Her aunt settled at the head of the table, tossing the ends of a lush silk wrap over her shoulders. She waited a moment, her fingers drumming against the tablecloth.

"Talk to me, dear."

Star didn't want to talk, didn't want to tell her aunt that the internship sucked. Eight weeks of utter boredom. She didn't want anything but tea—and sleep. The reflections had gotten worse lately—night and day. Cal filled them. Her sister, too. Maybe it meant something. She gazed past her aunt, beyond the bay window, through the bare tree branches that hung like dead twigs and imagined the marsh.

"Star?"

"It's just…I miss Alula."

Her aunt's hand clutched at her heart. "We all do."

"It's just weird." Star rubbed her neck. It ached almost as much as her head. "You know, the way she just —disappeared."

"Drowning is sudden and tragic."

The patronizing tone struck a raw nerve with Star. She took a long dreg of tea. Felt a little stronger. "But Dad was with her. I mean, he never would have let her… He'd have gone in, saved her."

Aunt Zoe stood up, swept toward the window. Star couldn't read her expression, but her voice was jagged. "Yes, that's what one would have hoped. But he didn't, did he? He just came home and cried."

Star looked up from the table to the glimmering chandelier overhead, her eyes glazing over.

"Why?"

"Why what?" her aunt snapped, impatience coloring her usually sweet tone. "Why did he take her out there in the first place? Why didn't he come home with her? Why did he let—let us down? I don't know. We'll never know. He took the easy way out."

Star shifted on the satin-covered dining chair and tilted her head to rest on her shoulder. The tea seemed to be losing its effect already, escalating the exhaustion overwhelming her. "I mean, all he had to do was jump in and save her…"

"What can I say? Much as it pains me to admit it, the man, at times, was weak."

164

Star massaged her forehead in slow circles, then slid her hands down to rest over her face. Her breath felt warm against her palms.

"He wasn't a good swimmer, was he?" she sighed. "Not like Cal."

Aunt Zoe huffed. "I told you to stay away from that boy. He's not right in the head. Nothing but trouble. Always has been."

"Don't freak. He's not interested in me. Not anymore."

"No loss. You can do better."

Star hated the words. No one was better than Cal. He was the best a person could be. But she'd been so stupid, taken him for granted. With her fingers still resting over her eyes, she parted them to glare at her aunt and was about to defend Cal when she saw something that took her breath away.

There in front of the window, in the jungle of plants that draped the frame and hung from the cornice overhead, her aunt stood fingering a copper band.

"What is—? Why are you wearing that?"

Star recognized the cool start in her aunt's eyes as easily as she recognized Alula's bracelet with the brushed copper finish and her set of initials.

"Lovely, isn't it?" her aunt said as she shoved the band beneath her bell sleeve. "A bit small, but I still wear it. Somehow, it makes me feel close to her." She dabbed at the wrinkled skin around her eyes and Star felt sorry for her. She forgot that Alula's death had been hard on all of them.

With a sniffle, Aunt Zoe leaned back from the window. "At times like this, it helps to talk about our feelings. But it seems you're bottling them all up. I'm here for you, Aster. Talk to me. You said you were having trouble sleeping. Bad dreams, perhaps? What's going on?"

Star just sat there, her head aching, the lights of the chandelier swimming before her eyes, almost into a watery blur… Her heart began to pound. "I'm tired now."

"Honestly, dear, you look hellacious. I'll get some more tea. Wait here."

Aunt Zoe swished from the room and Star sat there exhausted, yet somehow too wired to sleep. She looked up, the individual crystals on the chandelier kicking prisms of light into her eyes, until they seemed to spin. Star squeezed her eyes shut, tried to control her breathing. Something felt wrong. The room? The light? Her brain? No, it was Aunt Zoe. She'd gone the wrong way. Away from the kitchen. The opposite direction. Where the hell was this tea?

Star pressed her palms against the side of the table and pushed away, struggling to her feet, then wandered down an unexplored side hallway, wild with floral wallpaper and long on arched doorways. She heard rustling within one room and entered it, wide-eyed and amazed. Vines swung down from a glass-domed ceiling, leaves and potted plants spilled into the aisles while in the corner, Aunt Zoe stooped over a potting table, holding a heavy kettle, her fingers black with crushed leaves.

"A greenhouse, wow. What are you doing over there, making tea or mudpies?"

Startled, her aunt dropped the tea kettle with a bang. The contents spilled onto the tile floor. "Star, I thought I told you to wait in the—"

"And what's this? You growin' pot, Aunt Zoe?" Star grinned, pointing to a row of leafy plants four feet tall in terra cotta planters.

Her aunt remained focused on her task but let out an exasperated huff. "Cannabis. So much fuss over a mediocre plant. Really, so many other ways to feel better—and faster."

Closer by, Star noticed a tray of young plants tucked beneath the glow of a green, fluorescent light.

"What are these?"

"Herbs," her aunt said curtly, without looking up from the mess at the potting table.

Star brought her face close to examine the orange seedlings. They were unlike any she'd seen before, coiling up from the dirt on snakelike stems, then budding into multiple speckled heads. The tallest ones snapped at her like angry dragons.

She jerked back and hurried toward the next row, where a cluster of pots sat beneath a blue light. Inside the containers, she found not dirt but red-colored water. Black lilies crept out from each bloody pool, hissing as they bloomed, emitting shots of toxic-looking steam.

"What about these?" she asked, recoiling.

"More herbs," her aunt repeated, again not bothering to look up.

Star glared across the room, feeling dismissed, ignored, and deceived all at the same time. "And *these*?" Her index finger made a decided jab toward the rattan ceiling fan spinning overhead.

"More herbs," her aunt said absently. "I told you I'd teach you, but you said you had no interest."

"Sure as hell do now," Star muttered under her breath. With the weirdness factor of the place kicking up, she grew more focused. At the back section of the glass room, half-hidden by an angry-looking cactus, she spotted a short wooden door. She glanced at her aunt, still intent with the clean-up, walked over and yanked at the figure-eight handle.

The door opened just long enough for her to see the top of a spiral staircase and catch a dank whiff. Then it slammed in front of her. She looked back at Aunt Zoe who must have pole-vaulted over the plant tables to get there so fast.

"What's down there?" Star demanded.

"Nothing," her aunt said with a pant under her breath. "Your father used to work there, on occasion. But it's a mess, dear. Needs airing. Nothing in the room anyway except—sad memories."

But it was too late. Star had seen it. In the nervous blink of her black eyes, in the over-compensated curl of that fake pink smile, in the cold weight of the hand nudging her away, it was as plain as if her aunt had just slapped her across the face. Cal was right. Sweet Aunt Zoe was a liar. And that simple knowledge changed everything.

CHAPTER
TWENTY-ONE

Eva blinked at the computer screen, her gaze drifting sleepily toward the lower corner.

6:25 a.m.

It seemed absurd that Cummins required her to pour over every last detail before press time. It had been weeks since she had a decent night's sleep. She kept reminding herself though, that he was the guy with the major newspaper connections. If he liked her work, he'd hinted that he would use his clout to land her a summer internship at *The Buffalo News* or *The Democrat and Chronicle.*

Yawning, Eva reached for her coffee, which had graduated both in size and strength over the last two months. But it was a sloppy reach and, swoosh, hot coffee streamed everywhere—the desk, keyboard, her sweater. She bounded up from her chair only to send more coffee running down her clothes. Maybe this was why Meredith bailed.

From the outer office, Mr. Cummins saw the accident and rushed in to help with a stack of napkins. "No, it's fine," Eva said, yanking a stream of tissues from a nearby box. "I'll get some water."

Flustered, she edged around the desk, out the door and into the hallways, her footsteps the singular echo breaking the eerie silence. She brushed past the Wet Floor sign posted outside the girls' lavatory door and went straight over to the sink hoping to salvage her clothes. Behind her, the bathroom door slipped shut. Hearing a shuffle, Eva suddenly realized she wasn't alone. Gasping, she spun around, pink liquid soap dripping through her fingers. The automatic faucet shushed to a stop, and the room went silent.

"Fred, you startled me!" Eva exclaimed, her dry hand clutching her chest. It took a second for her to catch her breath. "You go ahead with whatever you're doing. I just need the sink."

"Looks like you got yourself a spill there."

Eva turned and faced the sink again, wetting down some of the smaller stains. "Yeah, coffee. Is there anything worse?"

"Hmm, suppose tea or grape juice might be. Nothing worse than crank case oil, though."

Eva didn't respond. She was working on the biggest stain now, the one split symmetrically between her thighs, scrubbing until the paper towel shredded into little white curds. Reaching up for another, she glanced in the mirror and saw the janitor kneeling on the floor with a dryer scattered in pieces on the tiles around him. He was fingering a large gasket and flipping through the pages of a manual. As she stood there, her head began to feel as upended as a toppled cup of coffee. She wanted to blame the achingly early hour, her soggy pants or an over-charged cup of caffeine. But it was more than that. Something somewhere was out-of-sync. It was like hearing a clock tick but not seeing the hands move. Her eyes darted around the room, but there was nothing here, just a bunch of sinks, a row of stalls, a couple of mirrors, a broken dryer and an old man staring at a manual like it was written in Arabic.

Leaning over the sink, Eva pressed the automatic faucet, cupped her hands beneath it and splashed cold water over her face. Feeling no refreshment, she hurried from the bathroom.

When 8:15 finally rolled around, it felt like midday. Entering Mr. Schlenz's class, Eva saw Henry VIII approaching the podium. Distraction. Good. Just what she needed. She plopped herself in the desk beside Lin and looked around for Tori.

"Getting your caffeine fix by osmosis?" Lin teased.

Eva glanced down at her jeans. "Do you think they're ruined?"

"Hopelessly."

"Where's Tori? Out again?"

"Didn't you hear?"

Eva leaned in for more details, but Mr. Schlenz's voice was circling nearby.

"No volunteers? Okay, then we'll have to draft a victim from the ranks. Hmmm, Eva Hughes, you look up for a challenge…"

After school, Eva rushed home. Tossing her books on the counter, she knocked the wet snow from her boots and unwound her scarf but didn't bother to remove her coat. As soon as she grabbed a quick bite, she was going straight over to the Emerlings to vet the wild rumor she'd heard, firsthand.

Scavenging for some pretzels and peanut butter, she found a package of sour gummy bears just as the side door rattled open. She looked up. Cal was standing at the bottom of the kitchen stairs, his jacket flecked with snow, his expression empty. In some ways, she hardly recognized him anymore. Something about his face…

"You're home early," he said, walking over and scooping out a finger full of peanut butter before she could stop him.

"Ditto," she huffed.

"Yeah, well, we were supposed to have practice, but Fred screwed up the pool again so we're heading over to Seneca East after dinner to use theirs."

Eva saw him eyeing the gummy bears and warned him off with a feral glare. He backed off and raided the refrigerator instead, pulling out a giant turkey drumstick that reminded her of the history lesson on Henry VIII. Rewinding her scarf, she started for the door. "I'm heading over to the Emerlings."

"Hey, I'll go with you. Bill wants to show me some new website he dug up."

"Probably porno," Eva grumbled, unhappy with Cal's suggestion. She didn't want him or Bill hanging around while she was trying to have a talk with Tori. "Do you have to go now?"

"What's the difference when I go over there?"

"Exactly, so go later."

"But I've got time now."

Eva rolled her eyes. The old Cal would have figured it out, read between the lines, caught the vibe that the girls wanted to be alone and that would've been the end of the discussion. Now he just kept looking at her, not with that blue stare that unnerved her, but with a dumb kind of what's-your-problem expression that, oddly, she found more aggravating.

"Fine, whatever."

Outside, the March afternoon seemed to be melting around them. The snow underfoot thick and wet, the air without bite.

"Weren't you supposed to shovel the driveway?" Eva asked, still trying to lose her brother.

"Yeah, but the snow'll be gone by tomorrow. Why bother?"

Unavoidably, their path took them past Mrs. Kenefick who was standing at the end of her driveway, her over-stuffed coat zippered to the tip of her bright red nose.

"Look at you two. Lovely, just lovely. Siblings taking a walk on an early spring afternoon. That's how I thought it would be for me and Hendrick, God rest his soul. Long walks, happy afternoons. We went everywhere together, even as children. Did I ever tell you about the time…"

Eva cut her off. "Actually, we're in kind of a hurry, Mrs. K. We're headed to—"

"The Emerlings. Yes, I know."

Eva exchanged a glance with Cal then looked back to Mrs. Kenefick, her lips wrinkled into a self-satisfied grin. "Well, give Deidre my best. Poor dear, such a lost soul wandering about. Let her know I've been thinking about her."

When they were out of earshot, Eva grabbed Cal's arm. "How did she know? I mean, you don't really think she's…"

Cal waved off the idea. "She watches this neighborhood like a hawk. Probably makes a hundred predictions a day. By dumb luck, she's bound to get a few right."

At the Emerlings', Bill answered the doorbell, then ushered Cal back to his bedroom, a lecherous grin on his face.

Alone in the entryway, Eva found herself gazing into a house that had lost its familiarity. Blankets, bed pillows and nightgowns dribbled from the couch as if it were a giant hamper. The closed drapes and muted TV gave the room an institutional feel. Bleach saturated the air but didn't hide the smell of dirty dishes or the empty medicine bottles staggering against each other on a side table.

Stepping into the living room, Eva realized she hadn't been there in a while. Thanks to her crazy schedule at the newspaper, she and Tori hardly shared the morning walk to school anymore. Afternoons didn't seem to work either. It had been weeks since they'd really talked. Last time was that night Mrs. Emerling passed out. Since then, Tori didn't have much to say in or out of school.

Eva approached the recliner, uncertainly. "Uh, Mrs. Emerling?"

"Don't bother," a voice blistered into the room. "She's—"

"Sleeping?"

"Sure. Call it that."

Eva turned and knew she should have called first. Tori's blonde hair hung raggedly over her forehead. She was still wearing a nightshirt and a pair of pink plaid pajama pants from the night before.

"Missed you at school today," Eva began, braving a smile. "You should have been there. I was Anne Boleyn to Mr. Schlenz's Henry VIII." Eva paused. "Er, how's your m—"

"The same," Tori responded flatly.

"How are you?"

Tori shrugged, her expression blank.

Eva slipped off her scarf and tossed it over a nearby ottoman. "I had a few minutes—finally—so I thought I'd…

"Lin told you, didn't she?"

Eva blinked innocently, then dropped the ruse.

"Well, yeah. Why didn't *you*?"

"Because I—"

"—didn't want to be talked out of it?" Eva removed her jacket. "Well, guess why I'm here?"

"Don't waste your precious time, Eva. Just go."

"No. We're going to have this out, right here and now." Eva looked toward the recliner and lowered her voice. "Let's go to your room or something."

"Um, it's kind of—a mess."

"Fine, we'll go to the kitchen."

Eva walked past Tori and marched up the steps to the next floor of the split-level home. Its hopeless clutter of dishes and old magazines offered no improvement. Tori followed, flip-flopping over to the kitchen's dinette table where she dropped herself into a chair, eyes lowered. There was a moment of silence. Eva took a breath—a quick one—then went for it.

"Why do you want to live with a guy who does nothing

but drift from concert to concert, rehearsal to rehearsal? All he cares about is music. He doesn't even have a phone. What are you going to live on, babysitting money?"

Tori's sunken cheeks managed a weak smile. "You'll make an awfully good mother someday, Eva. You'll drive your kids crazy."

Eva ignored the diversion. "How much do you really know about him? What kind of a guy—"

"Look, just 'cause you don't like him doesn't mean he's not a good person. He's kind and creative, not to mention totally hot. We get along really well."

"Yeah? If this guy is so great, why's he's asking you to screw up your life and move in with him?"

"He's not," Tori answered. "I'm asking him."

"*Why*?"

"Are you kidding?" Tori said, her eyes flashing. "Look around you! It feels like a funeral home and stinks like a hospital in here. I'm the maid, the nurse, and the counselor all rolled into one. I cook. I clean. I shop. I even started paying bills when final notices showed up."

"Tori, I—"

"Sometimes I think the next one kneeling over the toilet is going to be me. And coming home? That's the worst part 'cause when I open that door," her finger made a jab toward the front of the house, "I never know what I'm going to see on the other side."

Eva reached across the table, but Tori jerked her hands away, dropping them into her lap.

"Like that night when I came home and found her lying at the bottom of the stairs. I thought she was dead. I should've called 9-1-1 right away, but I went to your house because I was scared. It was stupid, I know, and I don't know why I didn't call the rescue squad first except…except maybe…" The grayness of her eyes grew wide and guilty. "Maybe I wanted her dead." She closed her eyes, dropped her head and grabbed a fist of hair at the top of her scalp. "I know that sounds horrible, but why else didn't I go straight to the phone? In the time it took me to run to your house and get your mother, it might've been too late. I could've killed her."

"But it wasn't too late, Tori. The ambulance came. The paramedics brought her around. You can't blame yourself. You were probably in shock. It's perfectly understandable."

"Good, then you understand why I have to leave."

Eva was stunned that Tori interpreted her empathy as a blessing to jump ship.

"But your mother needs you. Who'll take care of her if you go?"

"Billy," Tori answered coldly. "It's his turn to pick up the slack."

"C'mon, Tori, you know he won't."

"Well, maybe that's okay, too. Maybe my mom needs to stop lying around. Flowers, cards, phone calls—where's the incentive to get better? She never got this much attention in her whole life, certainly not from my father."

"You don't honestly believe that. Your mom has a serious problem. She needs help. Don't you care what'll happen if you leave?"

"Care?!" Tori slashed back. "I care when I'm mopping up puke in the middle of the night. I care when my mother can't remember where she's been all day. I care when the money in my wallet is missing."

"She steals from you?"

"When she's desperate enough. Billy started stashing his wad of cash—wherever that comes from—on the back shelf of his closet, but he's pretty sure she's gotten into it anyway."

Eva stared blankly at the kitchen table, understanding for the first time the quagmire of hopelessness in which Tori was drowning. Just then, Mrs. Emerling's voice beckoned from the front room.

"Tori? Tori!"

Numbly, Tori got to her feet. Eva followed. As she passed Tori's bedroom, she noticed a duffle bag open on the bed, clothes stuffed inside. In the living room, Mrs. Emerling strained away from the TV, her skin the color of dried paste, her eyes glassy. To Eva, it seemed she'd aged ten years in the last six months. The woman offered a half-hearted smile toward her before muscling up a curt tone for Tori.

"I asked you to run to Driscoll's for that cough syrup, didn't I? Now I'm all out and you'll have to go right away. No excuses! You know I have this terrible"—she let out a small, forced rasp—"cough."

Eva spied two empty bottles beside the recliner. It was a brand she remembered her mother avoiding because of its high alcohol content.

"I told you, Mom," and suddenly Tori sounded so tired, "they're closed today. I'll get it for you in the morning."

A great irritable expression flexed across Mrs. Emerling's face and she turned back to the television muttering something about a simple request and ungrateful children.

Eva grabbed her scarf and coat. "So, I'll see you tomorrow, Tori?"

"Whatever, sure…"

Tori's voice died out behind the closing door. As Eva walked down the snowy steps, she saw Cal waiting at the end of the driveway, his expression blank. Maybe it didn't bother him, but as the Emerling family imploded in the wake of the divorce, she felt a piece of the Hughes family crumbling away with it.

CHAPTER
TWENTY-TWO

Eva dug her fork into a kale and carrot salad, looked over to Cal's lunch table, and instantly lost her appetite. Harassment appeared to be the dish *du jour* this afternoon. It made her want to get up, walk over, and smack her brother for letting himself get roped in by those idiots. Even now, one of his minions was targeting a bunch of hapless freshmen with a can of shaken soda, the brown foam exploding over their heads as they sprinted for the door.

"...What I really want to do this summer," she could hear Lin saying, "is volunteer with an inner-city soccer camp. But I need money for college this fall. How 'bout you Tori, what's the word on the job front?"

"I'll take what I can get," she shrugged. "I heard Manny's is hiring. You got any prospects, Eva?"

"I'm counting on one of the dailies in either Rochester or Buffalo. I need a recommendation letter from Mr. Cummins, though. He said he was going to give it to me last week but..." Her eyes wandered back to the small crimes raging on the far side of the cafeteria. "He's been ...busy...I guess..."

"What *are* you looking at?" Lin finally asked.

"My brother. He's turned into such a jerk. Completely irresponsible. Last week, he forgot to pick up my mom from work and she had to walk home in the rain. All he cares about are his stupid new friends. He's always been annoying. Now he's brainless, too."

Lin shook her head. "Before, you didn't like Cal's friends because they were losers. Now you don't like them because they're the popular crowd. Face it, Eva, it's time to stop worrying about your baby brother."

Eva stiffened, stabbed another forkful of salad, but kept her eyes parked on the far side of the room. He didn't even look like her brother anymore—stylish shirts, designer jeans, shorter hair. What was he trying to prove?

"Besides, there are more important things to worry about," Lin said with a grin. "Like the Marsh Madness Dance."

Tori gasped. "You've been asked *already*? Who?"

"Jimmy Gugino. But he was just showing off in front of his goofball friends. I knew he was kidding."

Tori's eyes widened. "What if you thought he was serious and said yes?"

"Believe me," Lin said, straightening up and smoothing back her hair, "there was never any chance of that."

Eva followed her gaze two rows over to where Smitty and another guy from the cross-country team were nudging their way over.

"Hey, anyone want to donate their history homework for a worthy cause?" Smitty asked.

"What cause would that be?" Lin answered, her voice playful.

"Keeping ol' Smitty here out of detention," his buddy snorted, laughing just long enough to earn a jab in the ribs.

Lin's smile remained intact. "Well, save your groveling for another time, guys. Mr. Schlenz's out today."

"Again?" the boys said in unison.

"I know. I forgot how boring history class could be without him."

The boys nodded, stood around for an awkward moment then left the table elbow-jabbing each other all the way across the room.

Tori's eyes followed them. "Homework. What a ruse. It's all about Marsh Madness."

Lin shrugged. "I don't care if I go to the dance with a date or not. Maybe I'll just go solo and hang out."

Tori sighed, staring at the pieces of cut celery on her plate. "I don't have the nerve to go stag."

"What about Turk?"

"Yeah, well, we're sort of taking a break. Rehearsals, touring..." Her voice fell away.

"What about you, Eva?" Lin asked, her attention drifting over to the doorway where Smitty and his friends stood loitering.

"I don't know. Things kind of cooled off between me and Orrin, too. Ever since that internship. Said he's busy. We hardly see each other."

Lin jumped to her feet, grabbed her backpack and headed for the door.

"Hey, where are *you* going?" Tori asked.

"Oh, what the hell. I'll give him my homework." She shrugged, a guilty smile curving her lips. "I mean, it's already done, so why not?"

Tori's eyes followed Lin across the cafeteria to where Smitty stood brightening at her approach. She sighed wistfully into her lunch, then picked up a plastic knife and chopped a honey-raisin granola bar into a stack of cubes. "I don't know about you, but there's no way I'm going to that dance without a date. I don't care what Lin says."

Eva hardly heard her. Her attention had fallen back to the small tortures raging on the far side of the cafeteria. Cal's table, situated between the snack counter and the doorway, was an unavoidable hazard for students exiting the cafeteria. If anyone attempted to skirt the action, Jardo and his cousin were at the ready. With their long hair and acne-peppered faces, they looked like a couple of trolls guarding passage into safe territory. And there was always a price to pay.

Eva watched as a nerdy sophomore snapped open a bag of chips, only to have his precious graphing calculator swiped from his pocket and turned into a hot-potato that left him begging like a frantic puppy. He never got it back. Another student tried to keep it cool after the bullies nabbed his flash drive. But when they tossed it into the compost bin, he lost it.

Snap!

Eva jumped at the sound, then turned and glared at Tori.

"It's okay, I have a spare," Tori said, pulling out a fresh plastic knife.

Rolling her eyes, Eva's attention reverted to her brother's table. As Carol Zempke approached, the brood of bullies trained their eyes on her, staring until her shoulders had scrunched so far forward, she looked folded in half. Then Bill yelled, "Hey, your fly's open!" Carol grabbed at her crotch, dropped her sweatshirt and dashed off in tears, dirty whistles and comments flying in her wake.

Eva could hardly keep herself in her chair. Yet no one seemed to care, least of all Tori who continued to chisel away at her food and flip through a fashion magazine. Already another victim was heading into their trap. But this time Eva smiled. The goons were about to meet their match.

Star McClellan sauntered up from her solitary table in the corner, chains hanging from every section of her body, a black military jacket slung across her shoulders. Her entire mien said *I-dare-you*. At her approach, the table leaned in for a hurried huddle. Seconds into it, Eva could see Cal jerk back from the group, as if in protest. It was too late, though.

With the grace of ogres, Jardo and Ted shoved aside the chairs they had commandeered earlier and confronted Star. Her composure, however, was unshakable. In an instant, her blackened lips ripped them to shreds, accosting them with words Eva guessed they'd probably never heard before. Then, just as her vitriolic spew reached the boiling point, one cousin pinned back her arms while the other grabbed at her pierced ear and tore out a silver bar.

Blood, open flesh, and a scream poured from the other side of the room. The bell rang. Everyone dashed for the doors. In the middle of the chaos, Eva stood up, straining to see what happened. Where was Cal? What happened to Star, and why didn't anyone stop these creeps? She dropped back into her chair, exasperated.

"Did you see what just happened over there? I...I can't believe it!" The bullying that goes on in this school. It's as if nobody cares about anyone anymore. Everyone's so self-absorbed."

But Tori wasn't listening. She sat there working her knife into an apple, concentrating on the procedure like she was performing surgery. For some reason, the sight of it sickened Eva. An enormous ache started to pulse in her stomach, rising up through her chest until she was sure she was going to vomit all over the table.

"For God's sake! You and that stupid knife!"

She reached over and snatched it out of Tori's hands, snapping the knife in half. Then, on a hunch, she grabbed Tori's arm and scrunched up her shirt sleeve.

"What are those?"

Tori answered sheepishly. "I...I was babysitting Mrs. Kenefick's cats and got—scratched."

"I don't mean the scratches, Tori." Eva leaned in close. "I mean the *cuts*."

Tori's eyes grew wide, then tried to blink away her

surprise. "I don't know what you're…" But her mask withered. She snatched back her arm, pulled down her sleeve, and began to retreat. Eva grabbed her shoulder.

Tori turned. "*Please*," she whispered, her face anguished. "Not here. It's hard enough when people think you're normal."

"We need to talk," Eva said.

"All right. Tonight. Seven o'clock, the coffee shop."

———

That evening, Eva stood in the doorway of the Last Drop wondering if Tori would show. She slipped down the caramel-colored stairs into a room that felt like a giant cup of *café au lait* and smelled like a bag of freshly ground coffee beans. As her eyes adjusted to the dimmed lights, she looked around the circular room. Full house. On stage, a harmonica player stood testing the mike. After a moment, she spotted Tori and went over, slipping onto a cushioned armchair. Tori didn't look up but continued to stare into the pit of her coffee mug. Eva waited. The roar of the cappuccino frothier drew her attention toward the chrome and oak bar. On one stool, a guy who resembled Orrin flirted with the barista. Eva's stomach gave a twist.

"He's getting married."

Eva turned from the bar. "Who?"

"We met his fiancé at dinner last weekend." Tori's eyes remained in the pit of her mug. "*Naturally*, Billy and I have to attend the wedding. You know, I never really believed my parents would get back together. I mean, I hoped… Of course, my mother doesn't know. Yet. I'm sure it'll be the last straw for her. Was for me…"

She spoke in a dry, airless tone. The harmonica's bluesy

croon a funereal accompaniment to the fragments of broken heart falling from her mouth like glass from a broken pane.

"...or maybe the last straw was when Turk told me he didn't want me to move in. Needed *alone* time, he said. Then again, it could have been when my brother posted those photos of me on Facebook—as a joke. Or maybe it's feeling like I've lost my best friend because she's so busy I don't get to see her anymore."

Eva felt her lips part, her jaw drop.

"Oh, don't blame yourself, Eva. Like you said, it's as if nobody cares about anyone anymore. Everyone's so self-absorbed."

Now it was Eva's turn for downcast eyes. She was speechless. Ashamed.

Tori continued to empty her aching soul. "It's like everyone I've ever loved has let me down—simultaneously. I don't want much. Really, I don't. I just want everything and everyone to go back to the way they used to be, you know, before this miserable year started."

"That's not going to happen," Eva said, softly.

"Yeah, I figured that."

"It's hard to change people."

"Really? Then how come you're always trying to change your brother and when there's nothing wrong with him at all?"

"I...I'm not actually trying t-to *change* him," Eva stammered. "I'm just trying to figure him out. The guy is so mindless."

For a moment she glanced toward the door, half-wondering whether Cal would remember to pick up their mother after work. He seemed to forget everything lately. But the hum of the quivering harmonica brought Eva back to the room, its notes stirring the drops of a dozen different dialogues into a creamy swirl of background noise, lulling her into complacency. She struggled against its mellow vibe.

"Tori, you know why I'm here."

She shrugged, her eyes unmoved from her mug of cold coffee.

"Does it hurt?"

Tori's eyes lifted from the rim of her cup, wandering up and beyond the table to the faux-finish paint drizzling down from the lip of the ceiling.

"Sometimes. Depends."

"On what?"

"What I use, you know, a needle, a razor, knife—whatever."

"But *why* do you do it?"

Tori's wounded expression fell from the ceiling and landed squarely on Eva. "Because I'm tired of hurting on the *inside*. At least this pain I can control." She stretched her arm supine across the bistro table. "These scars will heal."

Eva looked at the crisscross marks over Tori's lower arm, many more than she had noticed in the lunchroom that afternoon. Some worm-shaped lines of dull pink, other wounds so fresh the scabs still buckled rough and raw above them.

"I watch them heal." Tori gazed at her arm with a disembodied stare. "Over and over again, a cut bleeds, then it gets better. It heals itself—*I* heal myself."

"But there are other ways, *better* ways, to deal with the crap that happens in life."

"Don't get all judgmental on me, Eva. You could never understand feeling abandoned by everyone that ever meant anything to you." Her voice cracked. "There's nothing that's gonna make this get better."

As the set ended and the musician left the stage, the sonic fabric of the room shifted—scraping chairs, clanking saucers, the microphone's hum—ripping through the thin cloak of privacy the two needed as their friendship hung in the balance.

Bumping up against their table, a pert waitress heightened the intrusion. "We're offering free samples of our new Himalayan mix tonight," she pitched. "It's a blend of five Asian beans that will *transcend* you!" She put a couple of thumb-sized cups on the table then receded toward the booths along the wall.

Eva grabbed one of the little cups and slugged it back. As the exotic coffee coursed down her throat, a strange idea sprouted, spreading its hopeful possibilities into every corner of her body.

"Tori, this might sound a little crazy, but hear me out. You can't always change the stuff that happens in life, but you *can* change the way you react to it."

Tori glanced up, her bangs hanging miserably in her eyes. "*I'm* the one who's supposed to change?"

"Look, you have every right to be disappointed in your family." Eva's eyes filtered downward, "Your friends, too. But even though you can't control them, you can control how you deal with it."

"Yeah. So?"

"So, let's take a yoga class."

"Nuh-uh. I've tried exercise classes before. They don't work. I'm not very—flexible."

"Pilates?"

Tori shook her head with more vigor.

"A spinning class, then. We'll learn together, we'll laugh together. If it helps, we'll cry together. Think of it: time out of the house for you, time away from the newspaper for me and a guaranteed night out for both of us."

Tori shifted on her chair, unconvinced.

"Come on, at the least, it might be good for a few laughs.

Who knows, we might wind up losing a few pounds in the process."

"We'll need to get some athletic wear," Tori said, a shadow of encouragement coloring her cheeks. "Something bright. And stretchy. I have this catalogue—" She stopped short, checking her enthusiasm. "Look, Eva, don't think this is suddenly going to change everything."

"So long as we're headed in the right direction, it doesn't matter. We'll spin all night if we have to!"

Tori smiled for the first time that evening. "Sure. I mean, why not? I'm a night owl. Kinda like your brother."

Eva cocked her head.

"I was up with my mom the other night, looked out the window and saw him. I think he was headed toward the marsh. Weird 'cause it was almost midnight."

CHAPTER
TWENTY-THREE

C al sprawled across his bed and glared at the wall. He could hear Eva chattering on the phone from her room next door. His foot made a nervous tap against the bedpost. She should've been asleep by now. For God's sake, she got up earlier than anyone he knew. Didn't she ever get tired? He could hear his father's bear-like snore across the hall and knew his mom would be out cold, too. Beyond his room, the rest of the neighborhood seemed quiet.

He stared at his phone and watched the minutes slip away. Eleven fifty-two, eleven fifty-three…

As soon as he heard Eva click off her light, Cal leapt up, tip-toed downstairs, and headed out through the kitchen, careful not to slam the door behind him. He didn't get far. Across the driveway, Mrs. Kenefick's porch lamp threw a raw shaft of light over half their yard. Great. Another night owl. He could see the old woman through the sheer curtains rocking in her chair, a cat in her lap, her face ghost white from the reflection off her TV.

Pulling up the hood of his sweatshirt, he crept past her driveway and made for the marsh's south side. As he crossed the boardwalk, he kept a watchful eye over his shoulder. It was a bitter night. No one would be out. Nevertheless, he stayed vigilant, careful he wasn't followed.

As he'd done every week for more than two months now, Cal slunk back to the piece of shoreline where he'd first seen the rare black water soldier and ducked down between the reeds. Even with his hands buried deep in his sweatshirt, they trembled so hard he could barely walk straight. His stomach rolled, and he felt like vomiting. With his breath short, he crouched down and waited.

The marsh was frozen now. The enchanted water soldier no longer floated through the grassy reeds like it had the first time but filtered up through a patch of broken black ice. He heard a cracking sound and his heart began to pound. A dark, shimmering shadow drifted below the frosty surface.

A second later, a small bud broke through the ice, pulsing on a plate of leaves, glittering in the darkness. As its black petals spread open, Cal fell to his knees and crawled toward it. His fingers gripped the ground, mud jamming beneath his fingernails. He shoved his spastic hands toward the luminescent blossom, then plunged them deep into the cold water, splashing it over his face and down his neck. Within seconds, his breathing eased up. His stomach settled. He steadied himself and stood up. The lily sunk out of sight and the marsh grew still.

From somewhere in town, twelve chimes struck the hour.

Cal turned away. With his hands calm, every step grew easier, and he felt stronger. But the elation he'd felt that first night was gone. He'd learned the enchanted cure was a fleeting one. Week after week, he needed to return to the marsh. If he didn't, his vision went on hyper-drive, the tremors grew worse. He was at the mercy of the water soldier.

Yet as he walked through the icy still of the night and the dark outline of his house came into view, he had little regret. A short-lived cure was better than none. Hell, in the past weeks, his life improved in ways he'd never expected. As long as he kept coming to the marsh and the black lily kept appearing, he could live a normal life. Best of all, the weird clouds of colored energy were gone. It was as simple as a walk across the bridge, a splash of water, and a walk back. Easy. Normal.

Sort of.

CHAPTER
TWENTY-FOUR

S
tar sat at her laptop Googling disorders of every kind, still trying to convince herself her problem was medical, curable—that the reflections could be medicated away. Beyond her door, she heard Aunt Zoe's determined gait, her dress heels tapping across the foyer's parquet floor. As the front door opened, then clicked shut, Star closed her computer and grinned. Garden Club meeting. First Tuesday, every month. 7:00 p.m. Her aunt never missed it.

She leapt from the chair, opened her bedroom door, then peered left and right. Coast clear. She jumped on the rail and slid down the grand staircase, her shirttails flying behind her, just because it was fun, just because it would piss off her aunt. She leapt off in the middle of the foyer and wandered through the wide-open spaces of well-appointed rooms. Too many rooms. Too much furniture. She walked through the den, the parlor and kitchen just to be sure the maid was gone, then made a beeline past the dining room, dashing down the narrow floral passage until she reached the greenhouse atrium. Finally. Her aunt had been careful to keep her away since that night when she stumbled in and caught her doing who-knew-what.

Intrigued, Star walked up and down the overgrown aisles, slapping away leaves or branches that dared get in her way. They seemed to actively climb and poke in her direction, like some carnivorous jungle. The place was just as weird as she remembered.

Looking around, she couldn't help but shake her head at Aunt Zoe. When was she going to figure it out? Homeopathy wasn't going to help her cure anything. No matter how many leaves, stems, and petals she pulverized.

Brushing past the plants that seemed more circus side show than garden-variety, Star aimed for the back of the room and the heavy wooden door now concealed by a trio of potted trees. With a gut-busting thrust, she edged each of the trees aside, one by one, then wrapped her fingers around the black figure-eight handle and pulled. Damn. Locked tight. Clearly, Aunt Zoe didn't trust her. She looked around the circular green house and spotted an iron skeleton key dangling from a loop at the side of the potting table.

She smiled. Clearly, Aunt Zoe underestimated her.

Star grabbed the key and slipped it into the keyhole using her full weight to shove the half-sized door open. Stepping through the low arching passageway, she stood at the top of the stairs, unprepared for what met her. The scent of worn leather and a softer, muskier smell, one she was sure she could only imagine, filled her with nostalgia. She could almost feel her father's presence, and it made her miss him all the more deeply.

She blinked back tears as a motion light switched on, then descended the stone steps. Peering through the dim circle of light that broke through the shadows, she saw furniture veiled in white sheets, cobbled walls. A single arched window at the end of the room offered a sliver of moonlight along with a chilly breeze that disturbed the draped sheets into a ghostly quiver. She walked toward a massive desk, piled with books and cluttered with papers, a laptop shoved to the side. She opened it but the battery was dead. No charging cord.

Her hand grazed the dusty shelf overhead, coating her fingers in a powdery gray film. Careful not to disturb anything, she tip-toed around books and files that lie helter-skelter across the floor as if the wild sweep of an arm had sent them there. Star shook her head in disbelief. If this was her father's room, he'd never have left it this way.

Curious, she walked over to one of the large sheet-draped pieces in the room, hesitated, then flung back the cover. Rows of petri dishes, tubes, and jars covered a lab table half the length of the room. They were full of—she didn't know what. Some held a whitish sort of film or chains of gossamer cells suspended in place. Others had larger oblique shapes, floating uncertainly while still others held a collection of listless blobs that appeared to stare at her.

She continued to lift one tarp after another, forgetting to blink or swallow. Whatever these containers held, it had been a long time since anyone bothered with them. Dusty lids, cloudy liquid. She felt a looming sadness here. It permeated the air. Was it the hum of the overhead light, the chill of the dungeon-like cellar, or the hopeless suspension of the matter in the jars?

She shivered and stared into the liquid, then began to feel it. Not one reflection, but many rushing behind her eyes. She squeezed them shut as a great rising sigh seemed to fill the room, whining and rushing like the wind. She spun away from the watery jars, pounded over the angry splatter of books and stopped short at the edge of the towering window, gasping as she reached up to close it. Her hand lingered on the window latch, then fell to her side.

It wasn't open.

After a minute, Star brushed back the hanging vines, cacti,

and potted house plants crowding the window seat along with a few books and slumped on the cushion beside them. A spindly spider plant poked at the top of her head and she knocked it back with a curse.

Staring through the window at the windswept yard, she spied a pair of leaves caught on an updraft and followed them as they twirled before the moon's pale glare. She thought of Cal with a sigh, fogging the glass and clouding her vision of the landscape below. But different visions replaced it, memories of that night last fall when she met him on the marsh bridge. It was the first time—the only time—she told anyone about her reflections. Didn't scare him off, though. Somehow, he refused to be put off by her. For some stupid reason, he accepted her unconditionally. Made her feel full of purpose and promise. He was the only reason she'd remained glued together this past year. Her smile hardened. That was until twelve weeks ago.

These days when Cal wasn't sucking face with Kelly Hanson, he was strutting down the hallway fist-bumping jocks, flunkies, and potheads. At first, she'd hoped his bravado would pass, a knee-jerk reaction to the attention he got after his suspension was lifted. But then she started to notice things. Things that didn't fit with her steady, unbreakable version of Calvin Hughes.

Like last Saturday, when trouble broke out at Ackley's Bend. Star remembered watching the whole debacle unfold from the footbridge where she'd been checking out a pond hockey game—watching and marveling at the collective stupidity of the skaters. Ackley's Bend was a windless armpit of the marsh. Home to one of its shallowest pools, it was the first section to freeze over and always the first to melt.

Sure enough, about two o'clock, with the strengthening sun beating down on the marsh and the temperatures inching up, the ice lid on Ackley's Bend gave way. It started with a crack, loud as a gunshot. Then all at once people went down, screaming, thrashing, diving for shore. On land there was a frantic grab for hockey sticks, branches, anything to extend into the icy water. For a few minutes, everyone actually forgot about their own selfish lives, rolled up their sleeves and helped out —except Cal.

Just before disaster struck, he had skated off from the main group with Kelly. As the icy water swallowed up their friends, he looked over his shoulder but never went back to see if anyone needed help. In the end, no one blamed Cal. After all, they said, he had to take care of Kelly who sobbed for countless minutes.

But there was one other person at the Bend that afternoon who seemed equally surprised at Cal's lack of action: Eva. Her green glare was just as visible yesterday at school when Star overheard a verbal throw-down between the Hughes siblings over who had rights to the car Friday night. Cal won.

As Star mulled over Cal's recent turn of character, she fought back the rumble of her conscience. Sure, she'd screwed him over last fall, but that was to save him from a fate that hopefully wasn't set in stone. In the end, she'd tried to set it straight. Sort of.

Her eyes fell away from the window, down to the clutter of books on the window seat. None looked like her father's science journals. These had weird titles like: *The Power of Plants, Herbaceous Remedies* and *Green Gold.* Among the scatter, one stood out. It lay open, a massive volume bound in worn black leather, edged in gold. With difficulty, Star hoisted it up and read the inscription on the opening page: To Zoe. With love, Ginny. Intrigued, she tried to leaf through the pages, but each time they dribbled through her fingers like a handful of water. Again and again Star picked at the page corners, but the moment she tried to turn one, it slipped through her hand.

Suddenly, her back stiffened. She could hear the groan of

the heavy door edging open at the top of the stairs. Her eyes dashed around for a hiding place—beneath the drapes, under the plants. But it was too late. Aunt Zoe was already in the room. Descending. Watching. Fuming...

"I noticed you weren't in bed, Aster. Hadn't drunk your tea." There was a pause. "What are you doing *here*?"

Her voice had a powdery false calm about it. Star decided to play the game.

"Just looking around," she answered. Maintaining a relaxed stance at the window, Star slipped the book back onto the seat cushion. Behind her, she could hear her aunt's breathing quicken as she circled down several more stairs.

"Tenacious, aren't you?" she croaked before softening her tone. "Just like your father."

"I hope so."

"Regardless, you're not allowed in this room. So, I'll ask you again, what are you doing here?"

"Looking up—stuff." Star's hand brushed one of the books on the window seat. "For school".

Aunt Zoe descended another stair.

"You're wasting your time, Aster. Some questions have no answers. Careful or you'll wind up like him—" Her chin lifted toward the large, disheveled desk. "Warped by intellect and ruined by conscience. Come along now."

"You never understood him or his work."

Her aunt turned and climbed a few steps. "I thought I did. Now let's go."

Star grew provocative. "What about my sister?"

The neat bob of gray hair snapped toward her, but Aunt Zoe recovered.

"Sickly child." She shook her head with fresh aggravation. "If I had known about their excursion...and with her weak constitution."

"But why did—"

"We've been through this a hundred times, Aster. When are you going to start moving on with your life?"

"When someone starts telling me the truth."

Her aunt gasped. Sensing for the first time that she had the upper hand, Star grew bold, daring to say something she'd suspected but never had the nerve to put into words.

"It had something to do with his research, didn't it? This room—"

Her aunt managed to maintain her prim composure, but in the faint drop of her jaw, Star saw that her wild guess had landed dangerously near the truth.

"You're losing your grip, Aster. Keep this up and you're going to lose your mind."

Even after the door slammed at the top of the stairs, Star stood there numb. Her gaze fell absently onto the window seat, to the leather-bound volume still open there. Staring at it, the writing on the page seemed to ebb and move like the tides. Suddenly she saw Alula's face rippling in the watery pages. Dark circles ringed her eyes. Tears stained her pale cheeks. Startled, Star slammed the book shut. Then she read the sweeping scroll written across the cover and staggered back: *The Dark Art of Reflections.*

CHAPTER
TWENTY-FIVE

S tar shoved a tray of instruments into the sterilizer, turned the lock and pressed the button, careful to avoid looking into the mirrored side panel. She'd had her fill of reflections. But when the timer buzzed, she just glared at the dial, making no move to retrieve the tray. Three months. The internship was as much a lie as Aunt Zoe's herbal tea.

"One more, Star, then you can go." A heavy woman walked in and slapped down another tray, popping her gum and chuckling. "Don't look so enthused. Somebody's gotta—hey, what's with your ear?" She leaned in, narrowing her eyes. "Ew. It looks all yellow and puss-like. Oh, and I found these on the floor by your backpack. You sure seem to go through a lot of 'um. Looks like Sudafed. You got allergies or something?"

Star snatched the tablets from her hand. "Yeah, allergies… Anyway, I was wondering if I could check out the centrifuge lab or maybe the frozen storage facility across the hall."

"Why?"

"Because it might be educational. You know, the reason I'm *here*."

The gum-chomper looked at Star, then let out a blast of a laugh.

"Ha! Fat chance, honey. You need top clearance for both. No one gets in there 'cept thems that are supposed to. What's a matter? You don't look like the sorta gal who'd get off on all that high-tech stuff."

Then the woman tossed her lab coat over a hook and walked out the door, chuckling and popping her gum.

"Sorry, I just thought it might be *interesting!*" Star shouted at the closing door. She threw down the last tray with a clatter and tugged off her lab coat. "They can do their own dirty dishes. I'm done." But reaching the door, Star stopped short. She could hear a pair of hushed voices across the corridor. Cracking the door open, she peered out and listened.

"And this is the long-term storage facility for frozen embryos you've been asking about. It's usually off limits, but I'm sure a quick look would be all right."

She recognized Dr. Malcolm, one of the top researchers at the facility. His guest was none other than the snake himself— Orrin Parker. Full of smiles and nods, he seemed ready to bend over and kiss the good doctor's ass if it meant getting behind that door.

Star waited a second, then made her way into the corridor. What the hell did Parker want with that lab? For him, the smug knowledge of getting into a place no one else was allowed might be enough reason. Still...

Preoccupied, Star forgot to take her usual escape route down the emergency exit stairwell. Instead, she shoved her way into an elevator filled with researchers and assistants and instantly regretted it. Sideways glances shot in her direction; eyes rolled. In no mood for moral or physical scrutiny, she made a quick exit at the next floor. Just a few steps down the connecting corridor, Star found herself—of all places—in the hospital maternity ward.

Passing the newborn nursery, she stopped and stared at the swaddled bundles. Some lie still and silent, others seemed to writhe and screech beneath their blankets. She sighed. So much pain in front of them...if they knew, would they bother with the struggle?

Turning from the window, Star made her way toward the closest stairwell, her army-style boots striking an intimidating echo behind her. As she neared the end of the corridor, the sharp wail of newborns again filled her ears. This time, though, there was no nursery window to show them off. She stopped in front of an office marked Women's Clinic, hesitated a moment, then turned the handle and walked inside.

"Do you have an appointment?" a voice asked from behind the desk.

Star glanced at the receptionist but didn't answer. Her eyes explored the room filled with young women. They sat paging through magazines or scrolling through their cell phones, a baby bump of some size above each lap. But no babies.

The receptionist waited. The patients shifted uncomfortably.

"Do you *have* an appointment?" the woman repeated. "We're booked this evening."

Star's eyes narrowed and shifted toward the inner offices on the far side of the room, then to the ceiling above them. She heard cries from somewhere, somewhere near here, but not exactly *here*.

The receptionist stood now, her eyes traveling over Star's fatigue-style pants, her black military jacket. Her hand inched toward the receiver.

"Uh, maybe we can fit you in. What did you say your name was?" she asked, her fingers stabbing at the phone.

Star stood there a moment longer, not so much staring as listening. Listening above the drone of the TV, the grunting fax machine and the gurgling aquarium. Listening to a sound, it seemed, from beyond this world, to cries so small yet so jagged they tore at her soul like metal teeth.

"—yes, the clinic on the second floor, hurry—"

Star stumbled back through the door, across the hallway, and down the emergency stairwell, pulling her hood around her face. Outside, a couple of security guards flashed by and she sidled off the main walkway, ducking into a memorial garden encircled by shrubs. With her heart racing, she scooted onto a stone bench and tried to look inconspicuous. After a moment, she lifted her head and looked up through the skeleton of trees surrounding the garden. The evening sky was softening with the last blush of day. As her pulse eased, she let her gaze drift toward town where the steeple of St. Francis looked like a giant lance poking at the swollen belly of the cloud-filled sky.

Closer at hand, she saw bushes sagging with snow. They looked tired, almost impatient for the sun to finish off their prolonged winter misery. Reaching out, she stroked a heavy branch and let the wetness drip through her fingers. She closed her eyes and massaged her forehead and the back of her neck. She was just starting to breathe normally again when a prong from one of her rings snagged at her ear. A jolt of pain ripped through her body. Even with her eyes closed, she winced.

"You should get that checked out."

Star froze. It was too good to be true. But as her eyelids slowly lifted, she saw him, the strands of his blonde hair stirring with the breeze, his jacket and shirt open at the collar.

"It'll heal."

"But faster if you get someone to look at it," Cal urged.

"I wouldn't need help if those felons you call friends had left me alone."

"They're not all bad."

"Yeah? I hadn't noticed."

Cal tried to joke away the tension. "Too many violent video games, I guess."

He smiled his crooked, beguiling smile. She steeled herself against it.

"Or maybe they're just assholes."

Cal's gaze drifted aloft, and he seemed to contemplate the clouds gathering in the dusky sky. "I tried to stop them."

In the awkward blue silence that followed, Star tried to embrace the moment—the smell of the warm March evening, the stir of bare branches budding overhead, the last ring of the seven o'clock chimes washing over town. She wrestled with the logic of Cal being here, despite all the ways she'd put him off. Here—with her. She started thinking about how the hospital wasn't on his way home—or anywhere else—and grew hopeful. When she spoke, she could hear the odd flirtatious note in her voice but didn't care.

"So, what brings you to the medical center?"

"I had the car so—"

Star held her breath.

"—when Orrin asked for a ride home, I told him, no problem."

Her hopes smashed in a spectacular inner explosion. She was just beginning to wrap her head around the strangeness of Orrin needing a ride home—he had a car—when a pair of security guards burst through the semi-circle of bushes, stopping so close she had to look up to see their faces.

"Excuse me, miss, can we see some ID?"

"Why?" she shot back.

"We have a report of someone causing a disturbance in the women's clinic."

"Lighten up. I'm an intern in the research wing. My supervisor can verify it."

"Some ID, please?"

Star reached for her pocket, then remembered ripping off her lab coat with the ID attached.

"Uh, I don't have it." She glanced at Cal.

"Then we'll have to ask you to leave the premises."

"Tools," she mumbled loud enough for them to hear. Before she could get to her feet, though, a call crackled over one of the guard's radios. An older woman, under the influence, was threatening a doctor in the ER. Seeing that Star was ready to leave, they hurried back toward the hospital.

Cal waited until they were out of earshot. "You have a thing for pissing people off, don't you? You need to lighten up."

"Says the guy who used to stress over everything."

Cal shuffled his feet in the snow, a hint of unease in his voice. "Maybe I've learned not to see so much."

"Really? I thought blindness was a disability, not a skill."

In the lapse that followed, Star sat back and hated herself anew. Why did every word from her mouth conspire against Cal's warmth? She didn't deserve a friend—a boyfriend—like him. Maybe it *was* their destiny to be apart.

As she tried to reboot the conversation, her attention drifted beyond the shrubs to a couple walking with a newborn baby wrapped in their arms. It started to cry. With an awkward motion, the young parents rocked the bundle before hurrying into a waiting car. Then, as her gaze followed them out of the parking lot, it started again. That sound. The small cries of the invisible. Slow and whiney at first, it became urgent, almost deafening, until she flattened her hands against her ears and cursed aloud for it to stop.

"Star, what is it? What's the matter?"

"I...I hear them," she said, her eyes welling with tears.

"Who?"

"It started upstairs. I thought the cries were coming from the women's clinic. But then it sounded like they were seeping through the ceiling, from the floor above—the long-term storage facility." She hesitated, her frayed nerves audible. "It was like…like I was hearing the sound of…of…" she struggled to say the words, "…limbo." Star felt her lip quiver. "The unborn crying for life or…or…maybe waiting for death."

She looked up. "Cal?"

But he just stared at her, his eyes a mottled blue fog. Star didn't see a shred of compassion, not a trace of empathy in them. For the first time since she'd known Cal, she felt truly alone.

Shifting her gaze beyond him, she observed the parking lot where the overhead lights bled a yellow glow over the pavement, slick and shiny now from a fresh drizzle of rain. She sensed he was anxious to leave and, turning her face up to the darkening sky, closed her eyes. As the rain coursed down her cheeks, Star wished it would wash away this existence that teetered between real and imagined worlds, between what was and what might be.

Then it began.

The feeling she got when boundaries became a watery blur. She fought it for a futile moment, but the duality overpowered her…

"You shouldn't be here, Cal," she began, her voice monotone.

"Yeah? I was about to suggest the same for—"

He caught her trance-like expression, her face lifted to the March night. "What do you mean?"

Star didn't respond. She sat there listening to the inaudible.

"What do you mean?" he repeated.

"You were supposed to be somewhere else?"

Cal shook his head. "No—well, yeah. But it's no problem. I'll pick up my mom after Orrin gets out. If she's in a hurry, she can walk home." He checked his watch, then glanced impatiently toward the hospital.

"Don't bother. She's on her way here."

From somewhere below, the wail of a siren whined through town.

CHAPTER
TWENTY-SIX

C al pressed his finger against the hospital window, tracing the raindrops that drizzled down the other side. Gray, hopeless. He let his gaze fall away toward the layers of gauzy bandage that wrapped his mother's skull, the long brown braid that lay over her pillow. Scooping a clatter of ice chips from a plastic cup, he dabbed them over her lips, watched and waited. Nothing. Just the shallow rise and fall of her chest. She didn't seem to be in this world. Wasn't in the next. Prisoner somewhere in between. And it was his fault.

He unzipped his backpack and pulled out a paperback, *The Great Gatsby*—one of his mom's favorites—and began to read aloud because the doctor said it would be helpful to keep her brain stimulated. A moment later, the door swung open and Kelly walked in.

"How is she?" she asked, clutching a small box of chocolates.

"Breathing on her own, pretty much."

"So, she'll be coming home—when?" The candy box became an impatient tambourine against her knee.

"When she regains consciousness, I guess."

Kelly bit her bright pink lips. "We're invited to Joe's party this weekend. You going?"

"I don't know."

"C'mon, Cal. We missed Ted's last weekend. I heard it was awesome. We never do anything anymore. You used to be fun…"

Her voice trailed off as she watched Cal fold a second blanket over his mother, then resume his bedside seat. She glanced at her cell phone, then changed course.

"Coach wants to know when you're going to show up. It's been a week." She hitched her hip. "If you don't get back in the pool, the team might not qualify for Sectionals."

Cal met Kelly's angry eyes and the pair of fake lashes that batted over them. "Coach said that?"

She tossed the box of chocolates on the bed where it landed between his mother's feet.

"He didn't have to, Cal. The whole swim team is talking about you. You missed the tournament in Rochester last weekend and they lost. Some of the guys"—her eyes narrowed —"think you're trying to tank the team on purpose, you know, get back at the coach for benching you last fall."

"Who?"

Kelly pursed her lips, glad at finally getting a rise from him.

"Well, Bill, for one."

Cal smirked. "Now there's a source."

"Look," she said, grabbing his shoulder, "I like being with you, but this is *not* working for me. You've—changed. I don't know if I even want to go to the Marsh Madness dance with you anymore."

She waited for some explosive effect to pass over Cal's expression. When none occurred, Kelly Hanson was the one to erupt.

"I don't go out with just anyone. I don't have to! I go out with guys that do things, guys that are fun."

Cal stared at Kelly. He could almost see the dark shades of selfish energy curdling around her like a rusty stew. But he couldn't be sure about that or anything else these days. His hands began to tremble, and he realized he was overdue at the marsh.

"I'll text Thornley tomorrow." He glanced back at his mother. "Or in a few days."

Kelly's fists curled in a huff of frustration. "That's too late, Cal. Too late for him and too late for me. We're through!" She stormed out, her heels striking an angry echo down the hallway.

Within an hour, the rain kicked up again, pouring down in a steady wash of misery. Cal's gaze drifted toward the window and the drops drizzling in serpentine patterns. He glanced at the clock above the door. It was after six. He wished Eva would show up. His dad would be there soon, but he wanted to see Eva. She'd been careful to avoid him since the car accident and had little or nothing to say when their paths did cross. Silence was her special sort of torment. But he wasn't looking for a long conversation. He just wanted to say he was sorry.

The door burst open. Cal looked up, hopeful. It was only Uncle Max.

"How's my sister today?" he boomed, addressing the patient. Then he bent over and planted a huge kiss on her forehead, nearly crushing a bouquet of lilies in his arms, the third bunch of flowers he'd brought that week.

"How is she, Cal?" he asked, his voice now hushed.

"Stable."

"Has she been conscious yet?" he asked, his moustache twitching.

"No. Last night the nurses were hopeful, but then —nothing."

"Progress." Uncle Max nodded. "That's all that matters." After several somber minutes, his business persona resurfaced. "Speaking of progress, I could use a hand at the restaurant this week."

Cal shook his head.

"Then a friend, perhaps. I've switched to a lower cost linen service and need someone to organize the tablecloths and napkins so they're ready for the weekend banquets. Pay's not bad. I was thinking, maybe, of that girlfriend of yours."

"I don't think so." Cal looked at his mother's face. "But I know someone else who might do it. Do you remember Mrs. Emerling?"

His uncle offered a slight smile. "Yes, lovely woman. But I heard she's…fallen on hard times, so to speak."

"She's trying to make changes."

Uncle Max's bushy eyebrows buckled skeptically.

"Really. She came to visit Mom a few days ago. We had a long talk." Cal searched for the right words. "She's—getting help. Went to her first group meeting." He paused. "At the very least, Mom would appreciate you helping her friend out."

His uncle glared at him. "Don't do that. Your mother used to use that same look on me whenever she needed a favor— usually for a hapless friend teetering on the brink of some unnamed disaster." He waved his fingers with finality. "Fine, I'll give her a try, but I'm not baby-sitting anyone. Tell her she can start Tuesday."

He turned and blew a kiss at his sister, then stopped at the door and cocked his head, "Hmm, Deidre Emerling…"

Shortly after, Cal's father walked in looking tired and drawn, a bag of fast food in his grip. He urged Cal to go home, do his homework, get some rest. Cal stood up, reluctant. He'd been so sure today would be the day his mother would open her eyes, wave aside the flood of apologies that would come streaming from his mouth and smile. But she wasn't moving now, might not ever again. He looked at her, lost beneath the pale endless sleep, then leaned over and kissed her cheek. From the corner of his eye, he saw a wave of indigo flare about her. In a second, it vanished, but Cal could feel it, just below the surface, her energy waiting for release. Without thinking, he reached down and cradled her bandaged scalp in his hands. His vision swam. His head pounded with fatigue. After a few seconds, he leaned back, said goodbye to his father, and left the room.

Downstairs, Cal caught a glimpse of Eva crouched behind—go figure—a rod and gun magazine in the lobby. He guessed it'd been the closest thing to grab when she spotted him stepping off the elevator. He thought about going over to her but, sensing the scene would end badly, kept walking out the door and down the front stairs of the hospital.

Pulling up his collar, he made his way through the misty drizzle of the parking lot and headed toward town. The humidity amplified every smell, from the stinking garbage piled at the curb to the fresh ground beans wafting out of The Last Drop.

Through the mist, Cal saw Driscoll's Drugs and the Playbill come into view, then St. Francis and its moss-covered stones exuding their own primeval scent. Walking past the church, Cal had the overwhelming sense he was being watched. He glanced over his shoulder and saw the flicker of votive candles wavering from the vestibule. The unsteady glow animated the figures in the stained-glass windows. They appeared to fidget and breathe, their eyes following him with unanimous reproach.

Then, from the corner of his eye, Cal thought he saw one of the statues beside the church stand and walk forward. Even in his peripheral vision, it seemed to hurry down the steps and call out to him.

"Cal, wait up!"

He stopped in his tracks.

"I've been waiting for you," Star panted, dashing down the slate steps and looking as anxious as the stained-glass saints behind her. "I didn't want to bother you at the hospital. Everyone's so—you know—wired up there." For a second, her nervous gaze dashed toward the church as if she, too, felt the presence of watchful eyes. "Anyway, how's your mother? Any improvement?"

Cal felt a strange tightening fill his chest, like a lump of soft clay drying too quick and too hard, and the thing he said next reflected its bitter turn.

"Shouldn't you be telling me?"

Star's silver-studded eyebrows wrinkled.

"Why don't you check your crystal ball or your little reflections or whatever you use to conjure up this stuff and tell me when she's going to get better?"

"How dare you!" she whispered. "You have no idea—"

"Yeah, but you did, Star. That night you knew."

In the distance, the sound of raindrops drumming across the pavement raced toward them. It pounded up the street until the storm seemed to stall and hover above their heads.

"You insensitive bastard! You think I get a bulletin with upcoming events?" Her chest rose and fell in heaves. "Sure, I see things coming. Sometimes. But I don't always know who or when until it's too late. I told you, I only get pieces, not the whole story. It's a watery blur."

"But you knew that night, didn't you?"

"Well—yeah. I mean, I knew, but it was only seconds, not even a minute…"

The rain continued to drench their clothes and pummel the pavement around their feet.

"It might have made a difference. *You* might have made a difference, but you chose not to."

"It's not that simple, Cal!" Star screamed above the roar of the rain, the plates of her pink-colored hair dripping over her shoulders. "You of all people should know it's not that simple!"

For several seconds Cal just stood there, blinking away the steady wash of rain over his eyes, gazing at Star who looked strangely heartsick and wounded.

"Listen, you've made it clear, you want nothing to do with me," he began, the edge in his voice softening, "and I've kept my distance. But no matter what stunt you pulled, I never stopped caring. I couldn't hate you if I tried. Still, I don't understand why you're hell-bent on making my life miserable."

Star's expression melted with his words. Her face awash with rainwater and tears revealed raw angst.

"It's because…because I've seen things about you…" She choked back a sob. "Bad things."

Cal concentrated on her. His vision showed him little more than a shadow of energy these days, still Star's was so radiant, he couldn't miss it. He looked for some hint she was trying to con him, but all he saw was that incredible band of silver gleaming like a halo. There was something else, too, something different—a small, frenzied fraying around the edges. Still, nothing to suggest her words were anything but the truth.

"Go on."

"I see you—and me," she continued. "Together—in trouble. And you know what you said about Aunt Zoe? Well, you were…"

A sudden movement from the church's side yard captured Star's attention. Cal had seen her eyes shift several times in that direction. This time, however, she began to shrink back, gaping as if the Devil himself were rising out of the darkened bushes.

"Star, what is it?"

He looked over his shoulder and saw Orrin rounding the back of the church, his neat oxford shirt barely dampened by the rain. Cal turned back toward Star, but she was gone, bolting down Main Street, the wisps of her gorgeous aura unraveling in a lustrous trail behind her.

"They ought to lock her up somewhere," Orrin snickered, coming up to Cal's side and watching Star dash off. "What a head case. So, what's her problem this time? Come on, I'm up for a laugh."

Cal shrugged off the topic and resumed his homeward trek, his hands at his sides trembling steadily. Orrin kept up with him.

"Hey, I got my car parked near the Last Drop. I'll give you a ride—but it'll cost you."

Cal's eyebrows rose.

"I want you to put in a good word with your sister for the Marsh Madness dance."

Cal shot Orrin a skeptical glance. "Why?"

"We sort of had this thing going and then I got busy and, well, things kind of unwound."

"C'mon. Really?"

"Yeah, it's this internship. Seriously messed with my social life. Check out the time. I just got out."

As he spoke, the church bells began to peal behind them. Cal glanced toward the tower, then back to Orrin who was covering his ears, wincing with each reverberation.

"Sensitive hearing," Orrin yelled, still agonizing from the sound above. "So, you'll put in a good word?"

Cal didn't answer. Something about Orrin had caught his eye, and it wasn't until the last bell struck the hour that he was able to refocus and respond. He shoved his hands in his pockets. "Uh, sure. I'll mention it."

By the time they reached Orrin's vehicle, the rain stopped and Cal used the turn in weather to beg off a ride home.

"Clearing up. Think I'll walk. Thanks, man. Some other time."

Cal figured things were cool between them, but he couldn't deny the rev of Orrin's engine or the furious squeal of his tires as he tore away.

CHAPTER
TWENTY-SEVEN

C al crouched among the reeds. He didn't want to be there. Not tonight, not on any night. He thought about getting up, walking away. But he was way overdue for a splash of the midnight waters and settled in to wait, evermore guilty. Staring into the black water, he shook his head. How the hell did his life sink this low? At first, it had been a no-brainer. A walk to the marsh, a quick dunk and, just like that, a freak no more. Losing his weird vision was beyond cool. What he'd always wanted.

Tonight though, as he argued with Star, his vision began to slip back and he got a glimpse of what he'd been missing—her beautiful energy faltering, fading. What's more, she finally seemed ready to open up, tell him something about Aunt Zoe. Even if she had, though, he doubted he could help her. Not anymore.

Then there was Orrin. The guy without an aura. Tonight, though, something about him seemed off. Cal wouldn't have noticed it if the water soldier's enchantment hadn't been wearing off. Yet as they stood there in the shadow of the giant steeple, he was sure he saw something around Orrin, a sliver of energy he'd never noticed before—

Cal's back straightened. He looked across the dark marsh. It was coming. He could hear it: the stirring of brushed leaves, the trickle of disturbed water. A moment later, he saw the black lily rise from beneath the surface of the water. It eased its way through the reeds, a slender bud on a plate of velvety leaves. Floating closer, the flower shivered a little, seemed to wait—for him. Cal couldn't help himself. He rushed toward it, stumbling through the reeds, his whole body convulsing. Thrusting his trembling hands through the weedy stalks, he strained to touch the erect bud. As his hand brushed its petals, the flower spread open and the whole surface of the marsh began to sparkle. He plunged his hands beneath the floating lily pad into the cold water.

Usually, Cal hurried away, but tonight he felt so spent he sunk back on his heels and just sat there, his head hanging between his knees. After a few minutes, he looked up. The enchanted lily had not re-submerged but was gliding across the surface of the water. In its glittering wake Cal saw odd creatures moving beneath the water, aquatic life he'd never seen before. Feeling stronger, he took a deep breath and stood up. Then, for a moment, he didn't breathe at all.

On the far end of the marsh, a woman in a dark robe stood waiting for the water soldier's approach. She seemed to have some command over it. As she lifted her hands, the lily glided to a stop. Crouching down, she scooped a measure of the sparkling water into a small black kettle, then reached for the flower. At her touch, the petals drooped and shriveled. She crushed them in her fist, sprinkled them into the kettle, then turned and walked away. Once more, the water and all the marsh fell dark.

Cal squinted, following the figure up the path that led through the willows and around the cove. It went toward Aunt

Zoe's house, hidden behind a tangle of vines and branches like some forbidden fortress. And Star was there, alone, unaware of the darkness that surrounded her. He had to warn her. But how? In some twisted way, he was part of the whole spell. Who was he to judge evil?

CHAPTER
TWENTY-EIGHT

Eva moved like a zombie through the empty school corridors, the malaise of early morning dripping off like rain from her red slicker. Friday. She was crazy to be here. There were no deadlines, no editorial meeting. She could have slept in, indulged in a real breakfast. But like a dumb dog that couldn't learn new tricks she showed up anyway. Of course, being here was really about *not* being somewhere else—home.

Until last week, Eva's testy morning mood had always been defused by her mother's ready smile and the smell of warm buttered toast. Now daybreak found an awkward emptiness in their kitchen, her father dashing off with little to say and nothing to eat, stress the mainstay of his diet.

Lately, she bolted out the door right behind him, careful to avoid Cal. If she hadn't hid behind that magazine rack in the lobby yesterday, they might have faced off in the hospital—and it would have gotten ugly. Oh, he'd be all apologetic, saying he was sorry about not picking up their mother, sorry a car nearly killed her as she walked home. Sorry! Well, it was too late for that. And what did he expect her to say? That it was okay, accidents happen? Well, they only happened if you were stupid and selfish and her brother was guilty on both counts. For now, being anywhere but home was the place she wanted to be. And if their mother didn't recover, she'd made a vow to avoid Cal for the rest of their lives.

Eva's wet sneakers squeaked further along the corridor until she stopped in front of a display case filled with photos from last year's Marsh Madness dance. Weird poses, garish tuxedos and a gymnasium wrapped in too much crepe paper filled the crazy collage. Despite what she'd told her friends, she wanted to go to the dance just as much as everyone else. With the hospital visits and the extra housework, though, it didn't seem like it was going to happen for her.

Then, Orrin called.

Things were awkward at first. He was polite and formal one minute, casual and familiar the next. As he tried to figure out where he stood, her tone made it crystal clear: on shaky ground. Finally, Orrin launched into an earnest apology about losing track of the weeks. He admitted being preoccupied with his internship and an extra project he'd been assigned at the medical center. He didn't mind the long hours, he said, except when they were a result of Star slacking off. Privately, Eva wondered how one girl could screw up so many lives.

Warmed by his honesty, she found herself enjoying the smooth roll of his voice again. He was sweet and engaging, complementing her on the newspaper, commiserating about her mother, and wondering if her brother had mentioned that he'd asked about her. Eva said no that it had probably slipped Cal's mind—like everything else lately. Then, sandwiched between all the chat, came a brief mention of the dance—it might be fun and would she go with him? The next day, flowers came—pink roses. She only wished she could share the news with her mother….

Needing a good cup of coffee—actually any cup of coffee—

Eva headed for the cafeteria. Hearing the din, a grin sprouted across her face. With just one week before the big dance, the place was buzzing with booths for pre-sale tickets, flowers and limos. She could hardly wait to tell Lin her big news. Tori, on the other hand, would be another story. Though spinning classes had worked wonders for her mental condition—and their friendship—she was pretty sure Tori didn't have a date for the dance and going to Marsh Madness meant more to her than anyone Eva could think of.

Bumping between tables, Eva found her friends standing in line for breakfast. Like everyone else, they seemed charged by the room's energy and burst out talking at the same time.

"Eva, we heard the news!"

"How about borrowing a dress?"

"What are you doing with your hair?"

Eva tossed her head, laughing. "How did you guys find out so fast?"

"C'mon, it's not that complicated. You told your brother, your brother told my brother, my brother told me." Tori's mouth made a popping noise. "Simple."

"Yeah, except I didn't tell my brother."

"Well then, he probably overheard you talking," Lin smiled. "The important thing is we're *all* going to the dance."

Eva's hand froze halfway to the bagel bin. "We are?" She turned to Tori, who was grinning with a smile that stretched longer than the ticket line. "Who?"

"He's over there, by the fresh fruit bar," she said, as she paid for a blueberry muffin and squeezed into a table against the wall.

Eva spotted the handsome, broad-shouldered guy in line, his boyish smile growing as he spied Tori looking his way. "Nice. Where did you meet?"

"Are you kidding?" Lin laughed. "He only sat at the end of our lunch table every day for the whole year. You know, the guy you used to yell at for drinking soda and eating junk food?"

Eva's eyes bulged. "That good-looking kid is Hank Towson? Well, this is Marsh *madness*. Seems everyone is going."

"Even Billy," Tori chuckled. "He's asked three girls. They all said no. But he hasn't given up."

"What about your brother, Eva?"

"Don't know. Don't care."

"Maybe you should," Tori warned. "What if he goes with St—"

Lin elbowed Tori so hard, her muffin popped out of her hand and flew over to the next table.

For Eva, the electricity in the room drained away. Her mind blanked, the voices around her turned to static. It would be inconceivable. Against all common sense.

"Incoming!"

She glanced up in time to duck as Lin's catching arm swung out and caught Tori's breakfast on its return flight to the table. Eva became aware of bickering—the muffin's edibility seemed in question. She had no desire to join the fray, but when she heard Lin bust on Tori for ruining the morning's good vibe, Eva piped in.

"Lin, it's okay. I'm done worrying about Cal. He can do what he wants."

"That's the spirit," Tori cheered.

But Eva hadn't meant a word of it. The very idea of Cal and Star—together—churned in her stomach all day, in the place where unanswered questions stumble and collide. Once again, she found that even thinking about her brother made the world feel unnatural and upside down.

CHAPTER
TWENTY-NINE

As Cal walked home from school Friday, reliving, regretting the events of the previous night, he stopped on the marsh bridge. Overnight, the wintry quiet of the place seemed to have melted off. All around him, new reeds and wildflowers sprung from the earth, bitterns and robins called out and the splash of young fish stirred the green water. He took it all in—the sounds, smells and sights—and smiled. Yeah, it was time. Time to head back to Oakwood. And he couldn't have been more ready.

He turned and hurried along the uphill path, his sneakers skidding over the soggy ground. A morning rainstorm—third one that week—drenched the area. The marshy creek now rushed like a river, the current wild, the banks submerged. But as Cal climbed, it became a distant blur, a patch of blue-green silk rippling at the bottom of the hill, and he found himself sprinting up the path. All at once, it felt like years, not months, since he'd been to Oakwood and he couldn't wait.

Rounding the final turn, though, an uneasiness sunk into his gut. What if Stan wasn't there? Even crazier, what if the graveyard was gone? A moment later, though, the gate that separated Oakwood Cemetery from the rest of the world came into view, its black points piercing his irrational fears as easily as they skewered the spring air. He yanked hard on the gate. It gave way with a recognizable groan.

Entering the yard, the familiarity of the place felt like a warm handshake to Cal, from the tombstones to the towering trees to the moss-roofed hut where he hoped the old caretaker would be tinkering away. As he made his way up the hill, he realized he'd never seen spring in Oakwood. A ceiling of bright green leaves branched overhead while sprays of white and yellow daffodils bloomed around the graves of the Young Ones. In centerfield, he saw Quinn's monument frost-heaved and listing to the side, like an old man who needed a hip replacement, and under the cherry tree, Hallie Lowe's grave sprinkled with pink blossoms and a fuzzy blanket of new grass.

"Well, helloa there, Cal!" Stan's voice sounded as he emerged from behind the shed. "I was wonderin' whether you'd come by again."

"Wasn't sure if you'd be here either," Cal said, grabbing the outstretched, iron-fisted grip.

"Where else do I have to go?" The old man smiled, back-slapping Cal so hard, it nearly knocked the wind from him. "But a handsome young guy with a guitar and a crop of friends? Well, I imagine that fella might have a few other things to do."

Somehow the caretaker always knew when Cal needed to get something off his chest, when his conscience needed clearing and at just those times the old man would toss out a comment as casually as he tossed grass seed about the yard. But Cal wasn't ready to go there, not yet. He rechanneled the conversation.

"There must be a million things to do around here. Where do we start?"

With a sweeping glance that seemed to take in every obstinate weed and overgrown patch of grass in the yard, the old man drew a mental list.

"Well, Cal, let's start where we ended. To the shed!"

They walked into the stone building, ducking in tandem beneath the garage door and the low beams toward the workbench. In a glance, Cal could see that everything was as they'd left it. Hoses on the reels, tools on the pegs, lawnmowers and trimmers aligned in the front end, miscellaneous boards and sledgehammers near the basin at the back. The tin box still sat on the shelf above the window, just where Stan had left it on Christmas Eve. The workbench, however, was cluttered with screws and bolts.

"Been here long?" Cal asked.

"Just come," the old man answered, "what with the snow and then all the rain."

Cal walked over to the window and smeared his hand across four months of filmy dirt. He looked out to the graveyard where a light breeze rustled through the willowy grass.

"If it wasn't so wet, we could mow."

"Nonsense!" Stan said, peering out the window. "It'll be fine. Follow me." He pushed one of the rattling mowers out of the shed, his arms barely flexing with the effort, then straightened up and pointed across the yard.

"Start cutting over the flush markers, then work your way down. Careful at the lower end by— what's the matter?"

"It's dry," Cal said, looking down. He stomped his sneakers on the grass. "Bone dry. But—but how?"

Stan's beaming smile popped up, stretching his cheeks into the far corners of his face. "Well, Cal, this is the high ground, after all."

For most of the afternoon, Cal bounced along on the rickety

mower, carving his way around the uprights and rolling over the flush monuments 'til the place looked like a park. Once or twice, he found himself thinking about Marsh Madness then wondered why he was thinking about it at all. Most of the girls he knew wanted to go to the dance. But Star wasn't like other girls. Hell, he wasn't even sure they were on speaking terms. Still, if he asked her, would she say yes or just walk away laughing?

As a new set of rain clouds ballooned up on the horizon, Cal pushed the mower back into the shed where he found Stan at the workbench splicing together a pair of hoses. Without disturbing him, he jacked up the mower, slid beneath the undercarriage and cleaned the blades using an old screwdriver to loosen clumps of grass clippings. Instantly, the scent of newly-mowed lawn spread throughout the workshop.

When he'd finished, Cal felt a familiar sense of melancholy creep over him. It was time to go but felt too soon to leave. He grabbed a broom. "So, what did you do all winter?"

"Oh, odds and ends," Stan replied, his knife working a steady slice around the hose's edge. "Went South for a while, soaked up some Vitamin D..." He laughed silently, his head shaking at the absurdity of his words. With a grin in his voice, he asked, "And yourself?"

Cal squirmed under the simple question. "Well, I pretty much did whatever I wanted."

"And how'd that work out for you?"

"Not so good," he confessed, a half-dozen images plodding through his mind. Pushing the lawnmower back to its corner, Cal wiped his hands on a ragged tee shirt and swept the last of the clippings from the floor. "What's on tap for tomorrow?"

The caretaker looked up from his work, gazing through the streak in the window marked by Cal's hand. "I suppose trimming, if the weather holds out. You got time?"

"Sure. Saturday. No problem. I'll be here right after I visit my mom."

Stan's large eyes popped over his bifocals.

Cal muttered a brief explanation about the car accident, then plucked his jacket off a nail and hoisted the garage door over his head. As he stepped beneath the shed's low opening, he paused.

"Stan?"

"Uh-huh."

"Last time I was here, you told me that story about how you got in trouble helping some guy you didn't even know. Well, I was wondering—"

"Yes?"

"I was just wondering, you know, how you moved on."

The caretaker sat back. Licking his plump lips, he considered the question with gravity. "For a time, I didn't. But then I realized there's a purpose for all. Leaders and followers. Thinkers and doers. Those meant to make things"—he glanced down at the knife in his hand and smiled—"those meant to fix 'em'."

"I don't think I'm meant for anything."

"Son, we *all* tip the balance. One way or the other. Good *or* bad. A fight ragin' since time began. We're never more than a few wrong steps from utter chaos, but we give it our best shot." His voice slowed and grew heavy. "Sometimes what we do doesn't help. But sometimes it makes a difference—sometimes it can change humanity."

For a moment, the world seemed to go quiet. As Cal stood there at the mouth of the work shed, nothing broke the spring silence. Not a cricket or a crow. It was as if the entire marsh were listening to the old man's words, absorbing the logic.

"Well, get along now," Stan finally said. "Gettin' late. Marsh is no place to be after dark. But then, I s'ppose you've figured that out by now."

As his yellowy eyes lifted above the bifocals, Cal was startled by the blaze that seemed to burn behind them. For a moment, he wasn't sure if it was the reflection of the bare light bulb hanging overhead or some deeper fire raging within.

CHAPTER
THIRTY

S tan knew.

Cal tried a dozen different ways to convince himself the old caretaker couldn't know about his midnight walks, about everything. But his gut told him differently. Those yellowy eyes said it all.

Getting out of bed, he reached for his jeans and made a vow: He was done with the black magic of the marsh. No matter the consequences. No matter the hassle. It was time to see what he'd been missing, embrace his weird vision, reconnect with Star—and figure out what had happened to Alula. Yeah, but could he hold out? In the few days since he'd seen the water soldier, his tremors had returned fast and furious.

Glad it was Saturday, Cal took a long hot shower, then made his way down to the kitchen, grabbed a bowl of cold cereal and set out for the hospital. Outside, he found his neighbor pacing her driveway, two kittens cradled in her arms.

"Morning, Mrs. K."

"No better than a wolf..." she muttered, glaring at the new pup yelping across the street. "May as well let wild rhinos roam the neighborhood!" And with little more than a nod, she let him pass without delay.

At the hospital, Cal followed the all too familiar path to his mother's room, subconsciously noting the posters that lined the walls, the hand sanitizers, the nurses' stations. Turning into the hallway near his mother's room, though, he noticed a shift in the unchanging scheme of things. Different sounds—too many voices—a commotion of some kind. His easy pace became a dash. He burst into the hospital room where the family huddled around his mother's bed.

"Mom?"

"Hello, sleepyhead. Glad you could make it."

He rushed to hug her and felt the warmth of her breath brush his cheek. Stepping back, he fell speechless.

"She woke up this morning and now doesn't want to sleep at all," a nurse said, walking into the room. "But it's time for your guests to leave, Mrs. Hughes. That is, if they want you home soon."

While the family shuffled out, Cal returned to his mother's side and took her hand. "Mom, I'm so sor—"

She pressed her pale fingers over his lips. "None of that, Cal, but thank you for what you did for Mrs. Emerling. Uncle Max told me." She sighed then caressed the side of his face with her hand. "Lucky are the people who stumble across your path."

Eva's voice shot in from the doorway. "Cal, you heard what the nurse said. Maybe if you'd shown up earlier…"

He glanced over his shoulder and saw Eva's raging green energy. The same way it'd looked years ago whenever she thought he'd gotten the larger slice of pizza or the first cookie out of the oven.

Moments later, the family left the hospital, moving off in separate directions, but no one with as light a step as Cal. Even the creaky boardwalk that zigzagged over the marsh like a giant zipper seemed unmoved by his weight. Flipping up the hood of his sweatshirt against the rain, he turned toward Oakwood, but his steps grew heavy. He ignored the toads leaping across his path, the warble of a reed bunting. By the time he reached the cemetery, his tremors were so violent he had trouble opening the gate. In the shed, Stan glanced over as Cal walked through the door, then reached up to a shelf and tossed something toward him.

"Might do you some good."

Cal bent over and picked up the cellophane package that had fallen through his trembling hands to the dusty floor. He expected aspirin or a couple of Tylenol. None of it would help.

He fingered the package. "Gummy bears?"

"Edibles. Work wonders," the old man said, grabbing a rake. "Never killed anyone anyway." He laughed, "That I know of."

Cal shrugged, tore open the package and shoved the chewy colored bears in his mouth.

As usual, time barely seemed to exist in Oakwood. For hours they raked and pruned, weeded and trimmed despite the on-again-off-again showers. As Cal's tremors settled down, the work grew easier. He didn't even mind the caretaker's lectures anymore, the casual bits of wisdom he tossed out like a dandelion shaking its seeds upon the wind.

Around three o'clock, just as his stomach began to grumble, Stan called him to the shed for a quick snack of cold pizza and pop. Cal grabbed a small bottle of frosty root beer and downed it in a single gulp then inhaled the pizza. Afterwards, they took to the yard with a couple of refurbished weed-whackers. Cal dodged between the granite markers with the ease of experience now, knowing just where the ground sagged and where it heaved up. There were just two rows left when his machine died out. As he headed for the shed to get the manual cutters, Stan called over to him.

"Don't bother, Cal. We'll call it a day. I'll finish up."

They were almost done, Cal thought. Why quit now? Glancing back, he saw Theresa Heyman's monument in the middle of the last untrimmed row and understood.

Back in the shed, it took a chunk of pumice soap, a couple of gallons of water, and ten minutes for Cal to lift the dirt and mud caked beneath his nails. As for the rest of him, there was no hope. His jeans and sneakers showed no sign of their original color, and his Pink Floyd tee shirt was stained with sweat. He had no idea how the caretaker managed his way through the afternoon with nothing but a scuff on his overalls.

"I'll see you tomorrow then," Cal said, pulling back his hair into an elastic band.

Stan looked up from the porcelain sink.

"Oh, right. Sunday. Then after school next week. Any day. Well, except Friday. There's this dance. I might… go…depends…"

"No problem. Just get here early next time. Things to do."

Cal wound his way down through the graveyard, past the cast-iron gate and over the path that hair-pinned down to the marsh. For a change, the sun was making a go at the burly clouds, blistering through the stubborn billows with shafts of light. The marsh brightened in swirling patches of olive green and blue. Every now and then, a flash of silver scales glimmered beneath the surface.

Closer to the shoreline, the sunlight shifted illuminating a portion of the marsh usually set in shade. Cal stopped in his tracks. Lounging on a large flat boulder near the water, he saw Star leaning back on her elbows, her face lifted to the sun, the straps of a dark paisley dress falling off her shoulders. He took a few steps closer. She opened her eyes as a pair of birds fluttered overhead. The dimple in her cheek deepened.

Damn. They hadn't talked since that fight in front of the

church. He didn't know how to approach her, what to say. He took a deep breath. What the hell. Go bold or go home.

"Red-winged blackbirds," he called out, his hands trembling gently as he pointed to them. "Every spring they head straight for last year's nesting location—no GPS, no Google maps. Cool, right?"

He jumped down from the path, came up and leaned against the other end of the boulder, trying to look more at ease than he was. Star glanced over, then casually returned her attention toward the water.

"Whirling beetles," she said, nodding toward the bank. "They have a special eye. Can hunt for prey above the surface and below—at the same time." She watched as they sped along the slower moving surface water. "Freaky, huh? Thing is, they all do the *same* trick. No one sees anything the others can't."

Her tone dripped with bitterness, but Cal focused on her energy. In the haze that had once dazzled with every color of the rainbow, he now saw erosion on a tragic scale, colors bleeding away like chalk from a sidewalk drawing left out in the rain. How long had it been that way? What else had he missed while indulging in the enchanted marsh waters?

"Anyway, enough on bugs. I came here hoping to catch you after work. I just wanted to say I'm sorry, sorry about your—"

"Never mind. It doesn't matter now. My mom's going to be fine."

"I know. I wanted to tell you that. But I guess…whatever."

Disappointment quavered in her voice and Cal wondered why they couldn't just have a conversation without some jagged edge erupting between them. Then he caught sight of Star's ear. He walked around the boulder, extended his arm, and brushed back the soft pink strands of hair from her cheek. She froze as his fingers probed the swollen area, hot to the touch.

"You really need to have this looked at," he warned, his hand gliding away from her face. "It's bad."

But Star seemed speechless, barely able to breathe. Cal watched as her tired eyes looked up from the water, scanning over his mud-caked sneakers, his dirt-splattered jeans, until they rested, finally, on his face. She stared into his eyes for a long moment, seemed to get lost in them, then blinked and turned away.

"Back to your old self again, I see. About time," she huffed, tearing away at the notes of concern in his voice, struggling, it seemed, to regain the toughness that kept her intact.

Cal hung his head. "Yeah. I guess I got—side-tracked." He picked up a stone and whipped it into the water. "For a while, it was easy to be normal. But there's a price for everything. I guess I just don't want to pay it anymore."

Star shook her head. "You sure? Cause I'd give anything to lose this stupid ability to see the not-yet."

Resting back on the rock, Cal fixed his gaze on the water where a water snake just swallowed an unsuspecting fishing spider. "I guess I've had it a little easier. I never knew any different. Since I was five, they were always there—the colors, the energy. In the beginning, I thought everyone could see them. Eva used to play along until, well, I guess she had enough of it."

A blue jay fluttered out from a nearby bush and touched off a flash migration around the cove. He looked at Star, hesitated, then asked, "Still seeing reflections?"

"Yeah. Alula is in them. You, too." She swallowed hard. "They don't end well. But that's the least of it—lately."

"What's going on?"

"Weird shit at my aunt's house. Secret doors, bizarre plants, creepy books and a lab that supposedly belonged to my father. I found research papers about cells and other scientific shit mixed with books on black magic. But what pisses me off most is this bracelet my aunt wears. Alula's bracelet."

"I knew it," Cal snapped, bolting upright.

"What?"

"She's looking for her. I knew it."

"What the hell are you talking about?"

"Some people believe if you touch an object closely associated with a person, you can connect with them. It's called psycho-something…psychometry…psycho-chemistry…whatever. It means she knows Alula's alive, and she's trying to get to her."

"But where is she? And why is Aunt Zoe pretending she's dead?"

"I don't know, but you have to steer clear of her 'til we figure this out."

Star gasped. "Alula alive. I…I can't believe it. I'm not sure I do."

He looked at Star, her face white, a confusion of energy writhing around her.

"Hey, you all right?" he asked, his voice pitching softer.

"I'm, uh—fine." She reached out across the smooth boulder and stroked his arm, her fingers lingering over his hand before withdrawing them. The warmth of her touch trickled through Cal's body, and he was unprepared for how it swept over him. For a moment he couldn't help thinking what would—should —come next. How simple this would be if only they were simple.

Star collected herself. "Hey, don't worry about me and Aunt Zoe. She may be tough, but she's nothing I can't handle."

"Listen," Cal hesitated, "about your aunt. There's something you should see. Meet me near the marsh bridge tonight —midnight."

Star turned her red-rimmed eyes toward Cal and offered a dimpled grin. "Wait, is this a date?"

He didn't return the smile. "Yeah, one you're not likely to forget."

————

As midnight approached, Cal neared the marsh apoplectic with shakes. Stumbling down the marshy bank, he settled in behind a cluster of osiers, hoping Star would be a no-show. Before he knew it, the black water soldier floated into view. The urge to reach out and touch its velvety petals was painful, overwhelming. Cal dug his trembling hands into the mud, rooted his feet to the ground. He sat close to the water—too close.

The water soldier stalled in the usual spot just inches off the bank and appeared to wait, impatient for Cal's touch. He kept watching, shaking, aching for it. Twice, he bent over and threw up, then looked up again. The lily pad glided toward the shore. Arm's length away. Just one touch, he thought. One quick dip in the water. Kill the tremors. Ease the—

"Don't do it."

Star had crept up behind him and placed her hand squarely on his shoulder. At once, the lily began to drift off, gliding away on its plate of leaves. The petals didn't glimmer, the water held no sparkle. Yet the moon was full and its light gave the marsh a dull luster. Still doubled over, Cal nudged Star. Just like before, a robed figure emerged from the shadows, kettle in hand. As the flower stalled on the far bank, the figure waved its hands over it. But the petals didn't open or wither. It just bobbed there. Ordinary. Nothing to harvest.

The hooded figure seemed to gaze in their direction, seemed to know they were there. He and Star slunk back into the shadows. The figure made a last attempt at the flower. When nothing happened, the kettle hit the ground and the enchanter stormed off.

Clutching his stomach, Cal couldn't even explain to Star what they'd just seen, but she seemed to guess his thoughts.

"Sorry, Cal," she whispered, "but that person—whoever it was—was not my aunt. She's in Buffalo tonight, accepting an honor for her donations to the Marsh Rejuvenation Fund."

In an exhausted whisper, he said, "J-just don't drink any more of her tea."

CHAPTER
THIRTY-ONE

What—the—hell? Star knew she should be rattled —no, entirely freaked out by the weird marsh escapade the other night. But when she was with Cal, nothing mattered. She closed her eyes and sighed at the memory of his electric touch. From the moment his finger had brushed her ear, she felt his white-hot energy course through her body. Waves of chills and heat seemed to heal her. And those eyes! Those deep sapphire eyes. When they looked at her, she felt invincible, like no one could mess with her.

And that stuff he'd said about Alula? Mind-blowing. Beyond crazy. She didn't even want to hope. But if Cal was right…

Leaning back against a stack of pillows, Star was less stressed than usual about staying awake. She'd thrown off the caffeine habit—too rough on her stomach. Red Bull tasted like acid and Monster made her gag. Turning toward her night-stand, she grabbed a few decongestion tablets and tossed them in her mouth. Her new go-to. They were a bitch to get hold of but kept her from the REM sleep she feared most.

Rolling over, she inhaled the deep scent of lilacs wafting through her open window. The fragrance crept up from the patio below, swirling in her head, numbing her out. She yawned. Her eyelids began to flutter and she burrowed more deeply into her pillow. But minutes later a sound jolted her eyelids open. She hesitated a second, then kicked off the bed sheets and tip-toed toward the window, listening as a voice shot into the air like a flaming spear.

"I told you never to come here!"

Star's eyes widened. Aunt Zoe? At this hour?

"Hey, it took three extra weeks at that hell-hole to get this, so pay up."

Her heart began to race. No way! Not that voice, not here, not in the middle of the night. She was already making excuses: exhaustion, a half-dream, a quirk of her sleep-starved brain. But her pounding heart wouldn't have it, wouldn't dismiss the sounds from the patio below. Slinking closer to the window, she edged the sheer curtains aside and looked down. "Shit!"

She slapped her hand over her mouth, then threw herself behind the casement, but it was too late. Orrin's gaze shot toward the window, half-forgetting, it seemed, the envelope extended in his hand. Remaining out-of-sight now, Star strained to hear the rest of the conversation. All she could make out was her aunt's knotted whisper ripping into Orrin, then his parting words:

"…Fine. Then I'll finish it off…"

Star staggered back from the window. Or did he say, *finish her off?*

Downstairs, the slam of the back door shook the house. Star waited for her aunt's stomp to disappear from the stairs, the slam of her bedroom door to die back, then peered outside again. She saw the outline of patio furniture and a fire pit, crystal clear beneath the wink of a half-moon. But the yard was deserted.

Next day, Star left early for school to catch up with Cal but he didn't show up. She overheard Bill say something about Cal's mom, trouble with headaches and that he'd stayed home to help out.

With no one to talk to, Star found herself brooding all day. Sweet Aunt Zoe. What had Cal seen—and tried to warn her about—that she'd missed all along? Why hadn't her reflections ever revealed anything about her aunt?

Around mid-day, Cal sent her a text. Sounded stressed. She said she wanted to talk with him but didn't mention specifics. Mostly because she had no f—ing idea what she'd heard outside her window or what it meant. But Cal would know, she told herself. He'd figure it out.

After school she pointed herself toward the boardwalk and the North side. At the very least, she wanted to tell Cal he'd been right about Aunt Zoe. As for as his buddy, Orrin? Well, on that count, he'd been wrong, dead wrong.

Fifteen minutes later, she double-pressed the doorbell at Cal's house and waited, relieved as the inner door rattled open. Then every muscle in her face tightened.

"What do *you* want?" Eva stood behind the screen with a poisonous stare.

"Is Cal home?"

"Why?"

Star cocked her head. Her eyes narrowed. "I'll dumb it down for you: Is—Cal—home? Now do you need that in sign language or are you just pretending to be deaf?"

"Get lost, Star. You've dumped enough misery into his life."

Star stepped closer, her nose pressing into the tiny gray squares of the outer screen door. "You don't get it, do you?

After all these years, you still can't see what's in your own f—ing backyard. Maybe the reason your brother and I get along so well is because I'm the only one who sees him for who he really is."

Eva rolled her eyes. "The problem is you don't know him well enough."

Star felt her nostrils flare, her fists curl. "You think you're such hot shit, so above it all, but you're just like everyone else in this stinking town. Too stubborn, too blind, too jealous to appreciate an amazing person like Cal until it's too late."

Eva glared at her for a few silent seconds then with a furious shove, slammed the door in Star's face.

With the bang of the door still vibrating in her ears, Star spun away, trembling with fury, her black leather boots pounding the pavement.

The witch! How could Eva have spent seventeen years living with the most intuitive person on the damn planet and not pick up a shred of human decency? Impossible that they were siblings, that they shared any genetic material at all.

As she crossed the boardwalk, though, her rage withered. Looking across the wet landscape, she thought about the dream she'd had again last night: the thick air, the sinking, suffocating moments before Cal broke through the fog and saved her. Then the clawing crowd, Cal vanishing and that same awful aftertaste when she awoke. Worst of all, the images were growing sharper. From past experience, she knew the hazy reflection would make its leap to harsh reality any day now. Time was running out.

Then, from somewhere in the middle of the reeds, she heard a rustling sound headed her way. She froze aware of the ready hiding places that fanned out all around her—the high grass, the sedges, the reeds, the underbelly of the walkway. Anyone could duck out here, unseen. She listened harder but heard only the plop of slow rain striking the boardwalk and the stream rushing below. Still uneasy, she sniffed the air. It stunk of saturated wood and soaked grass, but offered no clues as to what she'd heard.

Chill, she tried to tell herself. The sound could have been the flinch of a frog, the rustle of a beetle. But even if she couldn't see anything in the swamp-like stillness, she could *feel* it. Evil. So oppressive that it felt like the aftermath of her dream.

Suddenly, a violent sensation rocked her. Why was she standing out here in the middle of the marsh like a human bullseye? Maybe this was it. The beginning of it. The dream coming to life…

Gasping a little, she steadied herself along the rail and dashed for the other side of the marsh, paranoia gripping her like a fist around her throat.

But after arriving home, Star's focus quickly shifted to her dear Aunt Zoe. She watched her. Watched her with new eyes. The way the woman fussed over plants that didn't need fussing, concentrated over a pot of tea done brewing. All the while pretending as if there had never been a f—ing envelope delivered in the middle of the night.

"Why Aster, what is the matter? You're jumpy as a marsh frog."

Her aunt's rosy voice came from behind a potted palm near the tall French doors that separated the foyer from the plant-lined living room. Without answering, Star walked past and plopped herself onto a white settee, her muddy boots gashing the armrest with a wet brown smear.

"My furniture, please," her aunt huffed, forcing a calmness to her voice that was no longer natural.

For a while, only the snips of pruning shears broke the icy river of silence that rushed between them. Then, with a coldness that startled her, her Aunt Zoe spoke up.

"You think I'm stupid, don't you—"

Star nearly slipped from the cushioned chair.

"—that I don't know what this mood is about."

Star's throat went dry. She didn't expect this.

"Well, settle down, young lady. There's no need for hysterics. You're not the first girl to miss out on the Marsh Madness dance."

Star sighed with relief. Until the insult sunk in.

"I don't give a shit about—"

"But I'm here for you, dear, like I've always been." Her aunt turned and smiled, wide and shallow. It gave Star the creeps. "In fact, I know a young man who'd be delighted to take you out."

I bet you do.

Star glanced up through a tangle of pink hair that had fallen over her eyes and was startled by the sight of her sister's copper bracelet slipping from beneath Aunt Zoe's sleeve. She felt like going over and ripping it off. Restraint, she reminded herself. She still had that envelope to find.

So, Star dropped her feet to the floor—splattering the upholstery with more mud— got up, and shouldered past her aunt, shoving off the leaves and vines that, again, seemed to reach out and snare her. As she passed, Aunt Zoe's hand brushed over the petals of a bulging pink chrysanthemum releasing a pollen-like cloud that seemed to go straight to Star's head. She sneezed and grew dizzy.

"So then, shall I give him a call? Aster?"

Star stewed. The idea! That she needed help to find a date for the dance. Her thoughts began to jumble. Couldn't think straight. Her mind wandered: Would Cal ask her? He wasn't exactly the tuxedo type but...

"Oh, and tea's almost ready."

"I'm not thirsty," Star called back.

"But it's a new blend."

Star paused at the doorway, not bothering to hide the grit of her teeth. "Here's an idea. Why don't you take all that f—ing poison you call tea and dump it back in the marsh where it belongs?"

CHAPTER
THIRTY-TWO

The next day, Star dropped into her seat at the back of history class, wiped. She'd had that damn dream again. Apparently, Sudafed wasn't fool proof. Definitely *not* dream-proof.

She squeezed her eyes shut, rubbed them in circles, then blinked them back open. Standing at the front of the room, Schlenz posed, his floppy prospector hat wilting on his head, a pair of red suspenders slipping off his shoulders. Great. Another lesson aimed at the ADD crowd. Tuning out, she checked out the human landscape of the room. Craning her neck—a little further to the right—she saw Cal in his desk near the windows, his crooked smile widening as she caught his eye. She had to talk with him. Every instinct in her body vibrated with a sense that time was running out.

Half-awake and more than a little edgy, Star fidgeted with the cascade of black moons dangling from her ears and let the classroom discussion filter in:

"I wish West Shelby had a gold rush," Kelly whined. "Maybe then we'd get a little excitement around here."

"You want excitement?" Ted Weir said. "Move. Or join the army."

"On the contrary," the teacher said, "something extraordinary did happen here. About two hundred years ago. A gold rush of sorts—a spiritual gold rush. At one time, this section of the state was so coveted a territory for religious enthusiasts, that it got its own soubriquet: The Burned-Over District. Intense rivalries raged here among the Methodists, Presbyterians, Baptists and Quakers. In fact, the birthplace of the Mormon faith is less than an hour's drive away in Palmyra."

"Why here?" Carol asked.

Mr. Schlenz's eyes beamed at the question. "It's been said that West Shelby is located at a sort of vortex in the earth. Anyone care to guess what that means?"

"A vortex is created by spiraling energy," Star answered, surprising herself almost as much as her classmates. As heads turned, she glared back, then flipped off anyone who wasn't quick enough to look away.

"Correct," Mr. Schlenz said. "People once believed—and still do—that a vortex can only exist in a sacred place. It is believed they form a portal where humans can tap into their own higher-dimensional selves. Sensitive people are more apt to feel the effects."

"Are there other places?"

"Table Mountain in Cape Town, the Haleakala crater in Hawaii, Sedona, Arizona, Mt. Kailas in Tibet—to name a few."

Joe Felburs looked over at Kelly. "Kinda makes you want to stick around, don't it?"

The final bell rang and everyone began to shuffle out. Through the rain-spattered windows Star saw students dashing down the driveway, busses rumbling in idle. She felt a gentle squeeze on her upper arm and a whisper curl in her ear: "See you after class? Then I gotta run."

Cal walked toward the door and Star followed him, a growing sense of urgency pounding in her chest. They were arm's length from the door when disaster struck.

"Uh, Star, may I see you a moment?"

Her heart thumped to a halt.

"I have to go, Mr. Schlenz," she said, glancing toward the doorway. Cal was already past the threshold, pointing to his wrist.

"This won't take long. I promise."

Two minutes later, Star walked out of the classroom. She looked around, but no Cal. Shit. Panic began to trickle through her veins. She hurried out the exit. Big exhale. He stood waiting for her at the bottom of the stairs, a blue sparkle in his eyes. She ran down to meet him.

"I'm kinda late. You mind walking with me? Headed to Oakwood."

"Uh, sure." Star wouldn't have cared if he asked her to walk f—ing backward while spitting nickels. She just needed to get this off her chest.

"So, what did Schlenz want? You got detention or something?"

"Funny. You know, I'm not in trouble all the time. Only most of it. Anyway, nothing important. Some crap about a summer camp for advanced STEM students. But I got bigger issues."

"What's up?"

Flustered, Star struggled to answer. "I saw…I mean, I think that I saw…well, I definitely heard…" Then, giving her head a quick shake, she jostled her brain into focus and words came popping from her mouth, helter-skelter, like links from a snapped chain.

"Parker came over the other night—to see my aunt. She got pissed. He gave her some envelope. Don't know what it was. I couldn't really see it because I was hiding behind this curtain and it was dark, but then I think he saw me and he told Aunt Zoe he would finish something off, but I don't know what he meant and I'm afraid he was talking about me or Alula or maybe something else. Soooooo—"

For a moment, there was silence between them. Only the intermittent splash of the marsh heaving up and over its banks interrupted their footfalls on the boardwalk.

"So, I...I just thought...shit." Her black fingernails raked through her hair. "It's just that I don't usually get a vibe off people, not like you anyway. As far as I'm concerned, they're all pretty much assholes. But from the first time I met Orrin Parker, my skin crawled." She glanced over her shoulder. "Sometimes I even get this feeling he's following me. 'Course I'm the only one convinced Mr. Perfect's got a pointy tail jammed into those tight trousers. Everyone else thinks he's the greatest thing ever to happen to West Shelby."

Cal stopped short, so short, Star nearly ran into him. He set his hands on the rail and looked across the marsh. She scanned his expression, tried to read it. Couldn't, but she could see all the luster in his eyes had died.

"You're not the only one."

"What?"

"At first, he was good. I mean, *really* good. I didn't get a read on him at all. Every time I saw Orrin, there wasn't so much as a sliver of energy around the guy—until that night in front of St. Francis. Remember? We were arguing, and he showed up out of nowhere. That's when I saw it. Maybe it was the soft light from the stained-glass windows or maybe he'd just gotten careless, but that night, for the first time, I got a glimpse of it."

"And?"

He shook his head. "Blackness. Pure undiluted darkness."

"Does he know that you know?"

"I hope not, but I can't tell. There's nothing to see around him. No emotion, no depth, no color. No soul."

Star looked down into the churning water. "I wonder what was in that envelope. I'm sure it was something from the medical center, something my aunt shouldn't have her claws on. Something about Alula." Her eyes lit up. "Maybe it's time Aunt Zoe and I have a little sit-down."

"Don't." Cal glanced down at his phone. "Look, I gotta go. The caretaker was weird about me not being late today. Listen, whatever you do, don't confront Aunt Zoe alone. We need to do this together." She felt his gentle press on her arm, flashed her that amazing, crooked smile and disappeared up the path toward the cemetery.

And just like that, everything was okay. Star felt as if an army had just lined up behind her. With Cal on her side, she could do anything, even find Alula.

Still, she wished she knew where the hell that envelope was. She'd searched half a dozen rooms in the house, even the lab in the cellar, until Aunt Zoe wised-up and moved the key. She must've stashed it. But where?

CHAPTER
THIRTY-THREE

ight. How could he have spent most of his life watching human energy and not recognized the danger, the red flag when it was missing? He didn't know what to make of Orrin or that exchange with Aunt Zoe. But as long as the guy didn't know he was onto him, Cal figured it was cool. For now, anyway.

Walking toward Oakwood, Cal felt the rain kickup again, a straight curtain of water that wrapped itself around the marsh like a scrim. With his sneakers slipping over the gravel and mud, he remembered how he once trudged up to the cemetery as punishment, then because it offered him a sort of refuge from the staring eyes and wagging tongues of West Shelby. Now he was drawn there for the simple good company of a man who seemed to know more about everything and nothing than anyone he'd ever met before.

And those gummy bears. Damn if they didn't work. Definitely took the edge off. He felt stronger than he had in a while. Strong enough, anyway, to ask Star to the dance. He'd planned to ask her today, but the timing seemed off. She was flustered. He was running late. He thought about dropping over to her place when he was done at Oakwood, but then remembered Aunt Zoe. Bad idea. Plan B: ask her tomorrow after school. If she said yes, awesome. If she said no, well, he didn't even want to think about that.

As he hit the steeper portion of the trail, he peered from beneath his hood, looked up, and saw Stan at the graveyard's lower edge, his eyes surveying the watery wasteland all around. Cal picked up his pace, but even as he hurried into Oakwood and the gate closed hard behind him, the caretaker didn't move.

"Hey, sorry I'm late," he said, coming up beside him. "What are you looking at?"

"The water soldiers. They're early."

"Yeah, I noticed a few on my way. Usually come up closer to mid-summer, don't they? Maybe it's all this rain or global warming."

"Not a chance. Those plants are as precise as they are pretty. Each day their blossoms stay closed 'til the sun coaxes 'em open around noon. Then, as daylight fades, they close up again, sinkin' slightly into the water for protection."

There was a long pause filled only by the slap of raindrops tapping the shoulders of the tombstones behind them.

"Most beautiful flower on the marsh." The caretaker sighed. "Even in death."

"How's that?"

"Unlike most flowers that wither, the water soldier just disappears. When it's time is done, it sinks to the bottom of the marsh, drawing down on its long winding stem."

The old man stared a moment longer at the soggy marsh before turning to hike across the cemetery that somehow remained impervious to the spring downpours.

Back in the work shed, Cal got a shorter list of chores than he'd expected. He patched a hole in the compost fence, sharpened the mower blades, then oiled the springs on the garage door. Next, he took to the lawn, pushing around the old manual mower because the others were broken. From time to time, Cal glanced over at the old man. There was something about him today, something not right. His expression looked grim, hard, like the gravestones around him. Without his big, toothy grin for support, the skin around his eyes sagged. Even his body seemed off. Simple movements around the yard came with a half-limp and he groaned when lifting a coil of hose down from the wall. Cal chalked it up to old age or a bout of arthritis and did his best to lift the old man's spirits.

"So, I did the math on your old-time baseball players and found that Babe Ruth's $70,000 salary would be equal to about a million dollars today—nice chunk of change for 1927." He grinned at the caretaker and a half-smile finally surfaced across the dark, weary face.

"But he wasn't that kinda guy—none of them were. They played for the sake of the game, not for money or fancy goods."

"Didn't have much choice, did they?" Cal ribbed. "I mean, how many Model-Ts would a guy want, anyway?"

"Don't kid yourself, son. In any era, there are ways to squander money, to waste the talents the good Lord has given."

There were still hours of daylight left when they strolled out of the shed, chores done, hands scrubbed, the scent of dying forsythia a melancholy perfume behind the day's parting.

Cal grabbed his hoodie off a nearby branch and threw it over his shoulder. "What you'd do on your day off?" The care-taker shrugged, not seeing the playful glint in Cal's eyes. "You know, this isn't a bad gig for an old guy. A day off every week and time off all winter."

"I stay busy in the off-months."

"Doing what?" Cal teased. "Working on your tan?"

Stan laughed aloud, looking happier than he had all afternoon. Growing serious, he answered, "I help out at the senior center pool. Sub in for the lifeguards when needed."

"Yeah? I worked as a lifeguard last summer. Town pool."

"Ever have to save anybody?"

The caretaker's question was quick and direct, the yellowy eyes concentrating on Cal.

"Luckily, no. How 'bout you?"

"Couple a times. Years ago, when I was a lifeguard at Ocean Beach."

"Whoa, that's the big time. You really need your game on there. Ground swells, rip tides, bluefish and people everywhere. I wouldn't know where to look first."

"Well, there's a trick to it," the old man said, his eyes twinkling. "First of all, you have to be a good swimmer, but then you have to be a good watcher." He looked across the graveyard and the marsh beyond, motioning toward an invisible seashore. "As people come onto the beach, you watch 'em. You see how they move, how they react to the water, the tide. You watch how their bodies steady or tip with the waves, the way they react to other swimmers, a sudden splash or the lifeguard's whistle. Simply put, you find the weak ones and watch 'em, keep on watchin' 'til they're away from danger."

"It's all on you, right? Can't expect others to help out."

"Others." He shook his head. "Oh, they're around, sure 'nough. Lookin' for the same thing—weak swimmers. But they don't help. They just draw 'em out to deeper, darker water. Try and tip the balance their way."

Cal wasn't sure at what point the conversation had stopped being about lifeguarding, but after a moment Stan's gaze fell away from the graveyard, the beach he'd envisioned there. Growing somber once more, he pulled a worn piece of paper from the pocket of his work pants.

"Here," he said, his throat thick. "Your hours. You finished 'em off. S'all there, dates, times, everything."

Cal stared at the paper without reaching for it.

"Go ahead," the old man urged, extending his hand with the paper. "It's there. Everything listed and marked proper. I signed it on the back."

Cal smiled to himself. So, this was what the day, the mood had been all about.

"It's okay, Stan. You don't have to worry. Even if my hours are done, I'll still—"

"Here. Take it. Take it!" the caretaker demanded, shoving the paper into Cal's hand.

"Okay, okay, but it doesn't really mean anything to me."

"Well, it's gonna mean a hell of a lot to that judge when you show up without it."

Cal took the paper and shoved it into the pocket of his jeans. Then he looked up, a crooked smile growing on his face.

"So then, I'll see you tomorrow?"

Stan didn't answer. He pretended to be busy, fumbling with a rake propped against a nearby tree. Didn't the old guy get it? Coming to Oakwood had stopped being punishment, community service for him a long time ago. Still, from the weathered frown etched on his face, the caretaker's mind was made up: Cal had paid his debt to society and until some other kid screwed up, he'd be spending his afternoons in the graveyard alone, rusty tools and mossy tombstones his only companions.

Cal extended his hand. "Until next time."

Stan looked even sadder now, his eyes hanging like an old dog's. His handshake, though, was the same iron-fisted grip Cal remembered from the first day he'd come to the graveyard.

"It's been a privilege," the old man said before turning away. Then he sighed as if the day's goodbye would be their last.

CHAPTER
THIRTY-FOUR

C al's thumb had barely punched the message out when the reply came back:
Our rock? Do we have a rock? Sure, I'll meet you there Don't be late. I turn into a frog after dark...

Yesssss.

Cal glanced up from his phone with a smile, then hurried to help his mom settle into her chair at the kitchen table. He stepped back to look at her. The doctor said her color was improving, but Cal saw the *real* colors brightening in her energy field—a more accurate barometer.

A familiar tap-tap sounded at the side door. He hesitated. "Mom, if you're not up for this, I can tell her to go home."

His mother smiled weakly. "It's fine, Cal. She's harmless. Just bored."

Cal went to answer the door and came back a moment later with Mrs. Kenefick clutching his elbow.

"My dear! Now, don't you look"—she cocked her head—"hmm, well, certainly not as awful as you did the other day. Such an ordeal. It's a wonder you survived. No surprise though, at least not to me." She gazed up at the kitchen light as if it were a crystal ball. "In a week—no, six days' time—you'll be feeling measurably improved. "Mark my words!"

Cal pulled up a chair for her, but Mrs. Kenefick refused. "Have to keep a watch out. What with that beast barely leashed across the street." Yet before five minutes had passed, she eased into one of the kitchen chairs, asked for a glass of iced tea, and began spouting neighborhood gossip while trying to wheedle out an update on Mrs. Emerling.

"Her trouble is her health, that much I've divined on my own, but she is a curious gal. Secretive, too. Last week I caught her heading back from the marsh's west end where it widens to open water. You know, by those old, abandoned fishing cabins. I startled her when I asked her where she'd been." The old woman winked and tapped her temple. "Though I already knew."

"Who wouldn't want to go for a nice walk now that summer's almost here," Cal's mother said, deflecting the conversation.

"Summer!" the old woman spat. "Mosquitoes, ticks, fleas—nothing but trouble for my dears." She looked around. "And where's our lovely Eva?"

"Out with a friend."

"A young man, maybe? Well, well, and the big dance tomorrow night. Always trouble that Marsh Madness thing. Never fails." Mrs. Kenefick picked up her iced tea and gazed into the glass as if readable tea leaves were sunk beneath the ice cubes. "It'll be worse than usual this year. Mark my words!"

She turned toward Cal and fixed a prying eye on him. "And what about you, Calvin? A handsome fellow like yourself must have a date for the big dance, eh?"

Cal shrugged. "Not sure if I feel like going," he lied.

Mrs. Kenefick's hairless eyebrows stretched high into her forehead. "Well, well," she clucked, "a strong young man with a free evening on his hands. You know, I must have a dozen different chores…"

"Yes, and he *does* deserve a free evening," Cal's mother said, heading her off. "He's had so much on his plate lately— schoolwork, yard work, helping at my brother's place, community service. On top of all that, he's been taking care of me, too."

Though his mother couldn't have put it in nicer terms, their neighbor looked as though she'd just been slapped. Cal noticed Mrs. Kenefick's energy field curdle to a thorny brown. All at once, her gestures and words became like invisible grenades tossed into the air.

"Busy, hmm? Still working off that community service?" Her voice darkened. "Oakwood Cemetery, isn't it? Now what was the name of that old caretaker?" Her gnarled finger tapped at her chin. "Dan, Sam, Stan—that's it. Stan Heyman. Good heavens, he and I go way back, long before he worked at the cemetery."

Cal straightened from the counter he'd been leaning against, hairs prickling at the back of his neck. "You know him?"

The old woman turned toward Cal, her head rotating on her neck like a machine gun on a turret. Her eyes, hard and black as bullets, glared as she shot back a lethal reply.

"We met one December—years ago. The night he murdered my brother."

For a moment, only the random thuds of rain tapping at the screen door broke the silence.

"What happened?" Cal's mother asked in a hushed tone.

"It was a terrible night," Mrs. Kenefick began, "the weather ghastly. Accidents everywhere. Route 33, a sheet of ice. Our car slid into a van and then a car hit us. My poor brother, Hendrick —how he tried to hang on! I was in pretty bad shape myself and, well, it was already too late for my poor niece. Anyway, the ambulance was racing us to the hospital, when the paramedic—this Heyman fellow—failed to give Hendrick oxygen. I'll never understand why he didn't help him. Too stupid, too lazy—who knows? But because of his carelessness my brother died."

Cal wanted to tell his version of the story, a considerably different one, but his neighbor went on.

"Anyway, we got justice in the end. Managed to get a handsome settlement out of it, too. But that didn't bring back my poor Hendrick, now did it? As for the caretaker, I understand he had a miserable life afterward. Never able to forgive himself, I would imagine. Died a pauper, I'm told."

"Who?" Cal asked, thinking he must have zoned out during the conversation.

"Stan Heyman."

Cal stared into the air, a zombie. All the blood drained from his face. It was impossible. He saw the old man yesterday. But then he remembered how off he'd looked. Anything could have happened. He wondered if he'd passed away at work or at home.

"When?" Cal asked, his voice choked. "Last night?"

Mrs. Kenefick waved her hand. "Oh, my, no. It was—I don't know—maybe sixteen, seventeen years ago. And if I ever find out where they buried him, I swear, I'll go spit on his grave!"

CHAPTER
THIRTY-FIVE

et out. Go. Now.

The urgency of the idea burst into Cal's mind without warning. He concocted some half-ass excuse then bolted out through the kitchen door, his mother's voice unwinding like a spool of worried thread behind him. As soon as he was beyond her vision, he took off down the court, around the corner, across Alder Lane and Bittersweet Road, feeling nothing but the wild thump of his heart. His feet pounded over wet pavement, then clattered over the board-walk where he blasted through a swarm of May flies and skid head-first into a nasty clump of buckthorns.

He brushed if off and ran on, ripping up the path without so much as a sideways glance at the passing scenery. Yet somewhere in his peripheral vision he noted everything around him like drop pins on a Google map. As he did so, a strange desperate logic swept over his mind: if the rudds were swimming and the heron were fishing and the blue jays were flying and the lilies were floating and the reeds were stirring and the clouds were gathering, then all was cool and Stan would be at Oakwood like he'd always been before.

As for Mrs. Kenefick, her whacked out tale could have come from anywhere, a knee-jerk reaction to his mom calling her out. Absent, though, was that inner voice saying she was wrong, confused, a crazy old loon who couldn't tell the difference between a prediction and a pot roast.

Rounding the last turn, Cal looked down at the shrunken marsh and stream, the rush of water a muffled roar now. Chill, he told himself. Almost there. Soon he'd be opening the gate, hear that hearty *helloa* coming down from the shed, and all would be right in his world again.

A moment later, Cal did find a gate. But this one lay rusted, half-buried beneath the grass in its own sort of shallow grave. He stepped over it, scratched his head, looked around then glanced over his shoulder. Something was messed up. Maybe he'd taken a wrong turn. No way this was Oakwood Cemetery —some place like it, maybe, but not the Oakwood he knew. Here, the grass hadn't been cut—for months, maybe years— the gravestones lost beneath the hairy straggle of weeds that grew up and around their necks like frayed collars.

Turning three-sixty, Cal began to head out. Then something in the lower cemetery caught his eye. He squinted, walked toward it, and stopped short. Behind a sprawl of poison ivy, he recognized a memorable black tombstone. PEACE.

Impossible. Staggering over the tangled grass and up through the strangely unfamiliar yard, Cal tried to understand what the hell had happened. He thought about Stan, how he'd seemed off the other day. Maybe this was a mistake. Maybe the old guy tried a new fertilizer, forgot to read the directions and just dumped it on. It would take the better part of next week, at least, to mow the place back into shape.

Reaching the shed, he made a grab for the handle on the garage door. It wouldn't budge. Glancing up, he saw the last bit of daylight filtering through the trees. It'd be dark soon. Cal gripped the handle again and, with his muscles fully flexed, yanked the door open a grudging foot or two. Shouldering his way beneath it, he finally forced the door fully open, the wheels sticky and squealing—the same ones he'd greased just the other day.

Cal shuffled into the low-ceiling room, kicking up a cloud of dust that hung like a dense brown fog. He coughed, putting his sleeve across his mouth, then for a second didn't breathe at all. Hand tools and power tools littered the floor. Weed-whackers, hoes, and rakes collapsed into each other along the wall. A pair of garden hoses unwound and seemed to strangle the mower parked beneath them. Cal inched toward the workbench piled with rags and shook his head at the silent chaos of the place—trashed. A room once filled with Stan's gleaming work ethic, now embalmed in its own filth. The old man's gonna be pissed, Cal thought.

Had to be the work of neighborhood punks. Vandals. But Cal's theory failed on the spot. No one covered their tracks with dust or looped cobwebs from the ceiling. He ran his fingers over a half dozen trowels, each wearing the same rusty stubble of orange. And even the most clever thug couldn't oxidize metal—not in a day, not in a week, not in a year.

He glanced over at the window above the workbench. The same filmy layer of dirt that had settled over every inch of the workshop clung to it like a thin brown shade. Reaching out, he smudged his sweaty hand across the glass and leaned toward the window, gazing out over a scene that should've been so familiar but that he hardly recognized. He looked at the long grass he'd cut, the overgrown branches he'd pruned, the weeds he'd pulled, the broken fence he'd fixed. Then he looked at the tombstones.

Suddenly, he had an idea. In the place where reason and logic usually reigned, there was this idea. This ridiculous, terrible idea…

Cal tore out of the shed, striking his head full throttle on the low beam. It hardly slowed him. He raced down the sloping hill, running as if to escape the idea blossoming in his head like a poisonous weed. Veering left somewhere in the lower graveyard, he pulled up short in front of a tombstone, the one with the porcelain angel praying on top. With his chest heaving, he stared at the polished slab of granite and waited, waited for the courage it would take to do this thing, this thing that would solve it, solve it once and for all.

With his breath shaking, he knelt down and plunged his hand deep into the grass at the base of the tombstone. Brushing it aside, he read the inscription:

Theresa Heyman 1932-1999
Loving Wife

Then, moving his hand along the smooth base, he pushed aside the rest of the grass until his heart felt as cold as the stone upon which his hand now shook. He didn't read the inscription, rather it leapt into his consciousness, burning itself upon his mind, hot and painful like a brand:

Stan Heyman 1931- 2004
Devoted Husband

Cal didn't remember walking away from the grave or leaving the cemetery. He had no recollection of stepping over the prostrate gate or winding down the hill. He came to himself sometime later, halfway down the path, afraid to look back, sure the earth was swallowing his footsteps behind him. His brain ached over questions that had no answers. As the numbness wore off, the hurt sank in. By the time his sneakers oozed into the mud at the trail's end, he was left with one conclusion: he was crazy. Certifiably insane. How else could he justify hours of work he remembered in detail only to find it'd never been done, that there was no evidence he'd ever set foot in Oakwood? Still, it'd seemed so real…

"Cal! Hey, over here!"

And now he heard trees calling out to him. Man, he was sicker than he thought. Against his better judgment, he turned and walked toward a sprawling willow just off the path. Lifting his hand, he brushed aside the drooping branches.

"Star?"

"I waited on the rock for a freakin' hour." She got up, her long peasant skirt unfolding around her, and brushed back the tail of a linen scarf tossed around her bare neck. "Ducked in here when the skies opened up."

"Sorry. I…I forgot." He stepped inside the clearing, letting the branches sweep over his back.

"What's wrong?" she asked as he stepped closer.

Cal shrugged, his gaze moving to the landscape beyond the tree. "Nothing. Absolutely nothing. Just a place, a person, and a hundred hours—gone."

"I don't get it."

"Yeah. Neither do I."

Cal turned and disappeared behind the curtain of willow branches, a fresh shower of water drenching him as he brushed past. Star dashed after him.

"Cal? What is it?"

His gaze drifted skyward. For a second, he stared at the daylight falling away, the sky deepening into a starless royal blue. A perfect, uncomplicated blue.

He sighed. "For years I wondered about the stuff that made me *different.* You know, my vision, my hands. I wondered, why me? One day, after talking to the caretaker, I got the idea that maybe this is bigger than me."

"Bigger?"

"The Balance," he began, haunted by the echo of a familiar voice. "Maybe this weird ability or whatever you call it, is meant to make a difference, to prevent this world from barreling into chaos."

"What are you supposed to do?" Star asked, her voice a stunned whisper.

Cal cast his gaze into the gathering darkness, trying to snag the words that might help her understand. "Help those caught in between. The weak swimmers—"

Then his attention drifted toward the top of the hill, in the direction of Oakwood, and with a wave of his hand, he shoved the explanation aside. "But I was wrong. Crazy wrong. It's just me trying to make sense out of the madness that's been my life, out of something that makes no sense at all."

Star turned to face him, her eyes fixed, her chin set. "I don't know about all that balance shit, but when it comes to the world, I think you nailed it."

"Huh?"

"The world *is* a dangerous place. Not because of the assholes hell-bent on evil, but because of people who look on and do jack shit, who do nothing to stop them. Like the Uvalde tragedy."

Cal shrugged. "I don't get it."

"Albert Einstein. The history assignment, remember? His quote—give or take a few words—explains everything, about humanity, about you. When everyone turns a blind eye, you're meant to do something. Even when it seems crazy, even when it's impossible, even when it totally f—s up your life, you can't do nothing."

Silence settled over them, over the whole marsh. Cal gazed at the shimmer of energy beaming around Star, no less blown away than the first time he saw it.

"You're amazing, Star, and in ways you don't even realize."

He reached over, brushed back the strands of pink hair from her face, letting his hand linger on her cheek, then gazed more deeply into her cinnamon-colored eyes. She leaned into him and he felt a shiver ripple up her arm.

"When you look at me, Cal, what do you see?"

There were so many things. He didn't know how to put it into words.

"Light. Pure and radiant. It's always been there. For as long as I've had the ability to see, I've seen it around you."

"What does it mean?"

"I'm not sure. But you're meant for something great."

"Like what?"

"I don't know. Maybe to find Alula. Maybe something bigger. You have a soul that could part the seas."

Star smiled, her dimple sinking deep into her cheek. Then she reached up and curled her arms around his neck. His hands clasped her hips and pulled her in close. Their lips brushed, then closed over each other and the whole marsh seemed to pause and sigh in the moment.

Cal leaned back and smiled. "You good?"

"Uh, yeah. F-fine," she stammered.

He kissed her again, then offered a clumsy invite. "Um... I was thinking, maybe...the dance...if you weren't busy..." Cal's throat went dry as Star scrunched her nose. He felt his insides sink to his feet.

"It's, you know, not my kinda scene."

Train wreck. He shouldn't have asked her. How could he ever think she would go with him?

"But—maybe we could, you know, have our own marsh madness. Out here. Just us."

Her eyes blinked in a sleepy, sultry sort of way and Cal found it hard to let her go.

"Sounds like a plan." Unwinding his arms, he stepped back, turned and resumed his trek to the North side, waiting 'til he was around the bend before celebrating with a fist pump into the air. Only a few dozen yards down the boardwalk, though, he heard footsteps clattering over the boards behind him. Star reappeared out of the darkness.

"Cal, wait! What about you, what are you meant for?"

He looked at the tattered tail of Star's gorgeous energy, shimmering like a slivered sun, rising and falling on some invisible current, pulling toward, then away from him. He shrugged. "I don't know. Maybe to take care of you."

CHAPTER
THIRTY-SIX

She watched him dissolve into the darkness, the taste of his kiss still sizzling on her lips, her arms buzzing from his embrace. As soon as he was gone, though, Star lost her mind. Phantom figures seemed to ebb in and out of passing shadows, the wind became voices whispering doom. Her nervous steps became a glance-over-the-shoulder jog, then a full-on run. Even so, her sleep-starved brain plotted her next move: after creeping into the house, she'd make sure Aunt Zoe was asleep then prowl around—turn the place frigging upside-down if she had to—until she found whatever it was Orrin dropped off the other night. Then she'd dash it over to Cal's house for safekeeping.

But her timing sucked. Sneaking in through the front door, she found herself face-to-face with her aunt, just in from a late evening out. Star stood in the grand foyer, a swamp's worth of rainwater streaming off the ends of her fringe boho skirt. She listened to the drip-drops as they pooled in little brown puddles on the parquet floor. And waited. Any second, her aunt would open up on her. Deliver a shit storm of complaints.

It never came.

"Damp night, isn't it?" her aunt said, brushing rain droplets from her Burberry. "I'm chilled to the bone. I'll get you a nice cup of tea to warm up."

Star stood frozen in place, every hair on her arms bristling.

"Go along, Aster. Hurry into some dry clothes or you'll catch cold."

Star's eyes flashed around the room. For a crazy second, she even checked the door at her back, made sure no one was ambushing her from behind.

"Go on now," the raisin-sweet voice urged.

As a steady drool of muddy water poured off her clothes, Star climbed the spiral staircase, her aunt's forced smile following her every step. Through the jack-hammer ache in her head, Star knew something was off. Her gaze darted around the foyer: the palm tree in its brass holder, the gold satin side chair tucked in the arc of the staircase, the black marble table, an open handbag, the chandelier shimmering in tiers overhead and on the wall of mirrors opposite, her wet ragdoll reflection trudging up the stairs in multiple. And in the middle of it all, gazing up with that fat fake smile was dear Aunt—

The handbag!

Star made a mad dash for the manila envelope poking out from it. Aunt Zoe got there first. Their hands locked.

"Give it back you prying monster!" her aunt cried, her voice all vinegar now. "It's mine—give it back!"

Star snatched the envelope from her aunt's fingers, raised it above her head and tugged out the contents.

"What the hell is this? What does Parker have to do with it?" Star sidled away from her aunt's clawing hands. "Names? Addresses? Who are these people?"

The hands continued toward her, opening and closing with pincer-like snaps. Star pulled away, bolting across the foyer and up a few stairs. Her eyes flashed over the page and tried to make some sense of it, but there was nothing to make sense of.

"I don't get it. They're just names…names of people…"

"People whom your father trusted."

"Trusted more than you, I bet."

"Perhaps, but there was a time when he would have done anything for me—and did." An ugly grin filtered over her expression. "Alula was proof of it."

"Of what?"

For a strangled moment, Aunt Zoe seemed lost for words. She stood frazzled, hairpins jutting out at weird angles like small antennae. Then, with a boastful smirk, she began to unravel the lies she and her brother had spun around Star and the rest of West Shelby for years…

"As research director at the medical center, your father headed up the biogenetics team. His goal was to develop genetically-customized cells for therapeutic needs.

"But the political winds shifted. The government slammed the door on research. The promise for future disease-free generations would have to wait, he said, wait for a different administration, a different set of politicians." Aunt Zoe's lips tightened. "But I *needed* it now!" Her fist hammered down on the marble table and Star jumped. "I'd seen the ravages of old age in friends. In time, I'd suffer the same. So, *I* funded his research, pressing your father to steer his work in more aggressive directions."

"Aggressive?"

"It didn't take much. The temptation was already there, sitting in the lab, day after day, the spark of life quivering beneath his fingertips. Anyway, around this time, he and your mother decided to have another child—apparently, they were disappointed with their *first* effort." Aunt Zoe paused long enough for the insult to settle in. "But as fate would have it, they had trouble conceiving. They were forced to turn to in-vitro fertilization. That's when your father got creative."

Star gasped.

"In the lab, he extracted the nucleus from one of your mother's egg cells and replaced it with one from my own cells. Unaware that my DNA was now part of the forming cell mass, the doctor implanted the embryo in your mother. It gestated and history was made. Somatic cell nuclear transfer."

"I...I don't believe you. It's never been done."

"Until then. After all, Alula means *first leap*."

"My mother would never..."

"She didn't know. No one did. Except your father. And me."

"But then the baby—"

"Is my perfect twin. Complete with genetically identical, rejection-proof stem cells and tissues."

Star's mind whirled. It was crazy. The story was nothing but wishful thinking from a deranged, desperate woman. Yet, it connected all the puzzling dots in her father's notes. Still, she fought it.

"This is bullshit. My father wouldn't mess with mad science. Especially for you." But even Star could hear the weakness in her protest, the doubt in her voice.

"Mad, only if you can't see the brilliance in it." Aunt Zoe scowled. "Unfortunately, your father was not prepared to be a genetic pioneer. When your mother died during childbirth, he saw it as a sign, the consequence of his overstepping some invisible line." She sighed. "Then there were—the problems. The biology of it."

Star fumed. "Stop talking about Alula like she's some kind of science project!"

"In a way, she is. Those big freckles on her face? Age spots. Has blood platelet deficiencies, too. That's why even the smallest of her cuts bled excessively." Aunt Zoe grimaced at some unpleasant image before her eyes. "Your father began to obsess over potentially horrific outcomes, infantile ailments clashing with accelerated degeneration. In the end, he faked the child's death, then stashed her away somewhere. Shortly thereafter, he took his own life. Said he wanted peace. I suppose he expected his secret to die with him."

"He had his reasons for keeping you away from her."

"Certainly," Aunt Zoe said, her spirit strengthening as she inched closer to Star. "Your father feared what I would do as the child grew older and my needs advanced with age."

"You were supposed to be a homeopath, a healer," Star said, the paper nearly forgotten in her clenched fist.

"Yes, but when that failed me, I got *creative*." Aunt Zoe's eyes gleamed. "I learned plants can be used for more than healing."

Star gasped. "Cal was right."

"Of course, he was right! He was the first victim of my dark practice. That little punk picking the marsh water soldiers *I* needed. Made sure that never happened again."

"*You* caused his tremors?"

Aunt Zoe's mouth became a wicked grin.

"And his vision?"

The smile instantly shriveled. "Hmmm, yes. That vision. The curse was meant to keep his hands unsteady, unable to mess with my plants, but apparently there was this side effect. Unfortunate. Inconvenient, to say the least."

"How dare you! It's been more than *inconvenient* for him."

"Oh, not for him. For me. Thanks to Calvin, you were suddenly full of questions. When you starting nosing around about Alula's death, the situation had to be dealt with."

Star felt herself sway in place. "Dealt…how?"

"I conjured up—oh, let's call it a remedy—to erase his enhanced vision." Aunt Zoe shook her head, smiling to herself. "Ingenious, really. I knew the boy had an affinity for water soldiers, not to mention you, so I lured him into trading his ability—the one you convinced him was a liability—for normalcy. With no vision, he was out of my way." She made an impatient huff. "Unfortunately, he had aroused your suspicions and *you* became a problem. So, I experimented with the aftermath of the enchanted marsh waters. The spent lily petals and residual water—swirling full of Cal's erased vision—made quite a potent tea."

"Then it *was* you out there on the marsh."

"Most times. Anyway, after you drank it, your head was a confusing cocktail of your own thoughts and others. No one would understand your ramblings even if you did open up."

"*The Dark Art of Reflections*," Star muttered, recalling the strange book.

Aunt Zoe sneered. "In the end, your interference and Calvin's could not be tolerated. Alula was for me and me alone."

Star wiped her eyes, hot with tears. "Where is she?"

"Thanks to a resourceful young man at your school, I'm about to figure that out." Her aunt teetered on the stair below her, eyeing the paper in Star's hand. "And to think of the time I wasted rummaging around that basement lab when all along your father's secret was buried in the files at the research center."

"His secret?"

"The list of potential guardians for Alula."

"You monster." Star felt her voice growl up from deep in her chest. "I'll find my sister and never let you near her again."

"Not *your* sister. *My* clone."

"My father wouldn't…"

"Would and did." The wicked eyes held a new sparkle. "He was my brother. He wanted to take care of me. Now, I'll get that help after all."

With a quick snatch, Aunt Zoe ripped the paper from her hands, then turned and made a hurried hobble down the stairs. Stunned for a moment, Star didn't move. Rocked by the revelations that changed everything she'd ever thought about herself and her family, she felt numb. Then she caught sight of the paper—the key to finding her sister—gangling down the stairs in Aunt Zoe's determined fist. Star lunged forward, grabbing the paper with such force, it ripped in two and sent her aunt falling headfirst.

A shriveled scream pierced the air followed by the thump-thump of Aunt Zoe dropping from stair to stair and the snap-crackle of bones striking the parquet tiles. Star ran down and stood over the lifeless figure, arms and legs askew, a tangled marionette. She lay expressionless yet Star sensed malice oozing from every pore. Any second, she half-expected a pair of horns to sprout from the bloody scalp. Then, without warning, Aunt Zoe's head jerked up, as if on an invisible string, and she leered with a puppet's false smile.

"Go ahead, run! You'll never get away with this! I'll tell them you tried to kill me!"

"Yeah, you do that. In the meantime, I'll take this." Star reached down and wrenched the other half of the torn paper from her aunt's grasp, then stepped over her body and turned for the door.

"They'll send you away for good! You won't get beyond this street!" Aunt Zoe taunted. "They're already on their way." Her fingers reached beneath her blouse and pulled out a small device hanging from a band around her neck. "See?" she said, pressing the button franticly. "They'll hunt you down like a dog, treat you like the wild beast you are!"

Star walked out and closed the door behind her, the torn papers clenched in her hand like a lost treasure map. Aunt Zoe's threats couldn't tarnish the rush filling her heart because, finally, she knew what her dreams and Cal had been trying to tell her for months—her sister was alive.

Her boot barely struck the pavement, though, when a cop car came careening around the corner, blinding her with its flashing strobe light. From the other end of the street, she could hear another one closing in, its siren shredding the still night air.

Damn. So, the old bat wasn't bluffing after all. With blaring lights and sirens converging on the house, Star turned and bolted toward the back lawn. She ran without plan or destination, dashing across neighbors' yards, ducking between sheds and pool houses, sneaking around hedges and backyard gazebos, so lost that after a while she wasn't even sure if she was in West Shelby anymore.

She slunk from yard to yard like a marsh rat, traveling under some internal compass that offered only the most basic directive: go far, go fast, and don't look back. As the distant sirens rushed away from Water Lily Terrace, Star feared she was being followed, not by anything as loud and obvious as a patrol car, but by something more ruthless and relentless on foot. When this vibe took hold, she ran even faster, traveling in a blind panic through dark yards and over deserted streets, past places she'd never seen before, in neighborhoods she'd never been to.

Hours later, she stumbled along the marsh's edge and brushing aside the tall reeds, walked into a clearing. The stalks swayed back behind her, closing like a thick green drape. Exhausted, she collapsed to her knees, meant only to take a break, but within seconds her cheek was resting against the damp ground. Her eyes refused to stay open and, as she had no drugs to prevent it, Star fell asleep on the darkened belly of the marsh.

Around her, the swishing sway of the reeds sifted into her dreams, dreams of dogs and hunters, of puppets and pointy-tailed devils and eyes…and while the hours passed, she dreamt on…a lab became a greenhouse and then a lab again where bubbles floated to the ceiling, like champagne in a glass, then popped letting out the wail of newborn babies…and still those eyes, the ones she'd dreamt of over and over, laughing, leering, preying down upon her... Even in her sleep Star shuddered until, after several disbelieving blinks, she realized the dreaming had stopped and she was staring into the actual face of Orrin Parker, hovering over her, the torn list of names crushed in his hand.

CHAPTER
THIRTY-SEVEN

On Friday, Cal woke up, rolled over and stared at the sunrise struggling through his window blinds. Beyond his bedroom walls, he heard Eva's bare feet stomp toward the bathroom, the rush of water from the showerhead and, a few minutes later, the sound of her hurried steps pounding down the stairs, some excited talk about a new dress, then the slam of the door and Tori greeting her on the walk outside.

He knew it was late but couldn't drag himself from beneath the covers. He just lay there, gazing out the window, grieving the loss of Stan or at least the portion of his sanity that had created him. Then he thought about Star. Did he actually kiss her last night? Or was all that a mirage, too?

Cal swung his legs out of bed and looked out the window beyond the yard. More clouds loomed on the horizon, muscling out the fading sun. Great. Just what they needed—more rain. He glanced over at his backpack. If he had any sense, he'd skip out today. With the dance that night, school would be nothing but a time sink. He actually wanted to go, though. To see Star. To make sure last night actually happened.

He grabbed a pair of jeans hanging off the back of his desk chair and slipped them on. Shoving his hand into one of the pockets, he tried to unmangle the lining where something was stuck. It took a couple of seconds to wriggle the wadded ball out from the pocket, but when he did, his hand froze. The thing was damp, smudged with a mess of creases, but he knew it instantly. Uncrumpling the sheet of lined paper, Cal remembered how Stan had insisted he take it, how he said he would need it. And Cal *did* need it, but not for the court or the judge or any of the other reasons he'd thought the old guy meant. He needed this last souvenir of Oakwood for himself.

His gaze ran over the yellowed page—the one he now recognized from the lockbox on Christmas Eve. It was all there, all hundred hours of it, written in the caretaker's own rough script. As he looked at it, the sound of Stan's voice came rushing back to him, every sentence, every joke, every bit of advice mixing and jumbling so that the last word rewinding in his head was the very first thing the caretaker said to him: Boo. He remembered Stan asking if he was frightened, how disappointed he looked when Cal said no.

From downstairs, he heard his mom, something about breakfast and being late for school. Giving her an invisible nod, Cal folded the paper, first in half, then in quarters, and was about to stash it away in his desk drawer, when he noticed a note scribbled on the back. As he began to read it, a lump rolled to the back of his throat, the words swam before his eyes and he could hear the familiar cadence of Stan's voice echo in his ears as sure as if he were standing next to him:

Cal:

I am sorry I can no longer be with you. You have finished your community service and, in a different way, so have I. You did a fine job and I am grateful for every patch of grass you cut and tool you mended. After seein' the cemetery, you might think it was all a waste. Don't be discouraged. It'll come 'round again, though by other hands, hands that need to see the difference they can make among the dead so they can understand how much more they can do among the living.

Stan Heyman

For a long, long time, Cal stared at the worn piece of loose leaf. It didn't explain what had happened or why, but he knew now that the caretaker had been real—though on a different level, one beyond understanding.

When he got to school, Cal tried to find Star. So much to tell her. He tried all the usuals—homeroom, her locker, behind the track—no luck. His calls fell straight to voicemail, texts went unanswered. Then he looked around. Shaving cream smeared lockers, silly string splattered classroom windows, teachers patrolled the hallways while the principal threatened to cancel the dance if the pranks didn't stop. Cal shook his head. Mayhem. No wonder Star had skipped out.

Lunch played out the same way. Dodging an airborne tuna sandwich and a half-eaten hot pocket, Cal ducked too late—splat—to miss the sloppy end of a nutty buddy cone. He glanced down at the smudge of vanilla ice cream on his shoulder, then over to the far end of the cafeteria where his sister seemed just as caught up in the madness. Catching her eye, Cal grinned, pointed to his shoulder, then dragged his finger through the plop of ice cream and lapped it up with his tongue. Eva scrunched her nose and mouthed *grooooss*. Then she laughed, rolled her eyes, and looked away. Cal didn't. It was too rare a moment: Eva surrendering to a smile—marsh madness, indeed.

Just then, an apple core came hurtling through the air and struck her point blank in the temple. Her smile vanished. She got to her feet and was about to whip the chunk of fruit back, when Orrin sidled up from behind, wrapping his arms around her. Eva became mesmerized. Orrin spoke. She giggled. He leaned in to whisper, she cozied into his side. His lips touched her cheek, she blushed…

For a moment, Cal lost all sense of time and place. He sat there watching a cloud of black energy coil around his sister, menacing as a snake. Then, without warning, Orrin looked up and caught Cal's glare. A horrible understanding passed between them. A minute later—from somewhere far away, it seemed—the bell rang. Everyone stood up, Cal lost sight of Eva and it was over.

For the rest of the day, though, the image haunted Cal. He'd never seen energy so dark, so aggressive. Every neuron in his brain rattled. He needed to stop this. Eva and Orrin. The dance. Holy shit. He couldn't—he wouldn't let her go.

By the time he was crossing the marsh on his way home, Cal resolved that, whatever it took, he wouldn't let his sister spend another minute with Orrin—tonight or any other night. Yeah, but how? There was no easy way to make Eva see that blowing off the biggest dance of the year was the right thing—the *only* thing to do. Even if he tapped into one of her more reasonable moments, she was bound to ask him why. What was he supposed to say? That he saw it, that it was toxic for her—for anyone—to be near Orrin.

As he turned into Creeping Cress Court, his mind rounded a different, more troubling corner: Why didn't Star get back to him? Had she skipped out to avoid the Marsh Madness hype —or to avoid him?

At home, Cal paced his room, rehearsing different things he might say to Eva. When she wasn't home by dinner, he went downstairs and caught his parents just as they were heading out.

"Getting her hair done with friends," his mom explained.

"Must be running late, though. Should have been here an hour ago."

Great. Now he had a new hairdo to deal with on top of all the other stuff the evening promised. Why did this crap mean so much to girls?

Watching his parents' car pull out of the driveway, Cal anguished over how to move one of the most unmovable people he knew. By the time Eva burst through the door a half hour later, his nerves were as frazzled as hers.

"What a disaster! The salon was absolute chaos. Over-booked and understaffed. I barely have time to get dressed."

"Eva?"

"Lin got up and left. I should have, too, but I didn't want to leave Tori alone."

"Eva."

"Later, Cal. I'm running super late."

"It's important. It can't wait."

She pounded up the stairs and huffed back a frustrated sigh. "I'll be down in a few minutes. Whatever you want, though, it better be quick. I don't have much time."

Ten minutes later, Eva sashayed down the stairs, glamorous in a tight black sequined gown, a cluster of rhinestone clips tucked within the swirls of her dark hair. As she moved, they shimmered like fireflies on a warm summer night. Cal sighed. He was so screwed.

"So, what's so important it can't wait for my make-up to set?" she asked, her bright pink lips pursed.

"Um…"

"What? What is it already?" Eva's fingers reached behind her neck, fumbling to readjust the clasp on her pearls.

"Right. About tonight…I just thought, um, maybe—"

"Maybe what?"

Cal took a deep breath and exhaled his answer in a whisper. "Maybe you should stay home from the dance tonight."

Eva's head snapped up, dislodging one of the clips from her hair. It sputtered down her neck and clattered onto the floor.

Cal reworded. "Or at least go with someone else. Someone besides Orrin."

His sister's eyes flared, exaggerated by the liner penciled around them. Then, without warning, she burst out laughing.

"Calvin Hughes, stop being such a brother! What are you worried about, that I can't take care of myself?"

Cal jumped at this line of thinking. "Yeah, that's it. That's exactly what I think."

"Seriously? So just ditch my new dress, undo my hair, and have a sit-down with *you*? Or *maybe* this is about someone feeling left out, someone wishing he had a date for the dance tonight." She turned for the door. "Live and learn, Cal. Maybe next year you'll think ahead."

"Wait!" he called out louder than he'd meant to.

Eva turned in the doorway and glared at him. Her newly-polished nails struck an impatient rhythm against the frame of the screen door. Through it, the sounds of the neighborhood filtered into the kitchen—car horns, shouts, front porch laughter—while the ominous hint of thunder rumbled over the marsh. It heightened the tension rippling through the room and the words burning at the back of Cal's throat.

"I don't want you to go to the dance tonight because… because I think you're in danger."

Her fingers froze mid-tap.

"It's Orrin. He's…he's bad. Plain and simple. I don't know how else to put it."

"I don't have time for this, Cal. You're being outrageous. If you've got some proof, some evidence, let's have it. If not, I've got a dance to go to."

Black and white. It was so Eva. What did he expect, that she'd take him at his word and just go with it? Even now, her suspicious green-eyed glare was checking him over, looking for some ingenuous crack in his story—or his sanity. But he wasn't going to give up without a fight. Pulling out a chair, he sat down at the kitchen table and motioned for Eva to do the same. She hesitated, then plopped down in a petulant huff.

"Look, Cal, I'm not upending the biggest night of the school year because of some cryptic warning that my date"—she rolled her eyes—"is evil. If you've got something to say, say it. Otherwise, I'm outta here."

Outside, the intermittent roll of thunder grew louder. Cal lowered his eyes. Unconsciously, he began to trace the table's grainy patterns of wood. He was sure, any moment, that Eva would stand up and swish out the door. But she didn't. For the first time in forever, his sister seemed patient. That was something, anyway. And she was listening.

"It shouldn't surprise you, Eva," he began, his eyes still lowered. "Even when we were little, I suspect you knew. Knew that I wasn't like other kids. That I was different."

He glanced up and saw her pink lips begin to tremble.

"There's this…this thing about me. It's nothing I ever asked for, ever wanted…" He kept fumbling for words, always feeling as if he were falling short of what he wanted to say. "It's just that when I look at people, I see things. Light. It's energy, really. It changes and moves as thoughts and emotions change."

"What, is it like x-ray vision or something?"

The superhero idea distracted Cal for a moment, and he ran with it. "You mean, like, can I tell that you're wearing a black bra?"

Eva's eyes widened, and she threw her arms across her chest. Cal grinned and pointed to the black strap slipping down over her shoulder. She shot him a blazing glare and hiked the meandering strap beneath her gown.

"Anyway," he continued, his crooked smile falling away,

"because of what I see, I sometimes know stuff that other people don't."

"Like?"

"Remember the arson last October I almost got nailed for? Well, from the get-go, I knew who started it—Bill Emerling."

Eva's eyes bulged.

"The night before the fire, he'd spent the evening partying with a bunch of guys he wanted to get tight with. Next day, screening for the swim team rolls around and Bill freaks. No way he's gonna give a clean sample. So, he hatches this stupid plan to start a brush fire near the school. Nothing crazy, just enough for the fire department to show up, get after school activities—and the drug test—canceled."

"But it wasn't a brush fire. He torched Houdini's to the ground. And you knew about it?"

"Only afterwards. I saw his guilt—what little he had. He denied it, but I could tell he was lying. He eventually fessed up."

"Why didn't you turn him in?"

"It's so hard to explain..." Cal rubbed the lids of his downcast eyes. "Because of Mrs. Emerling. I just wanted to help her out. That night last fall, when we were at her house—when Dad was fixing the dishwasher—I saw her energy field imploding all around her. Mr. Emerling had just moved out; his affair was the talk of the town. She lost her job at the medical center and she'd started drinking. There's no way she could deal with Bill getting arrested. It would've finished her off. She was already so messed up. No one knew how much she was hurting."

"But you knew." Eva's voice was flat.

"Yeah. If a person's got issues, it shows up in their energy field first. Usually, it's just a dent or a chip, but if the problem festers, those indicators morph into gaping tears. Then the real trouble starts. A weakened energy field puts a person at risk for all sorts of lethal shit—cancer, infections, even mental breakdowns. It can trigger alcohol or drug abuse—I've seen it. And none of it shows up in medical tests or lab results until way too late."

He glanced at Eva, expecting an exaggerated binge of eye-rolling. But there was none. For a change, she didn't seem to be judging him with that older sister glare. He went on. "It's not that I *want* to know this stuff or see the things I do," he confessed. "It's just always been there, since I was five. At first, I thought everyone saw the light and energy—or at least that you could." The smile struggling at his lips faded. "I wished you could."

Eva seemed to harden herself against his sentimentality. "Does anyone else know about this?"

"No one—well, except for Star."

Her expression tightened. "Can this be proved?"

"Well, Thomas Edison discovered that the human body is surrounded by electromagnetic fields. Then in the 1950's, this Russian guy, Semyon Kirlian, developed an electro–photography technique which he said could record human energy. But it wasn't understood…or accepted…scientifically…"

He broke off. This was why he'd never tried to explain it to anyone. He was surprised Eva hadn't already stormed off.

"So, these colors"—her fingers quotation-marked the words—"what do they tell you?"

Cal sighed, "Everything. Pain, anger, love, revenge. That's why I sometimes do things that people—that *you* don't under-stand. It's hard for me to see this stuff and not react.

"Every day there are dozens of near-misses, disasters that don't happen because someone does *something*, tips the balance, even in a small way. Maybe it's a lunchtime wave-over to the kid who always eats alone or a smile aimed at someone who desperately needs that smile who's otherwise ready to blow.

"As for the different colors, well, they're like a map to someone's soul. Red and darker shades of orange…"

He went on, verbalizing the intangible, spilling the secrets that had nearly choked him over the years, trying to finish what he had to say while he still had words in his head that made sense of it all.

"Then there's—black. Technically speaking, it's not a color. It's the absence of light. And when I see Orrin, I only see black. What's more, I saw that blackness overshadow you today, trying to pull you in." He hesitated. "This energy—it matters. Even Kirlian, a hardcore scientist, thought the field of electro-magnetic light around humans was something special. Said it revealed the state of a person's soul. 'The spark of God', he called it, infused into humans at the time of their birth. And if there's no spark—"

"What about green?" she asked, cutting him off.

Cal retraced his explanation, knowing his answer wouldn't sit well. "Uh, generally, the swirl of green energy reveals jealousy."

"When we were young, you always drew me with a green haze around my head. Why?"

Cal was surprised she remembered. "I drew what I saw."

A great silence engulfed the kitchen then. Seventeen years of everything a brother and sister ever meant to each other, thought about each other, swam between them like a school of lost rudds uncertain which way was upstream and which way was down.

With the sound of thunder rumbling closer, Cal glanced up through his bangs. He watched Eva fidget with the clasp on her necklace, preoccupied once more with the evening's big event. Apparently, she'd had her fill.

Cal stood up, striking his head on the overhead light so that the whole kitchen seemed to lurch under its swaying glow. No way he was going to sit there and watch her walk out the door with Orrin Parker. As he turned for the stairs, he heard something like marbles strike the table and, glancing back, saw that Eva's pearly-colored beads were no longer around her neck.

"You're right, Cal," she began flippantly. "I have always known about you…" Her voice broke and tears began to glisten over her cheeks, bright as the sequins on her gown. "Known there was something, something that made you better than everyone else. Better than me. And I hated you for it, for being able to radiate the warmth of the sun. Even after all that's happened, all you've been through—" She glanced at his hands, "That hasn't changed. Somehow, you still manage to straighten the world with your crooked smile."

Once more, silence overwhelmed the kitchen. Nothing stirred, nothing sounded but the thunder that thumped and rattled against the screen door like a caged beast. It brought with it the smell of damp weeds, approaching rain and a marshy sort of melancholy that already enveloped the room in the aftermath of spilled consciences. The sound of tiny metal hairpins dropping onto the table added to the gloom, and Cal looked up to see Eva untangling the sparkly fireflies from her hair. Suddenly, he felt very sorry for ruining her beautiful evening.

"You want to go somewhere?" he asked. "You look too nice to stay at home."

Eva shrugged and continued to pull the clips from her hair.

"The Last Drop might be kinda busy tonight, but if you want to leave all this Marsh Madness behind, we could go to Manny's for something a little more—"

"Greasy? Sure, why not." She sniffled, looking relieved at the idea of getting out of town. "But I have to change first. No sense hobbling around in this all evening." She fluffed away a tulle puff poking at her cheek, then wiped a drizzle of black liner from beneath her eyes. "And I suppose I should call Orrin, make some excuse for blowing him off."

Cal got the car keys and closed the kitchen window against the pending storm. He needed to call Star now, knew he'd have plenty of time. Upstairs, he could hear Eva on the phone —Parker would put up a fight. Then, of course, there was the dress. He figured it would take at least the same amount of time to wriggle out of a thing like that as to slip into it. A moment later, though, Eva reappeared in the kitchen, formal wear still on, cell phone in hand, her brow wrinkled.

"That was weird."

Cal's heart began to pound.

"I just talked to Orrin and, strangely, he didn't seem to care about my dumping him last minute—jerk. Then he said the strangest thing. He gave me a message—for you."

Cal's mouth went dry.

"He said, 'Tell your brother I'm out on the marsh with Star and if he doesn't hurry, it'll be too late'." Eva stared at her cell phone, annoyed. "As if I would care about Star."

She looked up in time to hear the slam of the screen door and see Cal racing out into the looming storm.

CHAPTER
THIRTY-EIGHT

Tearing down the driveway, Cal hurtled toward the marsh for the second time in as many days, his mind careening all over the place. It's a hoax, he tried to tell himself, Orrin's sicko sense of humor, some screwed-up misunderstanding. But as his mind ran out of excuses, his feet ran faster, pummeling through the thorny overgrowth and pounding over the boardwalk. He saw the bridge in the distance brightened by the glow of party lanterns. They didn't throw much light. Squinting ahead, he saw movement. Two figures crushed-up against the railing. He couldn't see their faces, but they appeared to be struggling...

———

Waddling toward the kitchen window in her cinched gown, Eva watched her brother bolt down the driveway and across the center of the court, aiming straight for the marsh like a bullet from a gun. Then came the patter of slow rain against the roof, each drop a tiny nick against the wall of unease closing in around her. It gathered momentum, climaxing with a tremendous clap of thunder that shook the house and rattled the windows in their panes. Eva jumped and with it her mind leapt toward a disturbing logic: if it were dangerous for her to spend the evening with Orrin, then her brother shouldn't be anywhere near him either, especially not alone in the dark chasing him over the marsh.

Suddenly, she whipped off her shoes, scrunched up her gown and hobbled out the door after Cal. By the time her bare feet were padding over the boardwalk, though, her pace slowed. The path was darker than she'd expected—much darker. In the distance, she could just make out the strand of lanterns suspended above the bridge and wondered why the hell the decorating committee hadn't done more to light the place up. Moonlight? There was none. Looking around the dark, weedy path, she felt goose-bumps ripple across her arms. The boardwalk felt like one giant hazard. Every shred of common sense begged her to turn around, go home. But the crazed butterflies in her stomach urged her forward. Grabbing for the rickety railing, Eva hobbled on.

———

...Cal ran full throttle toward the two figures. As he got closer, he saw pushing and shoving, then heard a high-pitched squeal. Bounding forward, he wrenched them apart.

"Yo! Geh yer own date!"

Cal stumbled back. As his eyes adjusted to the shadows, he recognized a slurring Jardo and, ducking behind him, Kelly Hanson inching her gown back into place. She caught his glance, flashed a vengeful grin, then tugged at Jardo to kiss her again.

Less certain now, Cal moved on through the rain-spattered darkness. He groped his way along the path toward the distant glow of the green, orange, and yellow lights. Then, from somewhere below the walkway, he heard a whimper and moan. With flashes of lightning his only guide, he jumped down into the ankle-deep water. Feeling his way along the rushes and into the reeds, he searched beneath the boardwalk until he found the source: his neighbor's puppy trapped by the rising water. As it shivered and limped in circles, Cal inspected the end of the leash—it'd been cut. Mrs. Kenefick's handiwork, no doubt. He gave the dog's leg a quick rub, then it ran off with a furious wet shiver.

Soaked and stinking of marsh water, Cal leapt back onto the boardwalk. As he sloshed along, he began to consider the idea that maybe this was just a prank, a goof, Orrin's revenge for a ruined evening against the guy who ruined it. As for Star, Orrin's the last person she'd be with—out here or anywhere else. By the time he was rounding the last turn before the bridge, Cal convinced himself that he didn't give a damn what Orrin had to say—if he was out here at all. After all, Eva was waiting back home, and he'd promised her…

Crack!

Cal glanced up in time to see a huge spear of lightning jag down from the clouds. It struck something on the south side of town and illuminated the sky in an explosion of sparks. Rain began to pelt down as more lightning ripped the stormy air. And in that uneven light, he saw something so bizarre he thought it must be a trick of the strobe-like flashes. On the bridge, two figures appeared to be arguing, and he was sure he knew them both.

———

As the storm picked up, Eva winced through the rain and the darkness, searching for her brother. He had to turn back, she told herself. It was nuts out here. All the same, she went on, waddle-hopping over the boardwalk, struggling against the confines of her clingy dress. Frustrated, she began to cinch the gown above her knees. Then she stopped, her hands frozen mid-cinch. She heard something barreling down the board- walk. The rumble of the boards pulsed beneath her feet as it headed in her direction. Before she could scream, the thing charged through the darkness. She threw up her hands as violent waves of mud, water, and matted hair sprayed all over her. The dog raced past but seconds later something much bigger and louder came hurtling straight toward her. Eva had a second's warning to arch out of the way as Jardo hit up against the rail and vomited over the side. Somewhere behind him, she heard Kelly Hanson's slurred giggle. "Way-ta-go!"

Eva rolled her eyes and hurried away. Thunder crackled and rumbled in turns. She could feel the storm's current rippling through the air. Somewhere behind her, the dog started to howl, and she sensed that madness really had taken over the marsh.

Where *was* Cal? She didn't care about his weird vision or cryptic colors. She just wanted to see those reassuring blue eyes and know he was all right. She'd so much to tell him, things she should have shared over the years but held back. She blinked away the raindrops flicking into her eyes and against the deafening clatter of the rain, called for him: "Cal! Cal!"

————

Cal raced up to the bridge, then pulled-up short. The twisted horror of the scene took his breath away: Star, on her knees, half-strangled by her scarf, the other end wrapped tightly around Orrin's fist. A bulging blue bruise broke the skin on her cheek and her bloodshot eyes blinked raw fear. Cal felt his jaw clench, his breath hiss between his teeth.

"About time you got here," Orrin drawled. "I didn't think a

little *darkness* would slow you down—not with your vision, anyway."

"Get—away—" Star choked out. "It's a—trap."

Orrin grinned, his expression ghoulish beneath the crayon-colored lanterns bobbing above.

"It's going to be all right, Star," Cal assured, his voice falsely calm, "I think this is over now."

"Is it?" Orrin's eyebrows arched.

"Look, if you're pissed at me, Parker, fine. I'm here. Let her go."

"Go where? Back to her aunt?" Orrin laughed, then turned toward Star. "And in case you're worried about the dear woman, she's recovering nicely and anxious to see you again."

Cal didn't know why, but Star quaked at his words.

"I—I want that paper back, Parker!" she managed to rasp from beneath the scarf slicing into her throat.

"Ah, but it isn't yours," he answered, giving the scarf a good yank. Star doubled over coughing and Cal made a go for her, but Orrin's chilling voice stopped him mid-step.

"Any closer and she's done."

Even from where he stood, Cal felt Orrin's cold black energy, the dark swirl of his intent. There wasn't much time.

"C'mon, Parker. Grow up. You're playing errand boy for some old lady with a grudge? Get your kicks somewhere else."

The mocking tone pricked Orrin. His back stiffened, his eye twitched. For a moment, his focus shifted away from Star and toward Cal. His eyes seemed to dissect every inch of him, taking note of the smallest detail right down to the plank of wood beneath Cal's feet.

"He's—playing—you," Star cried, lurching under the pull of her scarf like a worm on the end of a muddy line. "Get the hell out of—"

Star's voice broke. She began to gag as Orrin tightened his

grip on the scarf once more. Cal's face flushed hot. The slight tremor in his hand vanished as it balled into a fist.

"Let her go," Cal demanded, inching closer.

"Now, considering you tampered with my plans this evening, give me one good reason why."

"*Plans?*" Cal goaded him. "You don't want Star and you never gave a shit about my sister, either. It's me you've been after. It's always been me. I know what you are."

Orrin cocked his head, again sizing up Cal and the place where he stood.

"Hmm, you *are* much better than any I've seen before. No wonder you've created a stir. So, what gave me away?"

Cal took a step closer. "That night. In front of the church."

"Ah, Good ol' St. Francis. No hiding myself in *that* light. But I had you until then, didn't I? Admit it."

"I got careless, maybe. Distracted..."

Parker grinned, and Cal felt the hair on the back of his neck tingle. He glanced at Star whose lips began to tinge an icy blue. "Let her go," Cal repeated.

"As you wish."

Without warning, Parker released his hold. The scarf's sudden slack slammed Star against the rail and nearly launched her over the side and into the turbulent waters below. She steadied herself against the railing. Orrin glared.

"Don't move."

———

"Cal...Cal..." But the clatter of the rain erased Eva's words as quickly as they left her mouth. "C'mon...where are you?"

Her mascara—or what was left of it—streamed into her eyes. She grabbed her gown, torn and mud-streaked, and gave it an awkward hitch. Beyond the next bend, she saw the bridge looking like some battered cruise ship with those hideous kitschy lanterns. Then she saw him. Cal. But he wasn't alone. Everything appeared civil, yet at the same time very tense and very wrong...

———

Cal rushed to Star's side. He smoothed his fingers over her bruised throat and looked into her terrified eyes. "Did he hurt you?"

She fell into him and in a croaky whisper said, "Get out... it's a...ploy...my dream..."

Orrin stepped back, hoisting himself atop the bridge railing. He sat and watched them with a detached sort of interest, like fish in an aquarium or animals in the zoo. Indifferent, almost bored.

"This ends now," Cal said, putting his arm around Star's shoulder. "He can't get to you anymore and neither can Aunt Zoe. I won't let them. It's time to go."

"Yes," Orrin echoed flatly. "It *is* time to go."

Cal's eyes darted up. Something in Orrin's words, the pitch of his voice.

"You don't need to do this," Cal said, trying to reason with him, with eyes that were as blank as a deadman's.

"Oh, but I'm afraid I do," Orrin said, his glare dancing between Cal's face and his feet.

"Why?"

"Because," Orrin whispered, "you're tipping *the balance*."

Then gripping the rail, he hammered down on the portion of the bridge where Cal and Star were standing. Instantly, the boards splintered and caved crashing into the turbulent waters below.

———

"Cal!" Eva screamed. Scrunching her gown above her knees, she sprinted toward the bridge, stopping just before the gaping hole through which her brother and Star had just fallen. Beneath her feet, she felt the weakened boards begin to teeter and cave and flung herself toward the railing. Tightrope-walking along the base, she scanned the water. In the eerie plastic glow of the bridge lights, she saw a head bobbing at the surface. It turned toward her, paused then submerged again.

"Cal! Hang on!" Her hands grabbed the rail, then Eva looked down at her skin-tight gown. "Damn it!" Glancing around, she realized she was alone. Orrin had managed to vanish and no one else…

Suddenly she heard voices and shouts, pitching high and wild over the rain. Classmates spilled from town, running up the boardwalk with a kind of hushed hysteria about a trans-former being blown out in town, the dance being canceled and now, this. There was a moment—and to Eva it felt like an hour —when everyone just seemed to stand and gape over the rail, looking down without any urgency.

"Someone save him!" she pleaded, grabbing tuxedo lapels and sequined shoulders. "I can't…my dress…" Cell phones were shoved her way. "No, no, there's no time for… He needs help now!" When no one headed for the water, Eva's panic stiffened to resolve. Ripping off the lower half of her gown, she mounted the bridge railing and swung her leg over. She was about to jump in, when someone grabbed her from behind.

"Get away! Let me go!" she cried, pummeling the air.

"Look!" someone called out. "In the water! I think it's Cal!"

"And there's Star!" another voice shouted. "She looks like she's in trouble!"

Everyone stopped, even Eva, and focused on the figures struggling against the frenzied black chop, the marsh-turned-raging-river below.

———

Cal crashed into the water and lost all sense of direction—the water so cold he couldn't even think. The shock pierced his body like a thousand needles of ice. Water surged into his ears, nose and throat. Gasping a moment too late, he sucked in a lungful of water. The force of the fall torpedoed him to the bottom. As instinct took over, he scrambled for the surface. All around him, the web of underwater plants snared at his hands and feet, slowing his upward progress.

He broke the surface, his lungs aching for air. Waves batted his head from every direction, side-swiping or blinding him head-on. Shaking the spray and wet hair from his face, Cal scanned every black inch of water. No Star. He glanced up toward the bridge, eerie beneath the carnival lights. Nothing. Afraid to waste another second, he kicked off his sneakers, took a huge gulp of air and dove back down.

Beneath the surface, Cal squinted through the curtain of murky water around him. Beyond dark. Impossible to see. Swimming into the blackness, he hazarded a couple of strokes one way, then the other, every decision a breath-draining risk. Then he saw it. The thinnest wisp of silvery light, floating a few yards away—Star's energy—giving shape and definition to the creepy underwater world of serpentine stems and roots. He stroked toward it and found her thrashing in place, fatally immobilized by her scarf. It looked like a fragile strand of seaweed floating around her but was actually strangling her.

He tore the garment away, then grabbed her waist and kicked upward. Breaking the surface with a lung-aching gasp, he could hear Star choking and coughing, swallowing more water as she tried to suck air in. He wrestled against the current to keep their heads above water. But the weight of their clothes submerged them again and again. Above the surface,

Star's breath came in pants. Cal could see she was crying as he struggled to hold onto her.

"I won't leave you!" he yelled.

She whimpered something back, but he couldn't hear. Even with just inches between them, the sound of the rain and the waves crashing over their heads drowned out her words. At one point, she slipped from his grasp and disappeared below. Cal dove after her, dragging her to the surface once more. Beneath the sporadic burst of lightning, she managed a few words.

"Get out…while you can…this is what she wants…too late…for me…"

Cal felt his muscles begin to numb, fatigue setting in.

"You have to hold on…" he said, his own breath coming in gasps now. "You're not done…Alula needs you…"

Star stopped the struggle. Even in the near darkness, Cal could see her gazing into his eyes. After a second or two, she nodded and began to doggie-paddle toward shore with him.

Then, without warning, several planks crashed down from the bridge, forcing a large tongue of water to surge toward them. Gorged with rainwater and debris, the stream rose up and swallowed them. Cal tumbled beneath the water for the longest time yet. He barely kicked to the surface in time for his lungs, burning and empty, to heave for air. Treading water, his eyes darted upstream to what was left of the bridge, the people gathering near it. Somehow, no one else had fallen in. He spotted Eva in the crowd, just as Star screamed from behind him.

"Cal! Over here! Help!"

He whirled around. In seconds, the current had carried Star downstream. Something beneath the surface appeared to be dragging her down. Cal's arms split through the ravaging water but by the time he reached the place where he'd last spotted Star, she was gone. He looked down into the foamy, black water. For the first time, he dreaded the thought of going under. Treading water for a second, he glanced back at the bridge and saw Eva swinging herself over the rail. She'd have been in the water if someone hadn't stopped her. As grateful tears welled in his eyes, he dove beneath the surface and disappeared from sight.

———

In the dreamy blur of the underwater marsh, Star found a black peace. Nothing like the chaos of the waves and lightning above. She began to sink into the airless gloom, lower, lower, deeper and deeper, surrendering to the fate she'd watched so many times before, but this time without the hope she'd wake up and walk away from it. Even as she saw the rush of Cal's arms and legs stroke toward her, her spirit caved, for this was exactly, tragically, how she knew it would end.

She felt a tug...then another...From somewhere far away she felt fingers crabbing their way toward her ankle, hands tearing at the coiled lily stem that tethered her to the marsh floor. But it was too late...game over. Expelling her last bubble of air, Star's eyes fluttered closed.

A moment later, she stirred as her ankle wriggled free, though on a leg that hardly seemed hers anymore. Cal's hands encircled her waist, then thrust her upward. As she broke the surface, a confusion of hands closed in around her, grabbing at her clothes, dragging her ashore.

So many people...so much water... Again and again she strained through the blur of people to see him. And still one more time. With a heart-crushing realization, she buried her face in her cold, muddy hands and sobbed. She knew that, just like her dream, the night had taken its final tragic turn.

EPILOGUE

Stan Heyman wasn't accustomed to visitors in his graveyard. Little happened there without his knowledge or consent. In fact, only one interloper had ever broken that unwritten rule. Now, as he squinted through the filmy layer of brown dust coating his workshop window, he saw that same person laboring her way up through the yard, a sling wrapped around her arm. He watched her pound over the ground, brushing past tombstones like they were in her way, her lips muttering silent curses. Preoccupied, she failed to notice him hurrying out of the shed to head her off, rake in hand.

"Lookin' for a plot?" he called out, an edge to his voice. "Somethin' for yourself, perhaps?"

"I'm here to see you, Heyman."

"I don't remember your bein' invited, Zoe."

"I don't need an invitation from you or anyone else," she answered. "Besides, I've been here before."

"I know," the caretaker boomed. "You had no business bein' here then. Especially when Cal was alone."

"And you have no business meddling in my affairs."

"But your business *is* my business," the caretaker said, a big toothy smile springing to his lips. "Or at least, undoin' it is."

She glared at him over a crooked row of tombstones that stood between them. "Look, I've come to make a deal with you. If you're smart, we can both come away winners."

"Ha! There are no good deals with the devil. Only bad bargains." The caretaker began to work the ground with sharp snaps, the rake's tongs scratching over several flat markers. " You can't win, Zoe. You wouldn't be here if you thought otherwise."

"Oh, I think I can," she said, her shoulders inching up with each metallic scrape. "In the short run, however, you have made my life unnecessarily difficult."

"That so?" The caretaker's voice rose as if her words were a compliment.

"Where's the girl?" she said through clenched teeth.

"Whatever do you mean, Zoe?"

"You're old, Heyman, maybe a bit confused but you know more than you pretend. Alula is not at any of the addresses on that safe house list. Where is she?"

"Why don't you ask your niece?"

"That useless waste of—"

"Word around town is she ran away." The caretaker glanced up from his work. "Can't say I blame her."

"I don't know or care where that little monster has gone."

"Sure you do. 'Cause you know she's out there lookin' for the same thing as you. Only she has a heart to guide her. You've just got your wicked old ways."

"Well, we've all had our disappointments of late, haven't we?" Her glare darkened to a condescending smile. "Shame about that boy drowning last week. Worked for you, didn't he?"

The strokes of the rake grew terse, but the old man's

composure remained unshaken. "Drowned, you say? Did they find his body?"

"Well, no. But, I mean, he couldn't have…it would be impossible…not after the fall, the storm…"

Stan kept raking. "If you say so."

"They had a memorial service for him."

"Well, Alula had a full-blown funeral, thanks to you, and you knew from the get–go she wasn't dead."

"But someone would have seen him. He'd be…" She stopped, craned her neck and peered behind a couple of tomb-stones. "Somewhere." Then she shot a suspicious glance uphill to the cobblestone shed.

He distracted her. "Now, if I were Cal, and I made it through that ordeal, I'm not so sure I'd rush back to West Shelby, especially if I found myself downstream a ways. Might be a bit liberatin' to take off, get away from the twisted folks around here. Especially with all manner of curses flyin' around." Stan poked reflectively at a leaf curled in the crook of a gravestone. "You oughtta be ashamed, Zoe. He was just a little kid."

She smoothed her fingers over her sling. "Cal got in my way—a lesson *you* could learn from."

"You don't scare me, Zoe. Anyway, the boy managed. You may have cursed him with those unsteady hands, but I gave him vision to live by."

Her black eyes narrowed. "So, it was you! What else are you hiding?"

"Not as much as you. That Parker fellow, for instance. Where'd you dig up a lowlife like him?"

"Ah, Orrin. A *weak swimmer*, for sure. It's nothing to draw that kind into deeper waters. The prettier they are, the easier they bend. I even taught him how to hide that dark glow around him—'til he got careless."

"You're a poisonous weed, Zoe. Nothin' more."

The craggy lips grinned. "Flattery isn't necessary."

Stan's eyes lost their warmth. Leaning back, he let out a belting yawn, more like a roar. Suddenly, the wind kicked-up, setting the graveyard into motion. Tall maples swayed like saplings, the gate rattled in its post and a thick sycamore branch blew over and whacked the back of Zoe's legs.

She kicked it off.

"Don't you have enough power in your clutch?" he asked. "Why pull the marsh into your dark swirl?"

She shrugged her cashmere-covered shoulders. "Because I can. Besides, who can resist a vortex? Especially one as potent as the one sitting under this marsh."

Stan Heyman stopped raking and stared at the woman, his gaze so intense it might have peeled back the false layers of her gentile façade—the neat bob of gray hair, the chalky makeup and floral print skirt.

"This marsh used to be a place where people came for peace and quiet, for healin'," he began, his voice somber. "Then your dark hocus-pocus poisoned the waters, enchanted the lilies. You and that hag, Kenefick."

"A loyal friend."

"No good, either one of you." He shook his head. "That poor young girl. You don't care about her, just what she is, what she represents."

"A rich opportunity. Never before seen by humankind. A cloned child, created not by God, but by man. And the soul? Well, how deliciously easy to corrupt." She glanced around. "But you and your little graveyard here keep getting in my way. So, enough stalling. Where's the girl? Tell me or there *will* be consequences."

The yellowy eyes narrowed to a pair of angry crescent moons.

"Don't threaten me, Zoe."

"I want what I want."

The caretaker straightened up and cleared his throat. Simultaneously, thunder filled the skies, shaking the ground in waves like an earthquake.

"This is not your place," he said.

The woman teetered on the unsteady earth, glanced at the sky but remained unmoved.

"Perhaps. But you can't stop me from having a quick look arou—"

Stan's expression became savage, his voice lowered. "You didn't belong here last November and you don't belong here now."

Then, one by one, he curled his fingers around the end of the rake. As he tightened their grip, Zoe McClellan grabbed her throat, coughing, struggling to breath. Her eyes bulged as she glared at the rake's handle.

A moment later, the caretaker's grip eased off. "So, you say you're *leaving*?"

Zoe straightened up and massaged her throat. "Not until we've come to an understanding," she persisted stepping back a pace or two .

"Oh, I think we have an understanding. Plain as the grass beneath your feet."

With that, the caretaker let the rake slip through his weathered fingers. It fell at Zoe's feet, heavy as a steel door. Instantly, the earth began to cave, opening a portal deeper than a grave right in front of her. "It's where you belong, Zoe," he pointed.

Again, thunder rolled, and the ground shook. More branches came tearing down from the trees. She shrieked, covering her head with her arms.

"Fool!" she hissed. "You haven't won anything here." But she was already halfway down the hill, scurrying off like a stink bug under an overturned rock.

He called after her. "And watch for them sink holes. Like

you said, I'm old and confused. You fall in, I might forget myself and bury you right there."

For all the time it took Zoe McClellan to make her way through the cemetery, the caretaker's yellowy eyes never lifted off her dark form. Not when she was passing the last row of tombstones, not even after she'd pushed her way through the gate with a stammering, "You'll be sorry," echoing up the hill. Even after she was gone, he went after her, plying his rake through the grass flattened by her footsteps as if to remove any residue left behind. When he was sure she was gone, Stan sighed. For one more day at least, he'd kept the balance from tipping toward the darkness she spread like an incurable disease.

He shook off the chill that settled in her wake and looked up. Sunlight filled the yard, filtering down between the leafy branches overhead and bathing the moss-covered shed in a hazy summer glow. He breathed it in, tossed his rake against his shoulder and whistled his way back uphill. The grass needed mowing and a pair of helping hands always lightened the load. And today, he was lucky enough to have two.

———

Don't miss your next favorite book!

Join the Fire & Ice mailing list
www.fireandiceya.com/mail.html

ACKNOWLEDGMENTS

This book would not have been possible without my writers' group: Chera Thompson, Lou Rera, Michael Marrone, Susan Solomon, Mary Ostrowski and dear George (we miss you). Your collective thoughts breathe through every chapter.

And to Mom for telling me it was okay to keep my head in the clouds so long as my feet stayed on the ground.

THANK YOU FOR READING

Did you enjoy this book?

We invite you to leave a review at the website of your choice, such as Goodreads, Amazon, Barnes & Noble, etc.

DID YOU KNOW THAT LEAVING A REVIEW...

- Helps other readers find books they may enjoy.
- Gives you a chance to let your voice be heard.
- Gives authors recognition for their hard work.
- Doesn't have to be long. A sentence or two about why you liked the book will do.

ABOUT THE AUTHOR

E. L. Werbitsky is a freelance writer and former news journalist with print and online credits including the literary journal, *WORDPEACE, Columbia Magazine,* and *The Buffalo News.* She is the founder of Buffalo Books & Brew, an organization that brings local readers and writers together.

Her favorite things to do are explore New York and Boston, listen to live music and read. She resides in Buffalo, NY with her husband, where she enjoys lake effect snow and, of course, the Buffalo Bills.

elwerbitsky.com

facebook.com/ELWerbitsky.author

twitter.com/EileenWerbitsky

instagram.com/elwerbitsky

Made in United States
North Haven, CT
07 March 2023

33712222R10173